# TIO

# JORGE

Also by Vincent Meis

*Eddie's Desert Rose (2011)*

# TIO
# JORGE
## A MEXICAN-AMERICAN
## SOAP OPERA

# VINCENT MEIS

The characters and events in this book are fictitious. Any
similarity to real persons, living or dead, is coincidental and not
intended by the author.

Copyright © 2012 Vincent Meis

Printed in The United States of America
Cover design by Martin Salazar and Vincent Meis
Interior design by Rose Rock

FIRST EDITION
Fallen Bros. Publishing
6010 Pacific Coast Highway #9
Redondo Beach, CA 90277
ISBN-13: 978-0615620237
ISBN-10: 061562023X

FOR

VIRGINIA C. MEIS

# ACKNOWLEDGMENTS

I would like to thank Antoni Gaudí and Edward James for their unique visions in architecture and design, and a singular way of living their lives. They provided the inspiration for the character Tio Jorge. I would also like to thank the people of Mexico for their graciousness and hospitality in my stays there while writing parts of this book, and Donna Hanelin for introducing me to the wonderful world of Oaxaca as well as her writing advice.

My family has been my bedrock of support. William A. Meis, Jr., Michael Meis, Mary Hardcastle, Monica Wellman, Marcia Meis, Morgan Meis and Marika Meis have all contributed in some way to this and other writing projects. I'd also like to mention Elaine Micus, Sabine Huemer, Stefany Anne Goldberg, Terry Hardcastle, Lesley Markoski, Lynn Wellman, and Jeff Cadwell for their support and encouragement. And my mother, Virginia C. Meis, who motivated us all to read, and continues to give herself to the world of books.

My fellow readers, Gilberto Leon, Nehemiah Lazo, Susan Herder, and Mike Raftery have inspired me with our book discussions, and Martin Salazar has, in addition, been a great help with cover design. Members of Guywriters have critiqued selected chapters, and a workshop with Benjamin Percy helped get the first chapter in line. I have also received editing help from Michael Kaye, Richard Hack, and Peter Master.

# 1: George

From high on a cliff, my body pressed to the ground, I peered down at her. She lay far below on a large, flat rock, a carefree girl with one leg curled up and the other dangling over the edge. The incoming tide lapped at her toes. A blue scarf had come loose under her chin, but was caught on something shiny, a gold chain around her neck perhaps, so that it whipped about her head like a flag. She might have been posing for a fashion magazine. Helen always did have a flair for style.

She wore a coy smile on her lips, and her arms were tossed open, ready to embrace the sky. Her bulky sweater was hitched up, revealing a bit of skin. On closer examination, there was something jarring about her attire, how her lime-green sweater clashed with her red-plaid stretch pants. I imagined her dressing in a rush to catch me on my morning jog, choosing her clothes in the half-light while her husband, Miguel, lay curled up sleeping in the warmth of their bed. The smile, her sad outfit, and her place at the water's edge painted a picture of vulnerability. I would keep an eye on her to make sure she was all right.

And then a wave slammed the rocks and crashed over her, plastering the scarf across her face like a veil. The brackish water rolled her toward the cliff, and then back as it receded. She didn't stir, didn't try to remove the scarf that seemed to be suffocating her.

Level with my eye a seagull hovered in the low fog. It screeched and the sound brought me out of my trance, making me aware of the gravel burrowing into my knees and the grass poking my bare legs. My ears ached from the wind, and my sweat had dried to a salty crust on my skin. What had happened flashed in my head—her scream followed by silence, my crawl to the ledge, and the paralysis that gripped me, seeing her fifty yards below on the rocks. How much time had passed? I scanned the rugged California coast and saw that there was no access to the beach where she had fallen. A climb down the sheer cliff face was impossible. Only a boat or helicopter could get to her.

I started to lift myself up, but the pressure of my hand on the eroding cliff dislodged a clump of dirt that cascaded down to where she lay. Bits of soil rained over her now-drenched clothes. I inched back and got up on my knees. Tearing at my insides was the notion that if I had reached out my hand a second sooner, I could have saved her. My head began to spin and bile rose in my throat. I leaned over and let it spew onto the dusty ground.

On hands and knees I got to the trail and grasped a branch of a small tree to help me up. I had to get back to the house, but for a moment was so disoriented I couldn't remember which way to go. I got my bearings and took off at a teetering run with the nightmarish sensation that I was making no progress.

After what seemed like an eternity, I emerged from the coastal scrub of lupine, manzanita, and coyote bush, and stopped short. The Craftsman house loomed in front of me, somber and intimidating, its overhanging roof putting a hush on the lawn and the squared-off hedges. I ran around to the side deck off the dining room where we always had breakfast. In a pocket of golden light where the sun had broken through, Miguel sat across from his five-year-old daughter, Rebecca. Conchita stood over them in a white apron and blue smock. She had her hand on the little girl's shoulder and pointed at the food on the table.

Miguel raised his head and gave me a half-hearted wave. He forced a smile.

Rebecca turned. "Hi, Tio," she said. "Have you seen Mommy?" She called me Tio Jorge, Spanish for Uncle George, though I wasn't really her uncle, or Mexican like her father, or even a native Spanish-speaker.

I stopped at the bottom of the steps leading up to the deck and took in air. "Miguel. Come! Quick!"

His face fell into a frown, and he looked at the upstairs window where Helen's parents slept. He spread his hands and pressed down on the air.

Rebecca giggled and put a finger to her lips. "Shhhh," she said.

"Miguel, please," I said.

He pushed up out of the chair and walked toward me. Rebecca started to get up, but Conchita squinted at me, sensed something wrong, and kept the girl in her seat with a firm hand.

Miguel lingered at the top of the steps. "What's going on? You look awful."

I backed up a few paces into the yard and motioned for him to join me. He cocked his head, not sure if he wanted to play the game, but then threw up his hands and descended the steps. "I'm not ready to talk about yesterday," he said in a low voice.

"Something happened," I gasped.  "An accident. It's Helen. Out there." I pointed to the cliff. "Come on." I started to move and then stopped. "Wait. Do you have your cell phone?"

"Helen? She just went for a walk. I don't—"

I grabbed his arm and put my face close to his. I could smell the coffee on his breath. "Helen fell. Onto the rocks."

He raked his fingers through his damp hair. A shadow gathered below his thick brows. "You left her there?" He looked down at my hand and pulled his arm away.

"I couldn't get to her. Give me your phone."

"What are you saying? Jesus! Is she alive?"

"I don't know."

His chest rose and fell in short breaths. "*Dios mío. Fuck. No puede ser.*" He pulled the phone from his pocket and handed it to me, stumbled back a couple of steps. I felt the lump of metal and plastic in my hand, still warm from the heat of his body. We stared at each other for a long moment. Instead of a mature 26-year-old man, I saw the small-town teenage boy I had met in Mexico eight years before.

I dialed 911, explained what happened, snapped the phone shut, and held it out to him. "The operator said we should go to the cliff and help direct the helicopter." When he made no effort to retrieve the phone, I forced it into his lifeless hand. "Come on. We've got to go."

Rebecca called out from the deck. "Papi, where are you going?"

He whirled around and jabbed a finger at Conchita. "Keep her here," he mouthed.

It was a ten-minute run out to where I had left Helen. Miguel was not a runner, and I soon heard his labored breathing behind me. I slowed down, but he motioned for us to keep going, pushing me slightly ahead of him.

By the time we got to the cliff, I could hear a helicopter buzzing the area, and it almost immediately came into view. I raised my hands into the air, waved frantically, and pointed at the rocks below. Miguel moved toward the edge.

"Stay back," I said.

"I have to see."

"You'd better get on your knees then. Crawl to the edge."

We both fell to our knees and crept over the pebbly ground until we could see down to the beach. She was the same as I had left her, though the water had risen so that she seemed to be rocking back and forth in a bath. Soon the surf would cover her completely. Miguel gripped the edge of the cliff, jutted out his chin, and zoomed in on her with beady eyes as if he were set to swoop down and lift her from the rocks.

The helicopter glided into position above us, and its updraft churned the dirt and dry grass, ruffled our clothes and Miguel's hair. His mouth hung open and it seemed that the moan of the rotor blades was coming from deep inside his throat. I tried to imagine what he was feeling, if he really loved his wife, if he had ever loved her. I wanted to reach out to him, comfort him, hold him in my arms, but his body was stiff, as if my presence repulsed him.

"I'm so sorry," I shouted over the din and then regretted it. It sounded like I was pronouncing her dead.

He said nothing.

We lay side by side in the whirl of the helicopter's storm and watched as the rescuer was lowered on a cable. Just before he got to her, a wave hit with a force that could draw her out to sea. He landed on the rock and grabbed her arm just in time. Then he felt for a pulse in her neck and lifted her eyelids before throwing his hands in the air and motioning for the stretcher to be lowered.

Miguel turned over on his back and looked up at the fog, a little higher now, but it hadn't cleared out here close to the ocean. He stared at a dull glow indicating the approximate location of the sun. I could feel a hint of warmth from it on my back. I angled my head to look at him, though he continued staring at the sky, pressing his lips together to keep them from trembling.

"Miguel, say something."

He turned his face toward me, and I reached out to touch it.

"Don't," he growled and pulled his head back. "How could you?"

"How could I what?"

He turned his face back to the sky.

"You don't think—" I began.

"Just don't talk, okay?"

The man strapped Helen to the stretcher and she was lifted with the cable. I scooted back from the edge and stood up, hunched over with the feeling that the chopper might lop off my head. "We should go back to the house," I yelled, and offered him a hand.

He didn't take it. Instead, he rolled over on his stomach again and grabbed a clump of dirt. He squeezed it until it crumbled in his hand. I wanted to point out how loose the soil was, how vulnerable the cliff face, how someone close to the edge could easily lose her footing.

The helicopter veered off. Its din faded. "I don't know what she was doing here," I said. "I looked up from my run and there she was. I know she was angry. She said terrible things. I told her to get away from the cliff. Then it just gave way and she was gone."

Miguel stood up and walked to the trail. He stuffed his hands into his chinos and bowed his head like a condemned man. I followed him, staying a few steps behind.

The driveway of the big house was full of black-and-white patrol cars. Police officers stood leaning against them in small groups, speaking in hushed voices. A pair of plainclothesmen recognized Miguel as the husband and took him aside, told him that they had just received a radio call from the helicopter confirming that his wife was dead. Miguel bobbed his head and stared at the rosebushes behind the police. He left me standing with them and marched toward the house, mumbling, "Where's Rebecca? Where's Rebecca?"

Two detectives escorted me across a manicured lawn to the guest cottage. We sat in the cramped living room on the heavy oak furniture with the light streaming through the lace curtains. They asked me questions, and I answered as best I could. In my running shorts and T-shirt I felt exposed.

The older detective, who did most of the talking at first, had a kind face and a polite manner. "Do you run every day?" he asked.

"About four or five times a week."

"Must get cold out there by the ocean."

"You get used to it."

The other detective, a young woman, looked at me with distrust, assessing me with her dark eyes. She nodded at my answers, but they were not what she wanted to hear. She fiddled with an engagement ring on her finger, turning it round and round, waiting her turn.

At a brief lull in the conversation, she jumped in. "The little girl referred to you as Tio Jorge." From her pronunciation I could tell she spoke Spanish. "Are you her uncle?"

"Not really. I'm a friend of the family." I chose my words carefully. "I've known Miguel since before he got married."

She stood up and made a dismissive cluck. She walked around behind me and peered into the bedroom.

"Going somewhere?" she said, pointing to my packed suitcases.

"Back home. I had planned to leave after my run."

"Where's home?"

"Mexico."

"You're not Mexican?" she said sourly. I had a feeling she might be and didn't like the idea of me being one of her people.

"I'm American, but have lived down there for ten years."

"I'm afraid you'll have to postpone your trip. We might want to talk to you again."

"Oh, I see. Of course."

At the door the male detective pointed to my neck. "What happened there?"

I felt a tender spot just below the ear and then looked at my fingers, but there was no blood. "A low-hanging branch on the trail. I wasn't paying attention."

"You might have someone take a look at it."

I stood under the hot water of the shower for a long time, but couldn't get the chill out of my bones. The day had begun with a feeling of hopelessness. Miguel had nothing to say to me since the previous afternoon when Helen opened the door of the cottage bedroom and found us sprawled naked on the bed, sharing a cigarette. It had left him split in half, unsure of each step, each breath, afraid to speak. I wondered if he still wanted me in his life, though I couldn't imagine not having him in mine. From the day he first showed up at my door in Mexico looking for work, he took me out of my selfish life and made me care about somebody else.

And then he had come to the States and married Helen. I had often fantasized that she would disappear. Now that it had happened, I realized that my chances of having a life with Miguel were diminished instead of improved. An hour earlier, when Miguel had grasped what had happened to Helen, I saw the fear in his eyes, a virus capable of destroying everything. Even after the tragedy of death and suffering had run its course, Miguel would remain crippled. He needed Helen on one side like he needed me on the other to keep him propped up.

I sat on the unmade bed and pulled on my socks. Though I couldn't leave town, I would have to move out of the cottage. My relationship with Helen's family would certainly become more difficult. I was tolerated as Miguel's friend and the person who had sent him to the United States to be educated at Berkeley where he met Helen. When the family was at the summerhouse and I was in town, they invited me to stay in the cottage. Now I needed to put myself at a distance, give Miguel the freedom to devote himself to Rebecca. I, too, loved Rebecca, as if she were my own, and felt deeply for her at an age not quite able to understand death, but certainly old enough to suffer the loss of her mother.

I went into the kitchen and began to search on my laptop for a hotel nearby. There was a knock on the door, and I saw two shadows behind the back-door shade. The detectives were back.

"Mr. Edwards, we would like you to come with us to the station," the woman said. She fiddled again with her ring.

I stared at her, trying to pull back the inane grin on my face. "I told you everything."

"Everything? There is a witness, said you two struggled." She barely covered a gloating smile.

"Witness? There was nobody there."

"We'll continue this down at the station," the male detective said.

I turned to him for a bit of sympathy, confirmation that it was just a formality, but he avoided my eyes. I would have to go along with them until the misunderstanding was cleared up. He took a firm grip on my arm.

I wasn't worried until I stepped out of the house and saw Miguel, who stood outside in the yard, his arms hanging like lead pipes at his sides. He looked as if he had joined the ranks of those who had already found me guilty. Behind him Rebecca burst from the big house and came running across the lawn. "Papi, I can't find Mommy." Miguel grabbed her and held her in his arms. She put her little fists to her eyes and rubbed away the tears. She looked up and saw me being led away. "Tio, where are you going?" she shouted.

"Miguel," I said. "You know it was an accident, right?"

He bowed his eyes and kissed his daughter on the top of her head.

I called out again. "Miguel. It was an accident. Miguel?"

"Watch your head," said the detective as he folded me into the car.

"What accident?" said Rebecca. She struggled to get free from his arms. "Papi, you're hurting me."

# 2: Rebecca

My graduation day from Stanford was a scorcher, not a day to be wearing a black gown for hours in the sun. Julia, my best friend, and I stood outside the stadium watching our fellow graduates begin to parade in through the arched entrance to Foster Field. We were waiting for our families to arrive before going in.

A giant dragon's head emerged from the crowd and thrust its shiny red tongue and sharp teeth in our faces. We screamed like schoolgirls in a haunted house, and she grabbed my arm as we danced away from the head that moved from side to side, the gold of its trim flashing in the June sun. The shimmering red and yellow fabric of its long body twisted and turned like a drunk serpent as the dancers under the canopy jerked first one way, then the other.

"Is this great or what?" Julia shouted over the clanging of cymbals and beating drums.

They called it Wacky Walk, and it was Stanford University's peculiar antidote to the boredom of conventional graduation ceremonies. It started as something of a protest, I was told, well before I got to Stanford, but had developed into a tradition, if you can call total bedlam a tradition. Most grads participated in some way, wearing bizarre costumes, carrying signs, and putting together props around fanciful themes. Julia had left me in charge of coming up with our graduation theme while she went off to Hawaii on a quick celebratory trip with her boyfriend after her last final. Since she came back with the glow of someone who had had lots of sex on an exotic island, she wasn't too upset that I had failed my mission. We threw the leis she brought back around our necks and put on rhinestone sunglasses. It was a little pathetic, but better than nothing.

"Hardly seems like graduation," I said.

"The thing is, Rebecca, we made it. We're free."

"Free? I'll be back here in a few months to start law school."

She turned to me, flashed a smile of brilliant white, and put her index finger in the middle of my forehead. "That's in a few months. This is now. Give the ol' noodle a rest."

Still holding on to my arm, she tried to pull me closer to the marchers just as a group of sheiks in graduation black came into view, their heads clad in the red-and-white *gutras* and black *agals* of Arab headdress. They sported aviator sunglasses and one lugged a boom box on his shoulder, blasting "Rock the Casbah" by the Clash.

"Rockin' the Casbah. Rock the Casbah," Julia sang. "Come on, Becca."

I repeated the chorus, though it seemed lame.

Julia stopped her bouncing, leaned close, and shouted in my ear. "Who's that?"

"Who?" I asked.

"That man over there." I followed her gaze across a group of people carrying balloons in Stanford's school color, cardinal red.

"I don't see anybody." I was distracted by a gigantic helium whale floating above the sea of balloons, a knowing smile plastered on its plastic face.

"Over there. He's staring at us."

"What are you talking about?"

"Look."

The crowd parted slightly and I saw him—a tall thin man in his fifties, slightly hunched over in an ill-fitting suit. He *was* staring, and seemed to be focused on me. The intensity of his stare made me shudder. I tried to ignore him and looked away, but my eyes were drawn back to him. At second glance it was not the stare of a rude person, but the faraway gaze of someone carrying the weight of the past. And then the tiny squares of recognition clicked into place. He was the man in one of the photographs that I kept on my bedside table, a friend of my father's who used to come and visit us. An old pain began in my gut and rose up into my chest.

"Wait here," I said.

"Where are you going?"

I dove into the middle of a marching brass band playing a discordant tune. The men had transformed their graduation robes into togas, and some had pushed them all the way down around their waists like skirts. I tried to ease past a saxophone player and felt my hand damp with sweat from his naked torso. I was halfway through to the other side. Just a few yards away I could see the stranger's blue eyes. Could it be him?

A dancing panda with a conductor's baton blocked my way, tried to take my hand, and pull me into a dance. Out of the corner of my eye, I saw the man moving off. I batted away the panda's paw and screamed, "No, wait! Tio Jorge!"

"No, wait! Tio Jorge!" echoed the panda in a mocking shrill voice, still dancing in my path.

I ducked under his arm and stumbled from the mob. The man was gone. I looked in both directions. He couldn't be far. I had to find him. Groups of parents and families milled about with doubtful grins as they watched the festivities. I scanned every face, every form. He had disappeared. Across the lawn I saw a tall blond man in the same wan-colored suit lean over to hug a girl with pink boa draped over her graduation gown. I ran toward him with my robe flying and my heeled sandals catching on tufts of grass. I lost my balance and fell into him, grabbing his arm. He spun around with a startled look.

"I'm so sorry," I said as I looked into the face of a much younger man. "I tripped."

"No problem at all," he said. He put his hand on mine and winked.

I retrieved my hand and smiled as I backed away. "Sorry, really. Enjoy your day."

The young man took a step as if to follow me, and I turned, scurried back to where I had left Julia, my eyes still sweeping the crowd for the shadow from the past. After several circles of the area, I was out of breath and sweating under the cap and gown, but I couldn't find Julia. I stood lost and confused, the clamor around me seeming to get louder and louder. Nearby a group of drummers with snare, bass, and conga drums beat a furious rhythm that made me feel that my head was about to explode.

I took hold of the lei around my neck, brought it up to my nose, and smelled its tropical sweetness. The edges of the plumeria flowers were browning, and I felt I should get out of the sun. I spotted some shade under an old cypress tree, but halfway there Julia and I caught sight of each other. She stood with a conservatively dressed older couple that I guessed were her parents. Though I had heard a lot about them, we had never met, and I was surprised how reserved they were, dull bookends to Julia's shining presence.

"Rebecca, over here. I want you to meet my parents."

I reached up to steady my cap, which had come loose from all my running, and lifted up the slick material of the gown as I walked toward them. Julia took a step to meet me.

"I've been looking for you," I said out the side of my mouth.

"Did you find him?" she whispered.

"No. I'll tell you later." I didn't want to say much with her parents waiting to be introduced.

"Becca, this is my mom and dad. *Papi, mami, les presento a mi amiga,* Rebecca Delon. You've heard me talk about her."

Being with Julia again had calmed me down, but when I heard her call her father Papi, it was another stab from the past. It was what I used to call my father when I was little. I stuck out a cool, clammy hand to them and each shook it tenuously as if it were a crab's claw. Their eyes darted from me to Julia. They sensed something was wrong. I felt my face going pale, and it seemed that my heart had ceased pumping.

"Becca, are you all right?" Julia said.

"I...I'm sorry. Just feeling a little faint, the sun, the pressure of the last few weeks."

"There's a bench over there. Why don't we sit down?"

Julia walked me to the bench under the cypress. "What's going on? Do you know that guy?"

"It looked like a friend of my father's, much older of course. I haven't seen him since I was a little girl. We used to call him Tio Jorge."

"You couldn't find him?" Julia said.

"He ran away."

"Why would he do that?'

"He was the man accused of my mother's death."

Julia gasped. "But I thought she died in a traffic accident or something."

"Not exactly. I never told anybody what really happened. Well, didn't know myself for a long time. That's all I can say now."

"Jesus, I'm glad you didn't find him."

"I don't think he's dangerous. It's complicated."

"You're sure it was him?"

"You know the pictures on my beside table? There's one of me as a little girl, standing between my father and another man, holding both their hands. The man I saw earlier had the same eyes, the same thin, blond hair and long face as my father's friend."

Julia shook her head in disbelief and I felt bad for never telling her, my best friend, the true story, or at least as much of it as I knew. I had left the circumstances of how

I had been raised by my grandparents vague, saying that my father had gone back to Mexico after mother died.

Before he left, he gave Conchita a few photos and told her to keep them for me. When I got older she showed them to me, and told me I could come in her room anytime to look at them, but I had to keep it a secret from Gran. Conchita and I had looked at the picture of Papi, Tio Jorge, and me many times. Later, when I started at Stanford she gave me the photos to keep.

Also next to my bed I had a formal portrait of my mother that showed her great beauty. Papi, Tio Jorge and my mother ruled over the early, happy years of my childhood. All three were taken from me when I was five— my mother by death, my father by sadness, and Tio Jorge by the police.

"What should we do?" Julia said.

"Nothing. Go back to your family."

"I'm not going to leave you alone with some madman running around. I think we should tell the campus police."

"Jules, really. I'm okay. My grandparents are on their way." My phone vibrated and I pulled it out from under my robe. "It's probably them right now."

"I'll be close by if you need anything," she said.

"We're here." Gran's voice boomed. She always thought you had to shout when you talked on a cell phone. "Sorry we're late. Jimmy stayed out all night, probably with one of his girlfriends." She drew out the last word as if she were admonishing him, but finished the phrase with a lilt in her voice showing she could never really be mad at her darling boy. "He arrived home late this morning a mess, unshaven and hung over."

"Are you surprised?"

"You would think on your graduation day he could at least—"

"Let's go, Margaret," I heard Granddad growl in the background.

"I'll meet you at the entrance," I said. "It's almost time for us to go in."

I sat a few more minutes on the bench, watching Julia with her parents. She constantly had an arm enlaced with one of them, or they were hugging, laughing, touching in some way. Every few minutes she glanced over to check on me. Julia was beautiful with her pale skin, reddish-blond hair and green eyes. She had been a prom queen back in Arizona where she grew up, and looked the part. No one would suspect that she had been born into an old but modest Mexican family from Monterey. I, on the other hand, was Mexican only on my father's side. I had his dark hair, brown eyes, and cinnamon skin.

When Julia and I went out to our favorite Mexican or Salvadorian restaurants, the waitperson would always speak to me in Spanish, and I would switch the conversation to English. To their surprise Julia would order in perfect Spanish. I sometimes joked that Julia and I had been switched at birth. She was a scholarship student. Her father was a plumber. I grew up on an exclusive cul-de-sac in Hillsborough.  My mother's family were all blond and blue-eyed, and at family gatherings I got tired of being the lone oak in a stand of beech trees. It was the same at school. So when I started high school at Crystal Springs Uplands, of which Patty Hearst was the most notable alumnus, I convinced Gran to let me dye my hair blond.

Still, other kids called me a beaner. It must have been a great blow to my grandparents—on top of losing their daughter—that they had to raise a granddaughter who looked so little like her. They would always tell me I had her delicate nose and thin lips, her svelte figure, avoiding any mention of my hair, eyes and skin.

I got up and walked to the stadium entrance. I wasn't looking forward to the drama that always found us on the rare occasions that Jimmy, my grandparents, and I got together. But they were what I had in lieu of a real family.

"Oh, Papi," I sighed. At important times in my life, I managed to put aside my anger at my father and wished he were with me. He would have made everything all right. After my mother's death and Tio Jorge's trial, the court granted my grandparents custody. Not long after that, my father went back to Mexico, never to return.

From a distance I saw them arrive, Granddad out front, rolling along like a bulldozer, and Gran on Jimmy's arm, lagging a little behind. I gave my grandparents airy hugs and turned to face Jimmy. He was my mother's younger brother and only eleven years older than me. Since we grew up in the same house, he seemed more like a brother than an uncle. And he more than fulfilled the older-brother role of being my tormentor.

"Love your outfit," said Jimmy, letting his eyes go from my cap down to my shoes.

"Thanks. Just hope no one shows up in the same one."

"I see you got lei-ed. What is that, Hawaiian safe sex? "

"Very safe. You might try it."

"Always safe, but I like to live a little. *You* might try it."

"You two." Gran moaned and shook her head.

Jimmy's blond hair shone in the sun, and his blue eyes sparkled with mischief. He had inherited the first-rate genes of the family that allowed him, in spite of his debauchery and lack of exercise, to be at thirty-two still boyishly handsome and in good shape. His charmed life also granted him a high-paying position in Granddad's firm where he spent as little time as he could.

"How about a hug for your uncle?" Jimmy said.

He leaned in to embrace me, and I backed up a step, making it an awkward half-hug. I still had a hard time being near him without remembering the night I woke up and found him hovering over my bed with a frightening leer. I was fifteen. I was groggy, just coming out of a dream, and he slurred his words. But I heard enough to know that he was saying something about my mother, a summer at the beach house. "You really believe she was killed in a traffic accident? Don't you wanna know the truth?"

I was petrified, but desperate to hear what he had to say. Granddad cut him off. He was a hound dog who could always sense when something was amiss. He came into my room, grabbed Jimmy by the collar, and dragged him out into the hall. I rolled my body up into a ball in the corner of my bed and listened through the closed door as Granddad threw him from wall to wall. Gran interceded to defend her only remaining child, saying he was confused. Drunk was more like it. I couldn't sleep the rest of the night, rattled by the question he had put in my head. All of my inquiries about my mother's death had always been quickly cut off. Was Jimmy just being evil or telling me something I needed to know?

"Most of the people have gone in." Gran said. "You'd better go, dear. We'll have a nice meal afterwards."

"And we've got something special for you," Granddad said. He was in a rare jovial mood, which seemed to happen when he was about to bestow another lavish gift upon me. There had been the pure-bred Afghan puppy when I was eight, the six hundred dollar bicycle when I was eleven, the diamond necklace when I was sixteen. The gifts always embarrassed me, though I tried not to seem ungrateful.

The one gift that I truly appreciated was the chance to go to Stanford. In the fall I would be returning to Stanford Law for another few years of torture, the kind of torture that many people would kill for. It wasn't greed or power or even social justice that pushed me. It was the conviction, ever since I had learned of the true circumstances of my mother's death, that something needed to be made right. Yet I had studied so hard the last couple of years, I had nearly lost sight of my long-term goal. Seeing Tio Jorge, at least thinking I saw him in the crowd, had shaken me out of my stupor and reminded me of my mission to fix the past.

Inside the stadium, the party atmosphere dwindled as we took our seats on the open field and steeled ourselves for the upcoming series of speeches. I panned the stadium one more time to try to spot him. In my constant search for information related to the case, I learned he had been released from prison. It had been nearly sixteen years since I had seen him. After all these years why would he show up at my graduation? How had he recognized me? I had the uneasy feeling that he was staring at me still from a lonely perch in the bleachers.

I saw Julia several rows in front of me stand up and crane her lovely long neck. When her eyes found me I made my best effort at a smile and waved. She still looked worried. Though the same age, she acted as my older sister, always looking out for me. She took out her phone and held it up. Then she sent me a text message: "Remember party 2nite."

She had taken on the monumental task of ensuring I had a social life. On weekends she would pry me from my books, drag me to a party, put a beer in my hand, and take me around to meet her friends. Several times she set me up with blind dates, shy ones that made me resort to counting the minutes until they took me home and suave ones that had a look in their eyes that they were going to bed me by the end of the night. They never did. Julia gave up on the blind dates project, and her increasing involvement with her boyfriend cut down the party invitations. Fine with me. I never enjoyed parties much.

As the speeches began, a balloon popped nearby and someone blew a single note on a trumpet. People laughed and then quieted down. I stared without interest toward the distant podium where small people gave long speeches. A fellow graduate wearing a cowboy hat was partially blocking my view. He removed the hat to wipe his forehead with a bandana, and then turned in profile. I slumped down in my seat and put my hand over my face. The man in front of me was Stuart Walters, a football player I had dated and lost my virginity to in high school. The girls at Crystal Springs Uplands had labeled our classmates as touchables and untouchables. I was desperate to be a touchable and when Stuart asked me out, I jumped at the chance. After he dumped me, I overheard him say to his friends at a party, "Don't let that blond hair fool you, man. She's not blond down there. She's a hot Latin bitch. When we're fucking, she screams, *"Más, más, más."*

I withdrew myself from the dating scene, and stopped dyeing my hair. But my mind was still full of childish notions and fears. The incidents with Jimmy, and later Stuart, made me determined to know who I was, where I had come from. On a winter rainy day in my junior year of high school, I went into Conchita's warm kitchen with the intention of blackmailing her into telling me my past. The grandparents had forbidden her to tell me anything about my early years and especially the circumstances around my mother's death. They also had forbidden her to speak Spanish to me.

Conchita looked at my hair and shook her head. It was a mess. The dark roots were growing out and the ends were a tangle of orangey-blond.

"What we do wit you hair, *hija,* make you pretty, huh?" she said.

I ignored her question and told her that if she didn't tell me what happened that summer at the beach when my family was destroyed, I was going to blurt out all the Spanish I knew at the dinner table, which at that time was about ten words. I told her I would say she had been teaching me all along.

Conchita put on a good show. "Why you make me say, *hija*? I can't. I can't." The truth was that she was dying to tell me, and I didn't feel completely cruel for twisting her arm. Still, she had been the only source of genuine love in that house and had embraced me as a daughter. I didn't want to put her on the spot. But I had to know.

"I remember weekend your mother come home from university, what called?"

"Berkeley."

"Beerk-lee, yes. She tell me she meet her future husband. 'His name Miguel and he from Mexico, like you,' she say. I tell her, 'O, por dios, hija, forget about it. You marry a Mexican, are you kidding?' For your grandparents we Mexicans belong in the kitchen or the garden. Period. But Helen is so sure, and I think she like idea of shocking her father. She and *el señor* both got the bad tempers. Your mother is stubborn like a *burro*. She want that boy and she gonna get him one way or other. As turn out, it be the other. She got pregnant." She chuckled and pounded the chicken breast filets with a flat-headed meat tenderizer. Then she was distracted by the sound of a car out on the road, and we both looked out the window in fear that it might be Gran coming home. The car went on.

"They good Catholics, abortion is no good. It a fast wedding and *la señora,* your grandmother, so furious, but she have go along wit it. To make more soft Mexican thing, Miguel say he from old Mexican Family. He have everyone fool but me. I know right away he is *campesino*, and when Tío Jorge come around, I know where he learn all his manners. Miguel so handsome and such a gentleman he impress lot a people, but for your grandparents, he still a Mexican even if he descend from Emperor Maximilian like he say. No, he no fool me for one minute, but I love him anyway." The chicken breasts were paper thin, and she stopped to look at them. "Oh, dear." She peeled one off the granite counter, held it up to the light, and then dredged it in seasoned flour.

"When wedding come, Miguel say his parents no can attend because his father bery sick. Tio Jorge represent of the family."

"Conchita, get to the part about that summer."

"I getting there, just give you little history. It is Fourth of July weekend and we all go down to Brookstone, that what they call house in Carmel. They sell it, don't want more after..." She stopped a moment and floured another breast, looking out the window. "Tio Jorge is up from Mexico for visit, so he go wit us. Everting okay but Helen and Tio Jorge very angry at dinner. He go out. It is next morning when it happen, when your mother leave us, poor soul."

"But what happened?"

"I don't know."

"Yes, you do. You were there."

"I am at the house, but who knows what happen out there on the cliff. After, there so much angry and sad, emotion. It is hard know what is what."

"Just tell me!" I screamed.

"I believe an accident. Your mother go off the cliff, poor dear. It is horrible. Tio Jorge is there, so they say he did it, that is murder. I no believe he can do that, but they have witness. He push her, they say."

"Who said?"

"The witness."

"Who was the witness?"

"I can't say."

"Damn it, Conchita. You can't hold back now."

"Don't make me. I don't even like a talk about it."

"Who was it?" I grabbed her arm and shook it hard. I think it scared her.

"Jimmy. It is Jimmy say that. Please, please, *hija*, don't tell *la señora* I tell you."

In her eyes I could see she didn't believe Jimmy. That was enough for me. I knew lying came easy to him, more so then, when he was just a teenager. With the revelation that Tio Jorge had been accused of killing my mother and that Jimmy had been the star witness, my life changed, not outwardly much, but inside my future was simmering like one of Conchita's slow-cooking stews. I studied harder than ever and gave up any semblance of a social life.

For a couple of years Conchita and I were mostly alone in the house. Granddad spent a lot of time working and Gran was busy with her civic luncheons and social events. Jimmy had moved in with a decent, but rather thick-brained rich girl from the neighborhood. Conchita and I became even closer than before. I started studying Spanish in secret and Conchita would help me practice. In her kitchen she would teach me the names of food and cooking utensils. I would also try out phrases I had learned in my books. Sometimes she would look at me as if she had no idea what I was saying. Other times she would laugh and laugh, and I would get so angry I would storm out of the room. She would call me back, apologizing and reminding me how bad her English was after twenty years in the States. "You doin' good, *hija*. I so proud of you." Then she would envelop me in her arms against her motherly breasts.

I got into Stanford and even though it was less than an hour's drive from home I insisted on living on campus. I was happy to get out of the monster house on Ashton lane, built to impress, not to live in. But I missed Conchita and would take my laundry home every week because no one knew how to wash clothes the way she did. Junior year I moved into an apartment with Julia and Karen.

The speeches came to an end as the president declared us graduates with all the "rights, responsibilities, and privileges." As a single body we joined in and shouted the words along with him. Then the merrymaking erupted in full force, and I went to find my grandparents. I knew they would be anxious to get away and go to lunch.

At the restaurant, Granddad stood up after his second martini, and gave a little speech. He fumbled in his pocket and pulled out a set of keys. He held them in the air like a solemn offering and explained that they were to a new silver BMW for the lawyer-to-be in the family, the granddaughter he was so proud of, Rebecca. I looked across the table at Jimmy and saw, in his steely blue gaze, the message that I was a lowly Mexican who didn't deserve to be part of the family.

Granddad put the keys in my hand, and then sat down with a heavy thump on the chair. I smiled and thanked him, but it felt false. Tio Jorge was on my mind, and beneath my smile was a seething anger at what they had done to him. I had no proof yet, but I was sure they had been instrumental in putting an innocent man behind bars. I couldn't wait to get out of the restaurant and meet up with Julia. I was afraid she had a bad impression of Tio Jorge and I wanted to explain.

## 3: George

There was a stillness to the fog-dampened streets of Horizons Mobile Home Park that seemed at odds with the chatter of birds high in the surrounding trees. It was a Northern California mobile-home park, and yes, we had trees, and bushes and flowers and even a creek running through it. But it was still a trailer park, which was tangibly obvious as I stepped out my front door and examined my single-wide of fiberglass and plastic. It had been a night of late May gusty winds, and I had awakened several times wondering if my roof was going to fly off. The downpours of the past winter had taken their toll with leaks causing the yellowing insulation to puff up and peek out through the cracks. And with the rains, flooding was always a danger, and I often pictured my home floating down to the river and out to sea, a romantic way to end it all.

I pushed one of the siding panels, where the cellulose was poking out, back in place and headed down the steps. I looked up and down the street with the hope that it was still early enough to take a walk around the park without running into any of my neighbors. They weren't a bad lot, retired people mostly, or like me retired from life, hiding out behind Levolor blinds and gingham curtains. On occasion a neighbor would introduce himself and two seconds later I would forget the name. I said my name was Simon. Tio Jorge was dead. I had no past.

My walk along Sunset Drive took me to the newer part of the park where people had double and even triple-wides. Through the open blinds of one window I saw a kitchen bathed in florescent light and I could hear the drone of talk radio. In another I saw a television flicker with the image of a bumbling president resonating the perfect pitch of mediocrity. But who was I to criticize? I was an ex-con. I had served seven of ten for manslaughter. I had been accused of pushing my dear friend's wife off a cliff to her death. In a fit of homosexual rage, the prosecuting attorney had repeated over and over, I had eliminated the competition. But because I was a model prisoner, I was let out.

It had been eight years since I got out, and I had substituted one kind of prison for another. I restricted my movements, ate on a firm schedule, allowed myself limited contact with the people around me, and locked myself in at night. When I left the large metal gates of the prison, I carried with me the habits of inmate life, yet unlike many of my fellow convicts I had options. I had money. Though I could afford better living conditions, I chose the mobile home park because I thought it would be a place where I could live in obscurity, a temporary situation until I regained enough self-respect to crawl out of my hole. But then inertia set in and the years passed. Now it was 2007. I could not account for where the time had gone. I was still adjusting.

Jim, my cellmate from prison, called the other night and said he had gotten out. He wanted to come and visit. I wished I had never answered the phone. I didn't want to be reminded of those days. Survival in jail, I had read in a pamphlet from the inmate library near the beginning of my term, was a matter of sheer will or dumb luck, sometimes a combination of the two. Since I had very little will to live after being sent to prison, my survival was more dumb luck. Jim was a yoga teacher, a teacher whose years of yoga practice and spiritual exercises failed him in the moment of truth. When a yoga seminar got cancelled, he came home and found his wife in bed with another guy. He went out to the shed and got a shotgun he had inherited from his father. Just the week before he had promised his wife he would get rid of it. It wasn't until he saw the blood on the living room wall that he realized what he had done. He said he didn't remember any of it—getting the gun, the shouts, the firing...just the blood.

But yoga helped Jim survive prison, and he convinced me to try it. I had been a jogger before, a daily ritual that ended that day on a cliff above the ocean in Carmel, the day that I was accused of ending Helen's life. The energy I used to expend through running was then balled up inside me. Jim showed me how I could release it. At first yoga seemed to do nothing, and with the awkward positions I felt foolish. My depression would quickly sap my desire to continue. But Jim had decided that he was going to save me, at times physically dragging me out of my bunk and compelling me to practice. After a couple of weeks I noticed that I wasn't angry all the time, that I could ignore the hard eyes of the inmates around me. Perhaps the greatest release was that I stopped dwelling in the past. I took each minute as it came, trying to look forward as much as possible, even if it was a looking forward to the next few minutes, hours, days. To think about any distant future would send me back into depression.

The authorities took me off suicide watch and gave me a job. Since I had computer skills, they trained me to do cold-calling to convince people to change their phone company. I hated it and wasn't much good at it. I would be amazed when someone would actually listen to my script, probably out of boredom or loneliness, and even more amazed when they would agree to switch. They were then transferred to someone on the outside as we weren't allowed to take their personal data. Several times people would delay the transfer, trying to keep me on the line. More than once a woman told me I didn't sound like the typical telemarketer and asked me for a date.

People began to emerge from their trailers, and I picked up my speed to return home. Jim said that he would stop by around noon. I needed to do my yoga and hoped to work a little more on a translation before he came.

On the living room floor I went straight into the *Bhujangasana* or Cobra Pose, and though distracted, managed to get through a short session before sitting down at my desk. With my knowledge of Spanish, and the Portuguese I had learned in prison, I got work doing translations. It was work I could do from home and I didn't have to answer the question on the job application if I had ever been arrested. On the screen in front of me was a proposal in Portuguese submitted by a Brazilian businessman. I tried to make sense of it, though it remained a blur.

I hadn't had a single visitor since I moved in. I looked around my cramped living room and wondered what Jim would think of the way I lived. It was an odd feeling since it had been so long that I cared what people thought. Jim and I were close in the way that people confined together become close. We never became lovers. It was a bridge he couldn't cross, but he respected my proclivities, knew most everything about me. In prison, I hadn't wanted to talk about my past, but we had to talk about something, and our histories had crept out little by little. We had spoken at length about our respective cases and I told him things that I later regretted. I got up from my desk and stood stupidly gazing out the window, dreading a visit from someone who knew so much about me.

Jim pulled up in a PT Cruiser, and I watched him saunter to the door from my kitchen window. Though still in good shape, his hair had turned almost completely gray. He wore it tied back in a ponytail. I opened the door and we hugged, something we had never done in prison. I poured coffee into the two mugs that I owned and we sat down in the two folding chairs at the little table wedged between the kitchen space and the living room space.

"I saw my ex wife," he began. "She remarried, but divorced again."

"And?"

"I don't know. She was...you know, open. I told her I needed to travel around a bit, stretch my limbs, but would keep in touch. I got one of those damn cell phones." He pulled it out like a kid with a new toy. "You can even take pictures and shit. I hold it out like this and take pictures of me in the Painted Desert or with the Golden Gate Bridge in the background. I send them to her right on the phone. Then she calls and we talk."

"How did you find me?"

"Remember? You sent me a postcard after you moved in here. I doubted you would still be here, but I called up the management company, and they gave me your number. Still doing yoga?"

"Every day. It's funny. My daily schedule isn't that different from when we were inside."

"That's your choice though. You've got options."

"True."

Jim set his mug with a definitive motion on the table and let his eyes skip over my meager surroundings. His eyes swept back and locked in on mine.

"No love in your life?"

"Oh, come on, Jim." I looked down into my empty coffee cup.

"Come on, what? I know you loved that guy, the Mexican, but you have to move on. What was the name of that one on block D? Ramon. He really had the hots for you."

Ramon was a Brazilian who taught me Portuguese. Despite his rough exterior he had a tender side and the disconcerting notion all Brazilians seem born with, that sex is good. He would even mumble sometimes in our furtive encounters that he loved me.

"I'd rather not talk about things that happened there."

"Sure, whatever. My point is that guys like you. You're an attractive man. You shouldn't be alone."

"Well, I am." I got up and went into the kitchen to get more coffee. The conversation was getting too close.

"All right. I just want the best for you, man. Have you had any contact with the girl, his daughter?"

The cup slipped out of my hand and crashed on the floor, sending a splash of brown over the cracked linoleum. "Shit!"

He rushed into kitchen. "I'm sorry, man. I seem to be upsetting you. Maybe I should go."

"Maybe you should."

"Here, let me help you." He grabbed some paper towel and crouched down to wipe up the floor.

I leaned against the counter and took a couple of deep yoga breaths. "No, I haven't contacted her."

He hesitated a moment with the soggy towel in his hand and a knowing grin on his face. I pointed to the cabinet under the sink.

"Do you know where she is?"

"Stanford."

"See, I knew it. You've been following her."

"She'll graduate in a couple of weeks."

"You should go to her graduation."

"And do what? Say, 'Hi, remember me? I'm the man accused of killing your mother.'"

"It's all about putting the devils of the past to rest. That's what I've been doing. People have surprised me. Look at my ex. You'd think she'd never want to see me again."

"How do you feel about her?"

"You mean, do I forgive her for cheating on me? I guess so. It was a long time ago. I'm trying. What I never told you is that the guy was my best friend."

After Jim left, I couldn't stop thinking about what he said. I really had no intention of showing up at Rebecca's graduation, but the idea got stuck in the back of my head. She was the one person on the planet that I wanted to see happy and well. As Jim had surmised, I had been cyberstalking her, amazed how much information I had gotten from the Internet, finding her on high school and college websites. But the idea of seeing her in person had been unthinkable, even if I kept my distance.

That night I lay awake for a long time with Rebecca on my mind. And then I fell into one of the recurring dreams that crept into my nights the way my cat came in and out of the house, passing through the cat door, without a warning, without a schedule. I dreamt of a woman on a cliff, whose face morphed into Miguel's. He was falling. I reached out to catch him, but it was too late. In another I was pushing through the branches of an overgrown trail on my land in Mexico. I saw Miguel ahead of me and I called out to him. He didn't answer. He was moving faster than me and I couldn't catch up to him. He disappeared into the jungle, the large green leaves of the elephant ear plants closing in around him, swallowing him up.

I woke up and threw on sweatpants and a sweatshirt. I went outside and looked at my worn-down trailer to bring me back to the harsh reality of my life. I walked around it, touched it, felt its artificial skin. And when I returned to my somber existence, I was reminded of the luxury of being able to go outside at 3:00 a.m. It was so quiet I could hear

the river on its way to the sea. A black cat crossed my path.
I smiled because it was mine. I didn't have to spit to
counter the bad luck the way Miguel had taught me. She
rubbed against my leg and I picked her up, cradled her
delicate bones and soft fur in my arms, nuzzled my face in
the back of her neck. When I headed for the door to go back
inside, she jumped from my arms, not ready to be closed in,
content to prowl the exotic regions of Horizons Mobile
Home Park. What if I did go to the graduation, just to see?

# 4: Rebecca

I woke up with a pounding headache and vague memories of kissing a man I had just met. Julia and a few friends had taken me out for my twenty-first birthday to a Peruvian restaurant in San Francisco, and then to a club. The night of dancing at a South of Market disco followed upon a string of graduation parties, a couple weeks of debauchery that I hadn't allowed myself since high school. I was a Stanford graduate now. I was supposed to be an adult. My partying was pure avoidance of the future.

Julia got me away from the man and dragged me off the dance floor.

"When I told you at graduation to let go, I didn't mean that you should turn into a slut. That guy is way below standard."

I stared at her with blurry eyes and a cloudy head. "An untouchable?"

"What?"

"Never mind. Take me home."

At the kitchen table with the cruel morning sun slicing across it, I poured some coffee and sat down. Julia and Karen had somehow managed to get up and go to work, and on top of my headache I felt guilty for being a slacker for the summer. There was a pile of mail on the table and I shuffled through it, coming across a birthday card from Conchita. It was in Spanish, a flowing message of tiresome platitudes with religious overtones, but I loved it because I knew she would never, ever forget my birthday, June 21, the day, she always said, that the sun stayed out extra long to see me being born.

There was also a formal letter from a lawyer named Patricia Mendez. I opened it with the silly notion that someone was suing me for something I did in my recent bout of bad behavior. But when I read the short, business-like letter, I sobered up quickly. The words "from your father" and "come see me at your earliest convenience" jumped out at me.

A few days later a secretary ushered me into Patricia's office. Patricia was a petite, raven-haired woman with burning eyes and a masculine voice. She was dressed casually and gave the impression of a temp who was filling in, someone who didn't quite inhabit the formal space around her. The walls were lined with law books, and the heavy furniture anchored the room with a sense of foreboding.

"Your father instructed me to give you this envelope when you reached your twenty-first birthday," she said in a bored voice. "You may open it now, in case you have any questions."

I sat with the plain manila envelope in my trembling hands. "My father? You knew my father?"

"I only met him twice. At our initial interview and then a few months later when he was on his way to Mexico."

I turned the envelope over and over in my hands. Patricia sat watching me, a monogrammed silver letter-opener in her outstretched hand.

I slid the blade under the flap and opened it, shaking out a note with a key attached. In my father's neat hand the note said the key was to a safe-deposit box.

"Did he tell you why he was going back?" I asked.

"It was some time ago. I believe he said his father had fallen ill."

"Yes, that's what he told me, too. He took me to the zoo and we sat on our favorite bench, looking at the monkeys. He bought me a stuffed chimp and some ice cream. I asked him to take me with him, but he said he would be gone just a short time."

I stopped and looked at Patricia, who continued to stare. "Sorry. I'm sure you're not interested in my sad stories."

"Go on. What happened?"

"That was the last time I saw him. He said he'd call me on my birthday. I was not quite six years old."

"Did he call?

"Two months later on my birthday, I sat by the phone all day. Nothing. I kept picking up the phone to see if there was a dial tone. A few weeks later, I got a birthday card in Spanish. The envelope was smudged and looked like it had traveled around the world. There was no return address for me to write him back."

Now, instead of staring, she seemed to be studying me. Her expression had turned from flat to interested. I wasn't sure, but I thought I detected something like mist in her eyes. "I'm sorry," she said in a tone halfway between caring and reserve.

"When he came to see you, was he...uh...sober?" I asked.

"I don't remember. Why?"

"I once heard my grandmother refer to him as a drunk, and I remember that something happened one day when he came to get me. My grandparents had custody, but he had me on Saturdays. That day he showed up acting ridiculous and Gran refused to let me go with him. I didn't understand what was going on and threw a tantrum. Gran yelled for our maid to come and help get me under control. After that he started missing Saturdays. He would always call and say he was sorry. I used to love those Saturday visits. They are my only happy childhood memories after my mother died."

"I guess he was going through a tough time." She picked up her coffee mug imprinted with the seal of Georgetown University, looked into it, and made a face. She set it back down. I could smell the remnants of coffee and I craved a cup myself.

"When were you informed of his death?" I asked.

"About five or six years after he left, I got a small package and the safe-deposit box key with instructions. It must have been a year or two later that I got a call from someone who said he was Miguel's brother. He told me that Miguel had been killed in a car accident. I called your grandmother right away and told her. That must have been hard on you, losing another parent."

I let out a big sigh and looked at her diplomas in weighty ornate frames on the wall. Her law degree was from Georgetown and I wondered why she had come all the way to the Bay Area to practice. I felt her eyes on me again as if she expected more of a reaction.

"I'm not going to cry if that is what you're waiting for. I never have."

"That's your business."

"They say he was very good-looking."

She shrugged. "I suppose he was."

"Don't you think that's strange?"

"What?"

"That I never cried."

"How old were you when you heard?"

"It was the summer before starting high school. I was in teen identity hormone hell. I hated everybody. I hated my grandparents for being so cold. I hated my mother for dying. And I hated my father for abandoning me. When Gran told me the news, I didn't cry. I sneered at her and said, 'I guess you're happy now.' 'Rebecca, what a terrible thing to say,' she said. 'Your father and I didn't always see eye-to-eye, but I never wished him any ill will.' I didn't know then what I know now, or I would have let loose with a few choice words. I simply said, 'Whether you did or didn't, I could care less. None of it matters anymore.' I went to my room and locked the door. Then I ran to my bathroom and threw up. When I started school in the fall, I was a blond and so skinny they took me to the doctor. I don't know why I'm telling you all this stuff." There was something about the way she sat there so coolly and didn't say much that made me open up to her. She was also the only person I knew who had had recent contact with my father. It meant something that he had entrusted important things to her.

"I hope you don't still feel resentment against your father. He was a troubled man, but he loved you." Patricia spoke with complete conviction.

"How would you know?"

"Because you were all he talked about. We didn't have much communication, the visits and then a few phone calls, but it was always about you. He got this glimmer of hope in his voice when he talked about you."

"He could have written at least."

"I think you need to take a look at what's in that safe-deposit box." She picked up her mug, and then, again, realized it was empty. "Would you like some coffee?"

"Love some."

"I'll ask Mathilde to brew a fresh pot." She picked up the phone and ordered the coffee.

"Do you know anything about Tío Jorge?" I asked.

"Who?"

"George Edwards, the man accused of killing my mother."

"Isn't he still in prison?"

"I thought I saw him at my graduation."

"You didn't talk to him?"

"He disappeared before I had the chance. I want to find him."

She looked at me with a sidelong glance as if she thought I might want to do him harm. "I have no information on him."

"He didn't do it, you know. He was only guilty of falling head over heels for my father. Just like my mother. Just like everybody, except my grandparents, of course."

"You know about the case?"

"I got our maid, Conchita, to tell me what happened. After that, I read everything there was to read—newspaper articles, trial transcripts. I even tried to contact his worthless lawyer, but he moved away. Haven't been able to locate him."

"Why are you so sure he didn't do it?"

"There is a lot about the case that doesn't add up. It was based on a public argument George and my mother had the night before her death, and the testimony of one witness, my uncle Jimmy, who is about as reliable as a crack-head looking for his next fix. Why did you give up criminal law?"

"How do you know that?"

"I do my homework."

"Your homework? You researched me?" She tried to sound annoyed, but there was a light in her eyes that she was flattered.

"Uh-huh."

"I don't think I was cut out for criminal law. I was losing most of my cases."

"They were some pretty tough ones."

She looked at me sideways again, surprised that I would know that much detail.

"If I can find Tio Jorge, I want to reopen the case. Maybe you can help."

Mathilde brought the coffee and we chatted for another half hour, mostly about law school. But I was anxious to get to the safe-deposit box and excused myself as soon as I could.

I went straight from Patricia's office to the bank. After making my request and signing a form, I sat in a room that was a suited banker's perfect 68 degrees and stared at the stark gray metal of the box. I was the only occupant of the room. It was still, cut off from the world, a vacuum. My heart beat wildly and I felt a slight headache when I looked up at the particles of dust dancing in the ray of sunlight coming in through a high window. I shivered as I ran my hand over the cold box. I should have brought a sweater. Opening a safe-deposit box, I had always imagined, would be something thrilling, anticipating jewels, money, secret documents. In this box I hoped for something much more precious—a link to my past and an explanation to the question that had tormented me for years: Why had my father abandoned me?

But I had delayed long enough. I jammed the key into the lock and threw open the lid. The first thing I spotted was a packet of letters, each one marked "Return to Sender" in Gran's shaky cursive. They were all addressed to me, and the oldest ones had a return address in San Jose, the rest an address in Mexico. So he *had* written...a lot. The case against my grandparents for how much they had interfered in my relationship with my father had reached, with this physical evidence, an unforgivable level. I wanted to strangle Gran.

At the bottom of the box was a fat envelope with $2000 in cash. There was no note or anything written on the outside. I surmised that it was a nest egg for when he might return to the United States. I desperately wanted to

believe that he had intended to come back. The final
envelope was a small manila one that had "To my dearest
daughter, Rebecca" scrawled across it in his neat hand.
Inside it was a letter to me and a smaller envelope marked
"Tio Jorge."

I held the letter in my damp palms, debating whether
to read it right away or take it to a place less sterile. I
thought about going back to the apartment in Palo Alto.
Julia and Karen both worked odd hours. I didn't want to
run into one of them and have to explain my sadness. At
least in the confines of this chilly room, I would be alone.
Wanting to preserve the envelope as much as possible, I
took a nail file out of my purse and slipped it under the
seal.

*My Dearest Daughter,*

*As you are reading this, it means you have reached your
twenty-first birthday and I wish so much that I could be
there to celebrate it with you. When I decided to return to
Mexico, I never intended it to be forever. But as time went by,
I thought it best that you forget about me. Maybe your
grandmother was right to return all my letters. I made so
many mistakes in my life that I didn't want to make another
by ruining yours. I have stayed away and even stopped
writing, but not a day goes by that I don't think about you,
wonder how you are getting along. I have a spy in the house.
I don't know if Conchita ever told you, I told her not to, but I
call from time to time and she tells me how you are
developing into a beautiful young lady. She tells me you look
like me, which makes me happy, though I'm sure it drives
your grandparents crazy. She tells me about your successes*

in school and it is what has kept me alive through all the pain. I sometimes feel that my life is spinning out of control.

Let me talk to you a little about your mother. She was a beautiful woman with many talents. I'm sure you got your intelligence from her. I think what drove her to me was that she longed to escape from the Hillsborough high life. It is ironic you ended up there. I know it has been difficult for you. I am truly sorry. Like your mother, I wanted to escape from my upbringing in Mexico. I think that is what brought your mother and me together like fleeing souls that bump into each other in the night. That is not to say that we didn't love each other. We learned to love each other because of you. You gave me so much joy that it was impossible not to love the woman who brought you into the world. But the truth of the matter is that I don't think we would have stayed together had she not met her tragic death.

That brings me to Tio Jorge. I know that you have inherited your mother's curiosity and have possibly read something about the trial. Jorge was not the man portrayed in the trial. He is kind and gentle.In the early years I thought my feelings for him were out of gratitude for what he had done for me. But the day they took him away, I had a sense of separation that I had never experienced in my life, an overpowering sadness. That day I held you in my arms as you struggled, but I needed you to make me strong. I was so close to running after the car that took him away, to touch him one more time. I can say that now.

It was at his insistence that we denied our relationship at the trial, which we knew they would bring up to establish motive. He convinced me that the only chance I had to maintain custody of you was to deny at all costs what we *had. I felt I was betraying him and in the end where did it get us? Your grandparents were granted custody anyway.*

*With this letter, there is one for him. Please find him and give it to him. I must live with knowing that I did not fight for the two people I loved the most. It is what makes life at times unbearable. Sometimes I can't stand myself. It seems that I have caused nothing but pain to the people around me. I was cruel to my parents, abandoning them. You see I never felt I belonged in that family, in that town, in that life. I would go outside at night into the front yard, look up at the stars, and dream of being in a distant, beautiful place. Well, it happened, but look at the mess I made of it. The only good thing about returning here was that I learned to appreciate my parents, their hard work, and yes, love them in a way I hadn't before. My fear is that it is too late to repair all the damage.*

*I hope you find it in your heart to forgive me. My one happiness in life is knowing that you have grown up to be a fine young woman as Conchita tells me. I know it has been hard growing up the way you did, but don't make the same mistakes I have, chasing after illusions. Chase after happiness. Find people who make you happy. Do things that make you feel good. And if you find Tio Jorge one day, try to open his heart. He can be stubborn, but keep trying.*

*Mi vida, try to recapture the memories of our early days together and remember me that way. You must believe that I love you with all my heart.*

*Siempre,*

*Tu papá*

The sadness was a monster ripping at my insides. The tears that I had held back for so long rushed out and I began to sob so loudly that the attendant who had brought me the deposit box came running. He picked up a box of tissues from a table by the door and carried it over to me. "Can I get you anything?" he asked.

"No, thanks. I just need to be alone."

My tears were followed by an anger rising out of the same well. I wanted to throw the metal box against the wall, upend the table. It was all such a fucking waste, the years of hurt and pain, and not knowing. Sitting by the phone when you are six years old, waiting desperately for a father who doesn't call, causes permanent damage. By the time I heard about his death seven years later, it felt like the blood in my veins flowed like an icy river, that I couldn't or didn't want to feel anything. In my darkest moments, I had even imagined that my mother's death and my father's abandonment were somehow my fault.

Now I knew my separation from my father wasn't because he didn't want me. The tragedy, the cruelty of my grandparents, and his weakness for alcohol had stacked up against him. I wasn't completely letting him off the hook. I was still angry that he couldn't overcome those difficulties and find a way to be part of my life. At the same time I knew my love for him was a thing that had its roots deep in my soul, something I would feel every day for the rest of my life.

And with the strength I gained from his words, I had no choice but to pursue my mission to help exonerate Tio Jorge of the crime. To seek him out also had its selfish side.

I longed to be in the presence of someone who might help me better understand the mystery of my father.

# 5: George

The knock at the back door caused me to spill the overly full cup of tea I was carrying from the counter to the table. Visitors were rare, and more so in the middle of a rainstorm. I lived alone on a plot of land carved out of the Mexican jungle, miles from the nearest town. The only other people normally on the property were the workers, and they had been sent home when the rain became heavy in the early afternoon.

I opened the door and felt the cool dampness infused with the fragrance of tropical green. The sight of the young man at the door made me take a step back. He looked like a deranged scarecrow that had been left out in the rain. His head was unprotected from the shower that poured off the roof as he gripped his straw hat in his hands. His black hair was plastered to his skull, and his white shirt with pearl snaps clung to his bony' frame, transparent to the skin, revealing a tuft of dark chest hair. He raised his eyes and I had to stop myself, as I always did in such moments, from being propelled into a fantasized future of extreme bliss. They were soft, brown and earnest, with lashes of exaggerated length. How many times had I let myself be led down an empty road by that look? My hand trembled on the handle of the door.

"Miguel Santos Ramirez, at your service, *señor*. I have come to humbly request that you find it in your goodness to give me work." His absurdly formal Spanish had the curious effect of relaxing me, almost to the point of laughter.

And then a small voice escaped from behind the waterfall. "Me, too." I had been so taken with the young man's eyes I hadn't noticed that he wasn't alone. A boy's head, more big black eyes than anything, appeared from behind the man's right hip, water rolling from his small round chin.

Miguel cuffed the boy on top of his head. "With respect, Vitico. Address the man as *señor*. Sorry, *señor*. I present my little brother Victor. We call him Vitico."

Rain continued to come off the roof and fall in a steady stream on Miguel's head and then down over his high cheekbones. He remained steadfast, unflinching.

"Please, come out of the rain," I said.

The boy started to rush forward, but Miguel clamped his hand on Vitico's neck and held him. He looked down at his shoes. His jeans were relatively new but a couple of sizes too short, giving a clear view of the black, rounded-toe tie shoes of the kind the locals normally saved for Sunday mass. I felt sad that he had worn his good shoes, now soggy and caked with mud. "We couldn't, *señor*," he muttered.

"I insist. Look," I said, pointing at the floor. "It's already dirty. This time of year I don't worry about it."

I ushered them into the kitchen, but they stayed close to the wall, dripping onto the mat where my muddy boots had been hurriedly discarded, one toppled over on the other. Miguel looked at my boots as if he was bothered by the disorder. I picked up the vagrant boot and set it upright. It was so quiet I could hear droplets of water from their clothes hitting the rubber mat.

"Let me get you some towels."

"Oh, no, please. Don't trouble yourself, *señor*."

"No trouble at all."

When I came back with towels, Miguel had a firm grip on the back of Vitico's collar. I imagined Miguel to be in his late teens and Vitico about six or seven. The boy's eyes were drinking in all the details of the room. And there was a lot to look at in my house of curiosities. While my new home was being built, I had moved into the "hacienda," as the real estate agent had described it, though it was more of a large cabin. I neither liked the location nor the style of what had been a summer retreat for one of the few wealthy families in Acalán. When I first visited the land, I got the idea to build a grand house near the waterfall, though I knew that would be a major project here in the jungle.

The distribution of rooms in the cabin was wrong, but the large open kitchen and dining area had become a repository for everything from construction materials to my unpacked boxes. Against the rustic walls my shiny stainless European kitchen gadgets—microwave, toaster oven, espresso machine, juicer, and blender—looked terribly out of place. There were braids of garlic and onions hanging from the walls next to framed art posters, and a large basket of fruit on the table. There were crystals hanging in the windows to catch the sunlight and throw rainbows on the walls, and cabinets full of Italian glassware. The sink was overflowing with dirty dishes, colorful ceramic cups and plates that I had collected in Spain. On the floor I had Turkish carpets, and several of my oddly shaped metal sculptures were hanging from the ceiling or propped against walls. In the corner were two canaries in a pagoda-shaped birdcage. I was sure the brothers had never been in a house quite like mine.

Miguel took one of the towels and rubbed the boy's head, and then dropped it over his shoulders. Vitico grabbed a corner and wiped his face. His eyes had gone from surveying the room to now watching my every move, suspicious of what kind of person could live in such exotic clutter. Miguel, on the other hand, only seemed concerned with trying to minimize their intrusion. He kept looking at the floor where they had dripped and tracked in mud, all the time having a watchful eye on Vitico lest he dart away and cause a disturbance.

"Would you like to see the birds?" I said to Vitico.

He nodded. I took his arm, gently pulling him away from Miguel, and led him to the cage.

"Don't touch anything," said Miguel.

Vitico looked at me with a little roll in his eyes. I winked at him.

When we got to the cage, Vitico asked, "Why don't they sing?"

"They usually sing in the morning, and they're shy when there are new people around."

I glanced back at Miguel. He had dried his own head and his shiny dark curls had sprung to life. He caught me looking at him and his eyes returned to the mess on the floor.

Vitico stared at the birds like a hungry cat, and the canaries flitted about the cage.

"How did you get here?" I asked Miguel from across the room.

"We got a ride in the back of a truck up to Alvarado Road and then walked." I shook my head. It was a two-mile walk from Alvarado Road on a steep gravel drive that was dangerous in the rain.

"Most days I only need five men and I have my regulars. Occasionally I have a big project where I need more. The work is hard."

Miguel didn't look very strong. We were building roads, clearing jungle, and laying the foundation for the new house. Things were moving slowly. It was the rainy season. I had gone down that morning to pick up the crew in my truck. A local named Juan had emerged as a leader and took charge of getting the workers, mostly his relatives. They were short, stocky and round-faced. He was very proud of his position and made it clear that next to me, *el patrón,* he was in charge. I knew he wouldn't think much of Miguel. Aside from being skinny, he clearly wasn't one of Juan's relatives.

"I can work very hard, *señor.*"

"I'm sure you can. It's just that—"

"Please, *señor,*" Vitico blurted out. "He's really strong. I want to work, too. Our father is sick and—"

"Vitico," Miguel warned. He motioned for Vitico to come back by his side. He gathered the soggy towels and held them out to me. "Sorry to bother you, *señor*. We will go now."

"Wait. I didn't say no. There's plenty of work. It's just the problem of the weather and getting supplies. I order materials and they don't arrive. I sometimes have to send the men home because there is nothing to do." I looked at Vitico. "Young man, I think you'll have to wait a few years. But what do you say I give your big strong brother a chance?"

Vitico cast his eyes down and twisted his mouth into a grimace. Miguel prompted him with a slight jerk to the back of his collar. "Yes, *señor*."

"I pick up the workers in the central square at 6:30 in the morning. If you're late, it's a long walk."

"You make me very happy," said Miguel. He stuck out his hand, still cold and wet, but the grip was surprisingly strong. A charge of anticipation went straight to my heart and flooded me with an overwhelming need to take care of him.

# 6: Rebecca

After reading my father's letter I had to talk to Conchita. I appeared at her kitchen door that same afternoon and she said, *"Hija,* what's wrong?" She knew my moods and quickly applied her usual remedy of food followed by a talk. She sat me down with a piece of freshly baked apple pie. I started to speak, but she held up her hand.

"Eat first."

I only made it through half the large slice and put down my fork. Then I told her about my visit to Patricia and the letter.

After a pause I picked up the fork and stabbed a piece of apple. "I know he talked to you over the years."

The light left her face. She got up from the table and started scrubbing the counter.

"What are you doing?" I asked.

She focused on the countertop and with each motion scrubbed harder. "You grandmother come back soon. I need clean."

"Conchita, really."

She twisted her neck slowly and looked over her shoulder. "You mad at me?"

"No. Why?"

"I no tell you about calls of your father."

"Conchita, stop that and come here." I got up and gave her a big hug. "How could I be mad? He told you not to."

"*Gracias a dios.* I no stand you be mad at me."

"But there is something you can do for me. I want to meet my Mexican grandparents. I need your help."

Her eyes got very big and she rounded her shoulders. "You are sure?"

"Sure about wanting to meet them, just don't know how. I have an address on the letters, but where is Acalán? I've never heard of it."

"I know," she said with a glint in her eye that told me she was holding back more secrets.

"You know where it is?"

"I been there...to your father's house."

"Okay. This has got to be good. *Explícame.*"

"You know I'm *chismosa,* nosey. On one my trips back to Veracruz, my town, I decide visit your father's village, which not too far away. I take bus there and visit your other grandparents. I have some pictures of wedding. They never seen any, and I also have pictures of you. You must about four year old. They thrilled, but sad they hear so little from Miguel since he leave. I never tell Miguel, I think he be furious. In the end, he go back to them."

With Conchita's help I planned my trip. I kept it a secret, only telling Patricia and Julia. I couldn't sleep at night and listened to my Spanish tapes constantly, cramming as if for the most important final of my life.

When I got on the plane to Mexico City, I was exhausted, anxious about my poor Spanish, and petrified of meeting the other side of my family, the part of me that Gran and Granddad had tried so hard to wipe out. Conchita assured me that they would want to meet me, but I had my doubts. Why would they be interested in someone who had never tried to contact them, had no knowledge of her Mexican roots, and barely spoke the language?

On the plane, and then on the bus to Acalán, I read all the letters my father had written to me over the years, the years I had been denied the pleasure of knowing that there was a father out there who loved me. After a time I could read them without tears and some I even found tedious, the same message of despair, lamenting his choices in life. I guessed that many of them were written when he was drinking as they were full of self-pity and a clear inability to take charge of his future. Yet it was all I had of him and I needed to savor every too-little-too-late word.

I also had a small packet of letters, separate from the others, that Patricia had given me later. She explained that Miguel's brother had included them when he sent a copy of the death certificate. These letters had never been addressed or mailed, only folded into plain white envelopes with my name on them. It seemed that he had stopped sending letters, but still felt the need to write them. I read with disbelief the date on one of them. It was written right around the time he died, possibly the same day. I had marked the day that Gran told me the news of his death as "Black Sunday" on my calendar and remembered it each year. I was unsure of the exact date of the accident, but imagined that it was a few days before. I had decided he died on the Wednesday before I got the news. Ever since I had heard the nursery rhyme that said "Wednesday's child is full of woe," I pegged Wednesday as a day of bad fortune. I was born on a Wednesday.

The unusually tense handwriting of the letter and the dark impression on the paper showed his fury in writing it. The tone, too, was bleaker than normal and he indicated that something happened that day, though he wasn't specific. "News from afar stabs me in the heart," he said. "It is a wound that not even the memory of your sweet smile can mend. Just when I come close to crawling out of my misery, I am thrust back into its waiting arms. How many barbs has life to throw at me?"

I knew little about what kind of contacts he might have outside Mexico, but I could make a good guess that the "news from afar" had come from California. The letter left me with a feeling of something crawling just under my skin. I stuffed it back in the envelope, but didn't forget about it.

I had to stop reading when the ADO bus from Mexico City to Acalán climbed into the mountains and began to edge its way around twists and turns that unsettled my stomach. The seats were comfortable, but the view was not, breathtaking drop-offs that would have been spectacular if I hadn't been thinking about the 20 tons of steel and glass trying to bend around hairpin curves. But it wasn't until I stepped into the small, spare bus terminal that I really felt the impact of moving out of my world of comfort and privilege into a world where people lived a subsistence lifestyle armed with little but hope. It was poorly lit and the benches were full of short, dark people surrounded by bundles, boxes, shopping bags, and bulging suitcases held together with frayed straps. The adults ignored me as I walked by, but the children looked up from the grimy floor with eyes like fat black marbles as if I were a ghost passing through the room.

When I asked the woman at the ticket counter about a hotel, she stared at me and with a clear lack of enthusiasm said there was only one, and it was in the center.

I took a taxi, an old beat-up Nissan, over potholed streets, feeling the heavy air on my face as I leaned out the window. The buildings we passed were one-story, basic brick or cinder-block construction with stucco facing, generally white with a few pastel colors mixed in. Most of the businesses were shut for the evening behind heavy metal doors. There were few trees and the streetlights were dim, everything a far cry from the Acalán that my father used to make up stories about. When he would put me to bed, sometimes he would abandon the books he read to me, and invent tales of his own about a boy named Miguel, who skipped to school each day by a town hall trimmed in gold. This town square had neither buildings trimmed in gold nor the flocks of white doves that circled over little Miguel's head in the stories. Around the square there were a few old trees and flowering bushes, but the fountain was dry, the pavement cracked, and the wooden benches were missing slats. Aside from a few young couples on the benches with their lips locked together, the only sign of life was the sound of a thousand birds perched in the old trees, chirping their evening song. They were definitely not doves.

The hotel, just off the square, was a three-story box in need of paint, its fading green façade dotted with rusty air conditioners that protruded from each window. The simple sign with Hotel Tropicana in stark block letters was comical, as there were none of the color or spice that the name conjured up.

I approached the deserted front desk of the small lobby, staring at the several places where the varnish was worn down to the bare wood of the counter. Then a heavy woman in a colorfully embroidered sack-like dress appeared from a room behind the desk. Her long hair was braided and arranged in an elaborate bun on the top of her head. Her eyes were jet black and suspicious.

*"Buenas noches, señorita."* She looked behind me as if expecting someone else to come through the door. A husband? A traveling companion? "Can I help you?"

"I need a single room, please," I said in a line of Spanish I had practiced a hundred times.

"Are you alone?"

*"Sí, señora."* If she was taken aback by a young woman traveling by herself and arriving at night in a small town at the end of a dusty road in a non-touristy part of Mexico, she couldn't imagine how much more strange it felt to me. My only trip outside the States had been to Europe, and that was with a chaperoned group of girls. This was no comparison. I stood up straight and rested my hands on the counter, but anyone could see that I was a bird on its first venture out of the nest.

After filling out the information card, I turned around and was startled by a man with a gaunt weathered face and arms like twigs standing just behind me. He already had one mottled hand wrapped around the grip of my bag. I was capable of managing my own luggage, but he looked so eager and in dire need of a tip that I couldn't deny him. I carried the backpack and he followed with my rolling bag, which he refused to roll. We trudged up the stairs to the second floor where he opened a room and stepped aside to let me pass. As soon as I entered I was slammed by a musty smell, and noticing my turned up nose, he hurried over to the air conditioner, clicked the dial to high cool, and hit the power button. It coughed to life as if awakened from a deep sleep. The man stood at attention and contemplated the floor. Then he raised his head and looked me straight in the eye. "*Está bien, señorita?*"

His question seemed out of character, such a diversion from his subservient silence that I stared at him dumbfounded. "Yes, I'm fine. Thank you. Just tired." I tried to smile as I put a bill in his hand.

He pointed to the phone. "At your service. Call if you need anything."

I put the chain on the door and checked the windows to make sure they were locked. I sat down on the bed and sank into it. I groaned in anticipation of a difficult night of sleep. The bathroom that I hadn't yet had the courage to inspect loomed like a dark cave on the other side of the bed.

I flipped on the bathroom light and saw several small creatures head for dark corners. I knew Mexico was going to be difficult for me, so I had come prepared with a small plastic spray bottle with my favorite all-purpose cleanser. I hit the sink and toilet with a scrub brush, and then got on my knees to tackle the tub. I was doubtful I could get rid of all the critters, but I believed that the strong antiseptic smell would discourage them. For me, cleaning had always been like a meditation, a way to get out of the day-to-day and forget my troubles. I got so caught up in scrubbing the bathroom that I forgot for a moment where I was and why I was making this trip.

Back in the bedroom, I opened a musty armoire and was debating if I should hang up my clothes when a vibrating noise made me jump. My cell phone danced on the small wooden table where I had left it. It was Patricia. Since that day in her office, we had gone to lunch a couple of times and had drinks after work one evening. We were becoming friends.

"I just called to see if you arrived okay."

"I arrived."

"What's the matter?"

"The Hotel Tropicana. It's the only gig in town, but I'll survive."

"Pretty bad, huh?"

"I guess I'm more nervous about tomorrow than anything. I wish my Spanish were better. What if they don't even want to see me?"

"Of course they want to meet you. You'll do fine. Anyway, I won't keep you. I know you're tired. Call me when you can, even if it's just for a minute to say that you're all right. Oh, by the way, I read some of the transcripts from the trial. You were right. George's lawyer was a jackass, but the judge was worse. We'll talk more later."

"Thanks, Patricia...for everything."

"Don't mention it. Bye."

I hadn't eaten anything since the Mexicana flight mini-meal and I was starving. I was afraid to go out, so I dug in my bag and came up with some lemon-flavored airline peanuts. With the air-conditioner rumbling, I sat in the cool dampness of the room, munching the peanuts one by one, washing them down with bottled water. I felt like calling Patricia back, just to have someone to talk to. The loneliness took over my body like a sickness, making me weak and doubtful about everything. I felt incapable of stopping my thoughts from spiraling downward through the various things wrong with my life. I dwelled a moment on why I had no significant other, and then slid down into a pool of anger at my father, my grandparents, the boyfriends who had given up on me. My life had been unfair. Negative thoughts continued to swim in the muddy water like bottom-feeders, and I wondered what could I possibly accomplish on this trip? I imagined a scenario of sitting around a big table with my Mexican grandparents and relatives, everyone staring at me like I was a freak. I would neither be one of them, nor the rich, sophisticated *gringa* they expected.

I worked myself into a depression that had no escape but to crawl into bed and hope for a better day. The fresh-smelling sheets offered no relief. It was a night of continual repositioning, on and off covers, trips to the bathroom after all the water I drank on the bus. Finally an early dim light came in the window and marked the end of any chance of sleep. I picked up my cell phone off the nightstand, and was at first shocked that it showed 4 a.m. until I realized it was still on California time, two hours earlier.

Out of the corner of my eye I spied the largest ant I had ever seen crawling up the wall, so large that, when I squashed it with my shoe, there was an audible crunch. I scraped the remains off the sole and glanced out the window. Daylight was bringing life to the street. Activity was still limited—a food vendor struggling with his cart, a woman with a bundle on her head, old trucks so loud as they changed gears I could hear them over the air-conditioner. A mangy dog crossed the street, miraculously avoiding the wheels of several vehicles, and sniffed at the heels of the woman carrying the bundle. I imagined the hunger of the dog, and then thought of my own.

After a quick shower, I debated about what to wear, and then settled on tight jeans, an embroidered Indian blouse, and sandals. I brushed my thick hair back and held it with a butterfly clip.

The café just off the lobby was opening when I got downstairs, and I could smell the day's first coffee brewing. It didn't smell like coffee at home; a slight cinnamon odor hung in the air. A man came in with a tray piled high with dry-looking pastries.

I ordered scrambled eggs and the Mexican *pan,* which begged to be dunked in the coffee. The woman who waited on me was short and squat, had a long braid of graying hair and served me with neither kindness nor contempt. I smiled at her and tried very hard to speak correct Spanish, even commented on the weather, but she remained impassive.

I opened a novel to hide behind as I ate my breakfast. I also needed to kill time until a respectable hour that I might show up unannounced, a stranger at my grandparents' door. Julia had decided that I should read García Márquez, and had given me *The Autumn of the Patriarch.* Though it was the English version, I still had a hard time following it. I would read a whole page and then realize that I didn't have the slightest idea what I had just read. My attention drifted to staring out the window and watching the street fill up with unsmiling people, stoic in their approach to a new day and its struggles. I was much more intrigued by the story unfolding in the real world outside than the one in the book. I saw in the dark eyes of the people around me, and those out the window, an ancient struggle that transcended the arrival of foreigners in their midst. I was just another person from another place, and I would soon be gone. It was as if they didn't see me, as if I didn't exist.

Mid-morning I asked the woman at the desk to call me a taxi. She sighed heavily and picked up the receiver as if it carried great weight. The driver arrived in a pair of minutes and informed me that the address was a good ways out of town. He apologized that he would have to charge me three dollars. I told him that it was no problem, but I had one request. I wasn't in a hurry and preferred that he drive a little slower. I had learned from the other taxi driver that the slow pace of life in a small Mexican town didn't apply to taxi drivers. He smiled at me through the rear-view mirror and answered in English, "No problem," though he paid little attention to my wishes, racing from speed bump to speed bump.

Since the town had been such a disappointment compared to my father's description, I prepared myself for the likelihood that his family home was not the hacienda where the little Miguel of the stories lived, with lush patios, tiled fountains, and a horse corral out back. But I wasn't quite prepared for the modest adobe house on a dusty lot, surrounded by a few scraggly trees. Several chickens clucked and got out of the way as we pulled up in front of the rusty gate. The driver turned around and stared at me with a questioning look. Conchita had been vague in her descriptions of the house. I thought perhaps the driver had mistaken the address until he asked if I was looking for Doña Miriam and I nodded. Miriam was my grandmother's name.

"This is the place then," he said.

I passed through the squeaky gate and had to knock several times on the heavy wooden door until it was opened by a woman in a sleeveless print dress that hung below the knees with a faded apron in a contrasting floral pattern over it. Her thick gray hair was cut relatively short and her handsome face was appropriately wrinkled for a woman in her sixties. She was medium height like me, her spine straight, though the hands folded in front of her had obviously seen years of hard toil.

"*Buenos días, hija. Estás buscando a Vitico.*" She asked if I were looking for someone named Vitico.

"*No. Es usted Doña Miriam?*"

She stepped outside and raised her hand to shade her eyes against the sun behind me. Then she took my arm with her other hand and pulled me into the shade of a laurel tree, staring at me intently.

"*Dios mío, mi nieta.*" She recognized me as her granddaughter and took both of my hands in her rough ones. *"Mi nieta, mi nieta."* Her deep brown eyes filled with tears.

*"Sí, soy Rebecca."*

"I knew it right away. You have the exact copy of Miguel's eyes. Come into the house out of the sun. It's not much, but it is yours. I have prayed to the Virgin for this day. I am so sorry your grandfather is not here to meet you."

"He..."

"He passed a few years ago."

"I'm sorry."

She patted my hand and shook her head as if casting away any sadness.

Despite the shabby exterior, the inside of the house was impeccably neat, simple but clean. The living room, dining room, and kitchen were all combined into one large room. She invited me to sit down at the heavy wooden table. The air smelled of homemade tortillas.

"Would you like some coffee?"

"Thank you."

She prepared two cups and then sat down across from me, gazing into my eyes with a beaming smile.

"I'm sorry my Spanish is not good," I said, "but I'm trying. I want so much to talk to you."

"Don't worry. The biggest part of the work is done. You are here. And you must stay for lunch. Jorge and Vitico will be here soon." She told me that Vitico was her youngest son, but I was thrown by the name, Jorge, and she offered no explanation. "Vitico still lives at home and he is a computer wizard. All day people are at the door with their computer problems. That's why I thought you were here...until I got a good look at you." She took my hands again. "Oh, Rebecca, your life has been so difficult. I'm sorry."

"My other grandparents treated me well, but of course I missed not having a mother...and a father."

"I told Miguelito a thousand times he must go to see you, be part of your life. He loved you so much and talked about you all the time. He just couldn't go there, especially in the later years when the drinking got bad." Her eyes became glassy and she squeezed my hands. "He didn't want you to see him that way, said it was better that you remember him as he was."

Up to that point I had done a brilliant job of holding it all in, but my quivering lips turned into a gasp and the tears started to flow. Abuela got up and came over to me. I stood up, too, and she held me as both our broken hearts wept. She smelled of honeysuckle and cornmeal as she embraced me with a love that I hadn't felt in years, perhaps since I was a little girl. She led me into the bathroom, again simple but very clean, and we washed our faces over the sink.

Back at the table, she showed me pictures. Some were of my father as a child, and then we jumped to pictures of my early years with Mom and Dad. I had noticed a photograph sitting on a table in the living room with a doily under it, a five-by-seven enlargement in a plastic frame of Papi and me when I was about four years old. A candle burned next to it. She gathered that one, too, and placed it before me.

We went through the pictures a second and third time while my grandmother told me stories about my father, mostly about when he was a boy. But a noise outside made Miriam get up and run to the door. "*Mijo,* come quickly," she shouted into the yard. "We have a very special guest."

When Vitico walked in, I could see the resemblance immediately, his face a little rounder, his body heavier, but features similar to the father I was getting reacquainted with in the photos. He was in his late twenties, about the age of Papi when I last saw him. Miriam had told me that she thought she wouldn't have any more children after Miguel. Years later came Vitico.

"Vitico, I want you to meet your niece, Rebecca."

"*De veras?*" He took my hand in both of his and glanced at the picture on the table. "Is that you? You've really grown up." He looked me up and down and grinned like a cat. "I can't believe it. Welcome." And then he released my hand.

Miriam looked toward the doorway and everyone followed suit. A boy stood there in his school uniform—starched white shirt, navy blue tie and pants. He had his hands buried in his armpits and the shy awkward smile of a teenager.

"*Mami,* aren't you going to introduce Rebecca to her little brother?"

Miriam looked anxious, as if the information she had left out suddenly made the walls close in on her.

"*Cómo?*" I said, not sure I had understood correctly.

"*Sí, mija.* I was getting to that part, but we didn't have time. This is Jorge, your *hermanito.*"

Jorge shuffled forward and took my hand in a quick, clammy shake, looking down all the while. He had my eyes...and Papi's. Neither of us knew what to say. Abuela put her hand on my arm. "Let's all sit down."

The four of us sat at the table in one of those friendly, protracted silences that grip strangers who have so many questions they don't know where to begin.

"You see," said Miriam, "Miguel was quite a catch when he came back from over there. Well, he would have been anyway, but all the girls in town were after him. He married Jorge's mother, Claribel, about a year after he got back."

"They weren't married," said Jorge sullenly.

"Well, not by the church, that's true. Anyway, my beautiful grandson was born. After Miguel...the accident, Claribel took a job in Mexico City. It was decided that Jorge should stay here and go to school. She comes to visit on weekends."

"Sometimes," Jorge mumbled.

"When she can," added Abuela.

Jorge stood up. "*Con permiso,* Abuela. Can I go to my room?"

"Of course. Do you have homework?"

"A little," he said, disappearing into the back of the house.

"It's been hard on him," said Vitico, switching to English. He was quite fluent and it was a relief not to have to struggle so much with the language. "He's a good boy. I think meeting you came as a shock."

"For me, too. I wish I had known."

Abuela hung her head again. "I told Miguel he should write you, but he said there was no point."

"No point?" I moaned. Vitico looked at me and tried to smile. He lifted his shoulders slightly. "I'm sorry," I continued. "It's great, really. I always wanted a little brother."

"Hopefully you can stay a while to get to know him, well, to know all of us," said Vitico.

"My plans for the rest of the summer are uncertain. I start law school in the fall."

Vitico repeated our conversation to Abuela in Spanish.

"Where are your things?" she said.

"At the hotel, the Tropicana."

"Oh, no. That's no good. You must come and stay with us. You can have my room."

"I couldn't put you out of your room." I had seen there were only two bedrooms, and I assumed Jorge shared one with his uncle.

"Don't worry about me. I don't sleep much. I will be fine on the sofa in the living room. I often take a siesta there in the afternoon, and it's quite comfortable."

Getting out of the hotel was tempting, but her offer also had its drawbacks. Aside from feeling guilty about putting Abuela out of her room, I had just met the family and was still getting used to the idea of having a brother. And though it embarrassed me to even think about it, I was spoiled, always living with comforts far beyond what I really needed. I imagined plumbing that didn't work right and scorpions in my shoes. But on the cleanliness issue, I was happy that Abuela and I shared a penchant for keeping things spotless.

"Your grandmother is serious," said Vitico, again speaking in English. "Nothing would make her happier. I know it's not the conditions that you are accustomed to, but it is better than that depressing hotel. She's also an excellent cook."

"It is generous of you, and I hope you won't be offended if I don't give you an answer right now," I said to Abuela. "I have already paid for tonight at the hotel. It will give me a chance to consult with my pillow, as they say."

"Whatever you decide is fine with us. We would love to have you stay, and you are most welcome."

I looked toward the room where Jorge had disappeared.

"Don't worry about him," said Vitico. "For years he has talked about meeting *'mi hermana Americana.'* Now that you are here, he doesn't know quite what to do."

"In any case, you will eat all your meals here. The restaurants in town are not worthy of anything. That reminds me, I must get back to cooking lunch. We eat a big meal midday. It's almost ready, so if you want to wash up, you know where the bathroom is. Vitico, get her a fresh towel."

Jorge's door was open, and he was sitting at a table that held an old computer with a bulky monitor and a small screen. I knocked lightly on the door. "Can I come in?"

He nodded.

"What are you studying?"

"Math."

"I'm pretty good at math. I was going to study computer science before I decided to be a lawyer."

"Really?"

"What? You don't think girls can be good at math?"

"It's not that," he said. "Here not too many girls study math. It's not considered...I don't know." His light skin, the lightest of the family, turned the color of a ripe peach.

"I know what you mean. What kind of math are you studying?"

"Algebra."

"My favorite. Let me see some of your problems, if you don't mind."

"I'm kind of stuck on this one."

"Let's see what we can do. Hmmm, that's a tough one."

We spent the next ten minutes working on algebra until Abuela called us to the table.

During lunch Abuela kept apologizing for the meager offerings—chicken with garlic and onions, rice, beans, tortillas and a salad of tomatoes, shredded cabbage and grated carrots. The tortillas were handmade, thick, not perfectly round, but tasty. I ate so much I felt like a stuffed pig. Jorge had loosened up, smiling and even laughing when Vitico told a story about a new female employee walking into the men's room by mistake at the cabinet shop where he worked. He was in there doing his business.

"I hope you didn't stink it up the way you usually do," said Vitico.

"Boys!" said Abuela. She hid a smile behind her hand and turned to me. "You know, a lot of the furniture in the house was made by Vitico. Look how solid this table is." She brought her fist down on the wood in a gesture so sudden it made me jump.

"Yeah, but my desk is crippled," Jorge said, laughing again.

"It is not," Vitico said, reaching over to cuff him on the side of the head. Jorge moved easily out of his way.

"It's a damn rocking horse, it teeters so much."

"It's the floor that's not even," Vitico concluded with a smirk.

"They're like kids," Abuela said to me. "I'm going to make some coffee." She rested her hand on Vitico's arm. "If Rebecca is tired, you can take her to the hotel on your way back to work. Then you can pick her up on the way home for dinner."

"Do you have a car?" I asked.

"Not quite. Just a small motorbike."

"What about Jorge? Doesn't he have to go back to school?

"No. The school's very crowded, so half the students go in the morning and the other half in the afternoon. He starts very early and finishes at noon."

Vitico unlocked the shed and rolled out a small, slightly beat-up motorcycle.

"What about a helmet?" I asked.

"Hmmm," he said. The exaggerated wrinkle of his brow belied his nonchalant gait back into the shed. He came out with something that looked like a World War II German military helmet stuck on his head. He took it off and scrunched up his shoulders. "Sorry, it's all I've got."

"Just one?"

"For you. I don't need one."

"Isn't there a law here?"

"There probably is, but nobody pays any attention. Hop on."

I donned the musty helmet and straddled the bike. God, if Gran could see me now, she would have a heart attack.

"You'd better hold on. The roads are bumpy. Don't be shy. I'm your uncle, remember?"

I put my hands gingerly at his sides, but he took them and wrapped them around his ample belly, chuckling at my timidity. Then we took off with a little jerk, quickly getting up to a pace geared to impress. I was forced to hold on tight, and pressed close to him. I caught a whiff of cologne wrapped up with his natural male odor. The combination, though not strong, was distinct and shot up into my brain. He smelled like my father. I was transported back in time, into a large overstuffed lazy-boy chair where my father used to read to me. I would fall asleep in his lap with my head in the crook of his neck breathing in his smell. I was warm and happy and loved.

"You're quiet," he shouted back. "You're not scared, are you?"

"I was just thinking."

As if reading my mind, he said, "I miss my brother a lot." I gave him a little squeeze with my arms. With the groan of the small engine under us, the movement across a repeated pattern of light and shadow as the sun cut through the trees, and the lazy warmth of mid-afternoon, it was easy to fall into silence. I was lulled into a world that felt vaguely like sex. I tried to shake myself out of it, but couldn't until we pulled up in front of the hotel and I jumped off the bike as if I were leaping from a burning building. I removed the helmet and thrust it towards him.

He started to take it, his hand touching mine, and then a grin spread across his face. The motor idled, and he kept giving it gas.

"Might as well hold on to it for the trip back. I'll pick you up around seven."

"Seven," I repeated, starting for the door. "Oh, and thanks."

When I entered the hotel, the woman looked past me and shook her head. "Watch out for that one. He's a heartbreaker."

"Don't worry. He's my uncle."

She twisted her mouth and moved her head back in surprise. "But you're not...Miguel's daughter?"

"Yes, I am."

"Oh, I see it now. God rest his soul. But your name..."

"My other grandparents convinced me to officially change it. I regret it now."

"So you are here to see the family. How is Miriam? I haven't seen her for ages."

"She knew who I was right away. I didn't tell them I was coming."

"Yes. She has kept the family together through all the hard times. She's a mountain of strength. I guess your life hasn't exactly been every day's bread either."

"How much do people know here?"

"Just about everything. People talk. Bad news travels fast and all that. Of course everybody knew Tio Jorge or knew of him. His place was just outside of town."

"Was?"

"He sold it a few years back to a developer who wanted to make it into some kind of tourist attraction."

"Did he come down here to sell it?"

"A local attorney handled the whole thing. It's a damn shame he had to give it up. He was well liked for the most part in the town because of the work he gave to people. The new owners brought in their own crew. Just a damn shame, all of it. Sorry about your mother, by the way. And your father, of course."

"It was a long time ago. I only have a few childhood memories of my mother, a few more of my father. Do you know the attorney who handled the sale?"

"This is a small town. Everybody knows everybody...and everybody's business. His office is not far from here."

With several hours before Vitico was supposed to pick me up, I walked the few blocks littered with trash along unshaded streets and stood outside a door with a sign above it. Faded lettering spelled out Licenciado Pedro Ramirez Salazar.

One of Granddad's favorite lines was that you should never put off until tomorrow what you could do today. But I wondered if I was pushing too hard. I had spent one day in Mexico and just a few hours with my Mexican family, yet I already felt there should be a new, more relaxed way of doing things. Trying to track down Tio Jorge could wait until tomorrow. And then I wondered if my hesitation was really a fresh way of thinking or if I was simply afraid, afraid that I would find Tio Jorge and be forced not only to confront my past, but to go forward with my mission to seek justice for him. I stood in a barren patch of concrete between my past and my future, staring at the door that held the information I needed. Was I prepared to go in and take it?

The windows and door of the man's office were covered with Venetian blinds and there was a monotonous drone from the air conditioner that protruded from a hole cut in the wall along the narrow passageway with small offices on either side. I could hear his voice inside with intermittent pauses, as if he were talking on the telephone. He was busy. I could come back another time. But would I? I waited a few minutes until there was quiet, and then knocked on the door.

A short, balding man with a Groucho Marx moustache and rheumy eyes opened the door. It appeared he had no secretary. He invited me into his cluttered office and cleared off a chair for me to sit down.

"I'm Rebecca Delon," I said, shaking his hand. "I wonder if you could help me locate George Edwards. I understand you handled the sale of his property, and I thought you might have an address where I could contact him." I struggled to get it all out in Spanish. At the same time, concentrating so hard on how I was saying it, relieved me of some of the stress of what I was saying, and what in fact I had set in motion.

"Nice to meet you, Ms. Delon," he answered in perfect English. "Of course I don't give out the private information of my clients, but if there is some business you have with him, I could contact him for you."

"It's a personal matter. I'm Miguel Santos' daughter."

His eyebrows rose as if they weren't quite attached and his face showed a twitch of pain. "I see. Sorry about your father. We were classmates. A fine man and a good friend. I feel profoundly the pain you must have." He took a deep breath. "But Mr. Edwards' instructions were clear that I am not to divulge his whereabouts to anyone."

"I understand your position. And I respect Mr. Edwards' desire for privacy. I also wish him no harm. I know quite a lot about the case. The thing is I have a letter my father wrote to him, given to me recently by a lawyer in the States. My father wanted me to deliver it to him in person. If you won't help me, I will have to hire a private investigator, but I *will* find him. I owe it to my father."

"You put me in a difficult position."

"I can pay you if that's what you want."

"No, please. Miguel was a friend." He paused and glanced at a file cabinet in the corner. His eyes came back to me and a smile crept across his face as if it were something that both pained him and gave him relief. "Tell you what," he said. "I am going to step out for fifteen minutes or so. I know things look like a mess, but I have an assistant who keeps the files relatively in order."

"Mr. Edwards doesn't have to know how I found him."

"It has been a pleasure, Ms. Delon. I wish you all the best." We both stood up and shook hands. Then he opened the door and a blast of hot air swirled into the office. He stepped out and left me standing in the middle of the room.

I easily found the file with Tio Jorge's address, and was stunned to see that it was in Monte Rio, California, just a couple hours' drive north of my grandparents' home in Hillsborough.

# 7: Rebecca

There was a knock on the door. Abuela paused in her washing of the dinner plates. Jorge was back in his room. Vitico held my hand and traced the line on my palm, predicting a long and adventurous life. The knock pinched his smiling face into a frown. He sighed and gave my hand a tender squeeze before releasing it. "I'll get it," he said, rising from the chair under the watchful gaze of his mother.

The dark-haired beauty at the door wore tight jeans, glittery-heeled sandals, and a low-cut tank top that allowed her ample chest to enter the room way before she did. She was carrying a laptop under her left arm as if it were an accessory rather than the purpose of the visit. She kissed Vitico on the cheek and pushed into the room. It seemed familiar territory for her. But when she saw me at the table, my hands gripping the edge ready to get up, she put on the brakes. Her manicured nails curled into claws as her mascara darkened and her red lips had a luscious shine under the overhead light.

Vitico hurried in between us. "Ana, this is my niece, Rebecca, from California."

"Oh," said Ana. She hugged the computer to her breasts like a shield.

I stood up and we shook hands.

"Vitico has been teaching me how to use my new laptop," she said. "*Buenas noches, señora.*"

Abuela was still at the sink. "*Buenas,*" she said, casting the greeting over her shoulder.

Vitico took Ana's arm and led her over to the sofa. "We won't be long. I'll take you back to the hotel as soon as we're finished.

"I can call a taxi."

"No," said Abuela, "he'll take you."

Vitico and Ana sat very close on the sofa, their thighs touching. She leaned forward, a good half of her breasts falling out of her low-cut top, and opened up the computer with a slow, casual hand. They began speaking in low voices, computer terms that became transformed in her mouth into sexual innuendos. He fell into her game and his face, cast in the blue light of the screen, took on the ghoulish air of a boy possessed by an irresistible spirit. I left them to their own little world and sat back down at the table. Abuela came over and laid the comfort of her hand on my shoulder. "Would you like some tea?" she said.

"Do you have any chamomile?"

"Your wish is my command, *hija.*" I leaned my head over and rested my cheek on her hand still damp from the sink. "Come help me prepare it."

I was thankful to be relieved of my voyeuristic duties though neither Vitico nor Ana seemed to notice when I got up to accompany Abuela to a far corner of the kitchen.

We stood by the cabinet where the teas were kept and Abuela whispered, "I don't like her. She's no good for him."

We heard a high, carefree giggle from the sofa and Abuela shook her head. "*Ves?*"

"Rebecca, tell your grandmother it's not polite to whisper," shouted Vitico in English.

"Right," I shouted back. And to Abuela I suggested we take our tea in to Jorge's room and see if he needed help with his homework.

We walked in his room and he quickly punched a key. The room, lit only by the screen, changed its color from a rosy red to cool blue.

"How is your math going?" I asked.

"I was just checking my e-mail."

"I hope you finished your homework first."

"Yes, Abuela."

Abuela sat down on one bed and I on the other across the room. I looked down at the beige bedspread with textured stripes of bright color woven through it and realized I was sitting on Vitico's bed. There was a single dark curly hair looped over one of the stripes. I got up and stood next to Jorge.

"Would you let me check my email?"

"The connection is really slow."

"Do you want some tea, *mijo,*" Abuela asked Jorge.

"Are you kidding? It smells like something horses eat."

I laughed and stuck the cup in his face. He pinched his nose and jumped up from the chair.

"I told you you could use my computer. You don't have to torture me."

I looked at Abuela, sitting up straight on the edge of the bed, her contented smile a thing of beauty.

"Is that your girlfriend?" I asked Vitico on the way back to the hotel.

"Not really. Why? Are you jealous?" The wind muffled his laughter, but with my hands laced around his middle, I felt his stomach jiggle.

"No, *Uncle,* I'm not."

"What if I weren't your uncle?"

I moved my hands to his sides. "Butcha are. So shut up."

"Shut up? Is that polite, *señorita*?" he said in an exaggerated Mexican accent.

"You're not being polite."

He laughed again and sped up. With one hand he moved my hands back around his middle. He had a sweetness that reminded me of my father, but unlike Miguel he had a cocky, a self-assured nature that was both annoying and charming. Despite their differences, I felt in his presence the spirit of my father, and the need to gather all he could tell me about his brother became a physical yearning, a need so strong that new questions rose up from the well of my brain every time I saw him. Though the flirtation was fun and seemingly harmless, I looked forward to a time when we might have a serious conversation.

In front of the hotel we got off the bike. "Do you have any free time tomorrow?" I asked.

"For you I'll make time." He cocked his eyebrows, his voice shaded with innuendo.

"Forget it." I was tired of his jokes. I turned to walk away.

He grabbed my hand. "Sorry."

"I just wanted to talk."

"About what?"

"Miguel. Away from Abuela and Jorge."

His face lost its spark. "Sure." He chewed his lower lip and his eyes narrowed. "I don't work tomorrow. Why don't we go and look at Tío Jorge's old house? There are lots of nice places on the land to walk and talk."

"I'd like that."

"I'll pick you up about ten."

His face had fallen yet again into a distant, sad memory. His head was slightly tilted as if he were going to kiss me. Not an uncle's kiss. I looked over at the light coming from the lobby. The woman at the desk was craning her neck to watch. The shabby hotel stood like an inner city flophouse in front of me, and I hated the thought of spending another night there. But the confusing glint in Vitico's black eyes, which at times seemed almost inhuman, made me wonder if moving to Abuela's was a wise choice.

"Well, goodnight," I said, stepping back.

"Can't I give you a hug? An uncle hug?"

I allowed him to envelop me in a strong embrace. His whole body sighed.

I stiffened and tried to pull back. He dropped his arms and pulled a long face.

"Goodnight," I said again.

"*Está bien.* See you tomorrow." He jumped on his bike and stared at me a moment before taking off. I cradled the helmet under my arm and mounted the steps, bowing my head to ward off the inquisitive looks of the woman.

"I haven't been up here in a long time," Vitico said as we pushed our way along overgrown trails. We came to a clearing and sat down on a curvy cement bench that was embedded with pieces of broken tiles in a mosaic pattern. At one end several pieces of tile had come loose and fallen to the ground. "I guess the new owners haven't had the money to keep things up. Tourist revenues aren't what they hoped for. It's so hard to get to. On the other hand, I like that the isolation preserves the natural beauty of the place."

It had taken us an hour on a narrow windy road through lush mountain vegetation to get to the valley where Tio Jorge had built his whimsical tropical paradise. He called it Parque Escondido. We walked along the trails and each plant and tree seemed to ooze moisture, giving the impression that we were walking through a giant greenhouse. Long chains of sleepy red and yellow acanthus blossoms hung alongside ivy ready to retake the trail. And then we would come upon a clearing, similar to where we were now, with benches, a respite from the dense jungle.

"I've never seen anything like this," I said. "I feel like Alice in Wonderland."

"Most of his ideas came from Gaudi." Vitico pointed at the tile patterns on the bench and indicated the organic shapes by curving his hands in the air. "Tio Jorge lived in Barcelona for a while and fell in love with the Gaudi stuff, especially the big park there called Parque Güell."

He explained that the main house we had seen at the entrance, built of rough stone with a chimney shaped like a mushroom and covered with ceramic tiles, had Gaudi influences. It had the tile pattern around the windows and doors, but he had incorporated some elements of Mexican hacienda style as well. It was single-story around a central patio. The caretaker had told us that the house was closed for repairs, so we couldn't go inside. They were renovating it to turn it into a bed and breakfast.

"Have you been to Barcelona?" Vitico asked me.

"No, my grandparents sent me to France with a group of girls for a few weeks one summer. Made it to England and Switzerland, but not Spain."

"I only know Gaudi's work from a book Tio Jorge gave Miguel. I'll show it to you when we get back home. Wait until you see pictures of the church he was building, La Sagrada Familia. It was never finished. That guy was flipped out."

"Did you ever come up here as a kid?"

"Miguel brought me a few times. I was about six or seven, and he must have been around seventeen when he started working for Tio Jorge. He put a lot of guys to work. I wanted to work, too, but they said I was too young. You know, Miguel wanted to be an architect. He started doing manual labor here at the park, but it wasn't long before he was doing a lot of the design as well. Tio Jorge recognized that he had talent and decided to send him to school up there. Well, you know the story. He met Helen. She got pregnant with you, and that was the end of that."

"It was my fault, then, that he didn't become an architect. Did he ever talk about it?"

"If you mean, did he regret having you? Don't believe it for a minute! He was crazy about you. I was a teenager when he first came back. I didn't know my ass from a hole in the ground. I thought he was so cool because all the girls were after him. He used to get on my case all the time about studying and staying in school. I didn't listen and it made him so mad. As I got older, he talked to me a lot. He was going to get sober and go back up there. He wanted to be near you. Sometimes I would catch him staring at that photo of you and him on the living room table with tears in his eyes. But then there was Jorgito to raise, and he couldn't stop drinking, couldn't stand the pain of it all."

"Even as a little girl I think I knew he was unhappy. I would catch him with a frown and say, 'Papi, smile.' After Mom died the unhappiness just took over."

"I didn't really understand all that went on up there. I couldn't figure out why he was like that. He was smart. He was handsome. He was so cool. He had girls after him. How could he be unhappy? God, I worshiped him." His voice was shaky. Our hands were almost touching on the bench, and I moved mine on top of his. "It nearly killed me when the accident happened. I went wild for a week. But one day Abuela sat me down at the kitchen table. 'I'm not going to lose another one,' she said. 'It's fine if you don't want to study anymore, but you're going to have a trade. On Monday you will start as a carpenter's apprentice to your uncle.' She didn't give me a choice, and the pain in her eyes was so deep, I couldn't disappoint her."

"How come she didn't have more kids? Two is kind of a small family in Mexico, isn't it?"

"After Miguel they told her she better not risk having more children. When she got pregnant with me years later it was like a miracle, but the doctors said she had to stay in bed for the whole pregnancy. Can you imagine Abuela in bed for nine months? *That* nearly killed her."

"I guess she wanted you bad."

"That's what my father always told me growing up. He was a good man, waited on her hand and foot while she was in bed."

"I'm sorry I never got to meet him." I removed my hand from his and slapped a mosquito on my arm. It splattered red. "Let's get moving. The mosquitoes have found me. Fresh new blood."

A flock of parrots started screeching in the trees above us as we moved along the trail to a bridge over a creek with a waterfall feeding into it. In the middle of the creek, just below the falls was a big rock. Atop the rock was a giant lizard done in the same broken tile mosaic style as the bench. Beneath us the water gurgled over the shiny stones as we leaned on the rail of the bridge, taking in the dense tropical air. I had the sensation that the bridge was moving, that we were floating down the stream in a boat. Then I heard the dentist-drill buzz of mosquitoes around my ear and started swatting.

"Too bad Tio Jorge had to give up all this," said Vitico.

"It would have been difficult for him to come back after the trial, prison, and everything. I suppose people were pretty hard on him here."

"People believe what they want to believe. After it all came out, some said they never liked him, that he was a bad influence. Others appreciated the work he gave to men in town. Miriam always defended him, said she didn't think he was capable of causing your mother's death. She can be hard sometimes, but she's got a heart that recognizes the good in people. She had decided that Tio Jorge was a good person and that was that."

"I don't believe he did it either. I'm going to find him and make it right if I can. I can't bring back his lost years, but I know Papi would want me to do something."

"What can you do, though?"

"I'm starting law school in the fall. I have a friend who's a lawyer, used to do some criminal stuff. We might be able to reopen the case."

"Miguel would be so proud of you. Damn, there's so much in life that isn't fair."

It had taken a while, but I was seeing him serious, opening up a little and not constantly using humor and flirtation to deflect. I had a feeling that the capacity to love, the thread of human kindness that I saw in my father and Vitico came right from Miriam. And I hoped there was at least a drop of that humanity in me. When you inherit the kind of openness my father had, people handle it in different ways with different degrees of success. He tried to please everybody, juggling the people he loved and hurting all of us. Vitico handled it by taking on the role of jokester and flirt, though he wasn't hard to see through. He desperately wanted love and affection, and I didn't like him falling into the easy trap of women like Ana.

We listened to the run of the river and I felt as if the water were flowing through me, cleansing me. There was no doubt in my mind that coming here to meet my Mexican family was the right thing. It was awkward at times and painful bringing up the past, but it was right. In the process I was becoming a whole person though I still had a long way to go.

"Rebecca, you scare me sometimes. You're so serious. Do you ever have fun?"

"Life hasn't been much fun since I was five."

"There's a lot of pain in life. That's why I think you've got to enjoy it best you can."

"Shit," I said, swatting a mosquito on my neck. "Can we go?"

"It's going to be dark soon."

The ride back to town was quiet with a steamy mist that arose from the jungle floor and seeped out onto the highway. The streets of the town were dimly lit and empty by the time we got there. Vitico stopped the bike in front of a place called Cantina Rosa. There was a striped curtain hanging over the arched entrance and we could hear the ra-ta-ta trumpet of Mariachi music flowing out into the street. Aside from a few barking dogs it was the only sign of life in the town.

"Have you ever tried mescal?"

"It's like tequila, right?"

"Not the same. From the same plant, but the process is different. Made in small batches."

"Can I go in there?"

"You might be the only woman, that is, except for the bartender, Rosa."

A drink sounded like a good idea. Maybe Vitico was right and I needed to loosen up. Five shots of mescal later—Vitico had more—I wondered if enjoying life was all it was cracked up to be. The first couple of shots were to try the stuff. I had the impression of drinking turpentine, so I was sucking a lot of lime wedges dredged in spicy salt. The next three were to help me forget after Rosa casually mentioned that Papi used to hang out there.

"Did you have to bring me *here*?" I whined to Vitico. My eyelids were heavy, and my head felt improperly attached to my shoulders.

"It's the only place in town. I didn't mean to make you feel bad."

"I know."

Rosa had her back to us, polishing glasses, but she overheard our conversation. "I told him not to get in his truck that night," she threw out without looking at us.

"Rosa, *por favor*..." said Vitico with an anger I hadn't yet seen from him.

"I'll have another one," I said.

"No you won't. We're gonna dance." He pulled me off the stool. There was a salsa song playing and the melody seemed much too joyful for the hangdog expressions of the rest of the five or six patrons, hovering over their beers or shots of mescal.

Normally I would have refused the dance invitation, but I felt like putty at that point, ready to morph into any form. It seemed that the new me was beginning to take shape. "I'm warning you. I've got two left feet."

"Just follow my lead."

I had never liked partner-dancing much and usually preferred free form if I danced at all. But I surprised myself and let him take charge. Among his talents was dancing and he knew how to lead. With my hand tucked in his, and his other hand firmly at the small of my back, he had me swirling and moving my hips like I'd seen people do on TV. Then dizziness got the better of me and I begged him to stop. "At least I got a smile out of you," he said.

"I thought my mouth was doing something funny."

Vitico paid the tab and we staggered out the door. He headed for his bike. I grabbed his arm. "No, no, no. No way. You're not driving that thing."

"I can do it." He stepped sideways, a bit off-balance and struggled to get the keys out of his pocket.

"God! Men! No means no. Give me the keys."

"What are we going to do then?"

"Walk. The hotel can't be too far."

"It's not."

"We'll get you a room."

"I could stay at Ana's."

"Is that what you want? Let that viper get her fangs in you?"

"Listen to you. Talking trash." He started laughing and I did, too. We stumbled down the street holding each other up.

As we passed under one of the dim streetlights, a toe-sized cockroach ran across our path and Vitico stomped on it.

"Yuck!" I said, and then started to sing. "*La cucaracha, la cucaracha, da-da, da-da, da-da, da.*"

"You don't know the words," he laughed. "*La cucaracha, la cucaracha, ya no puede caminar.*"

We sang the line together.

"But wait. It gets better. *La cucaracha, la cucaracha, Ya no puede caminar, Porque no tiene, porque le falta, marihuana que fumar.*"

"No marihuana to smoke? Poor cockroach," I said.

We sang several rounds of the chorus. With each round I felt better, allowing myself to go deeper into the world of silliness, a world foreign to me. And with each round I had the sensation of getting drunker. We walked along, and several times Vitico had to take hold of me to keep me more or less going in a straight line.

"Miss Ana," I shouted in the dead quiet street. "Here comes your lover boy. And he can sing!"

"*Cállate,*" he said, giggling.

"Don't tell me to shut up."

"Anyway, I ain't going."

"Go, I don't care."

"Yes you do."

"Believe me, I don't."

We got to the hotel and Vitico still hadn't made any real attempt to separate himself from me and head for Ana's. I kept telling myself that it would make things easier between us if he would go do his macho thing, even if he was sleeping with a woman that I knew he didn't love. It was none of my business, and yet I cared enough about him to want to save him from her claws.

Our mescal-infused brashness on the street turned to sheepish grins as we entered the hotel lobby.

"*Hola, Berta,*" said Vitico.

"Just what do you think you're doing?" she said.

"He needs a room," I said. "He can't drive home."

"Apparently you two didn't see the tour bus parked out front. Group of evangelicals on their way to Tampico for some kind of convention. Had mechanical problems so they're passing the night here. Every bed is taken, even the rollaways."

Berta's image wrinkled in my vision, a blur before my eyes. Vitico leaned on the counter for support. We stared at her with our mouths slack.

"There's always bundling," I said to Vitico.

"What?"

"Put a barrier down the middle of the bed. Way for unmarried people to stay warm in cold climes."

"It's hot here."

"Or lack of bed space. I don't know. It's Ana or bundling. You choose. I have to go to bed."

Berta threw up her hands. *"No entiendo de que estan hablando."* She gave me the key and disappeared into the back.

"Well, let's go," said Vitico.

"I mean it. Bundling."

I had trouble getting the key in the door. On my second attempt I dropped it. We both leaned over to pick it up and bumped heads. I fell back and landed on my ass while Vitico laughed so hard he doubled over like a man in pain.

"That hurt," I said. "Help me up, you jerk."

Inside the room we fell on the bed with our clothes on. I kicked off my sandals and he followed suit with his Nikes.

"Can I hold you at least?" Vitico said like a five-year-old boy.

I karate-chopped the bed in the middle. "That's your side, and this is mine. Don't cross the line."

"You're so cold."

*"Buenas noches, tío."*

I woke up with the sun in my face and a hairy arm across my stomach. There was a dark critter on the wall and I watched it creep up toward the ceiling. I picked up Vitico's arm and dropped it like a dead weight on his side of the bed. My head was a bowling ball with a little gnome inside that was relentlessly pounding with a hammer. I went to the bathroom and threw up.

There was a light rap on the door. "Are you okay in there?" said Vitico.

"Is this what enjoying life is all about?"

"Like everything, there is a price to pay."

"I've just paid in great quantities! Did you call your mother?"

"I'm an adult in case you haven't noticed. I can stay out all night if I want."

"I mean she might be concerned about me."

"Can we not have this conversation through the bathroom door?"

"Just don't look at me. I'm a mess."

"How 'bout I go get us some coffee?"

"Great. I'll be out in a minute."

I splashed some water on my face and tried to do something with my hair. God, I just slept with my uncle! All right, nothing happened, but it could have. No, it couldn't have. Even drunk, I never lose control. What was I thinking? No, Vitico was a mover, but he would never let it get to that point. I knew he respected me. It was just a friendly hug. Maybe it was myself that I didn't trust. There was a moment, that dusky, half-conscious moment in the morning, when I felt warm and protected, a gentle arm around me. It was a second of feeling good, floating down a lazy river. And then reality hit me, a craggy rock just below the surface. It quickly went from being something lovely, on the verge of erotic, to something queasily inappropriate.

"Coffee's here."

I splashed some more cold water on my face. "I'll be right out."

# 8: Rebecca

I woke up to the smell of honeysuckle in Abuela's bed. I had checked out of the hotel at noon the day before, having become convinced that escape was a necessity when Vitico and I were surrounded by serene evangelicals at breakfast. They occasionally looked up from their quiet conversations and glanced at us with the wide eyes of shepherds on sheep who have lost their way.

It was comforting to be waking up far from the center of town and there was something sweet about sleeping between Abuela's crisp fragrant sheets. I certainly didn't miss the squalor of my hotel room, though I still had my doubts about staying in the same house with Vitico.

I put on a freshly washed robe that Abuela had laid out for me and headed for the bathroom. Jorge had already gone off to school. The door to their room was open. Jorge's bed was unmade, but it looked like Vitico's hadn't been slept in. I had heard him go out after dinner, and I fell asleep before I knew if he came home or not. I leaned against the doorjamb and stared at the bed. It looked as though Ana had won out in the end. Abuela came around the corner from the kitchen and caught me in my mood.

"*Buenos días, hija. Dormiste bien?*" She looked at Jorge's bed and then Vitico's.

"*Sí*, Abuela." I turned to give her a morning kiss.

"I haven't had a chance to clean up in there yet. I didn't want to wake you."

"Jorge should make his own bed."

"He's always in such a rush, leaving so early." She looked at Vitico's bed again and shook her head. "I wish he would settle down. He just doesn't seem to meet the right girl. Ana is not the right one, but my boys have never listened to me."

"Maybe not in their choice of mates, but in other ways."

"It would be nice to have more grandchildren. I'm so happy to have Jorge here, and now you. I want you always to think of this as your home. Don't forget us when you go back there."

"Never. You're all part of my life now. How could I forget you?"

"Come on. I'm going to show you how to make tortillas."

She had already made the dough and it was resting in a red plastic tub on the counter. She made me wash my hands, and then showed me how to knead the *masa*. Putting her hands on top of mine, she guided me in the proper technique.

"Abuela, I want to ask you something, but I don't want to upset you. It's about the day my father had his accident."

She stopped working the *masa* and gave me a half-smile. "Ask, my dear. I'm sure there are things you want to know."

"I've been reading his letters to me and I came upon one that was written around the time of his death." I stopped and assessed the contours of pain on her face, the fading light in her eyes. But I had to go on. "He said that he had received news from far away that hurt him very much, but he didn't say what it was or from where. I just wondered if he mentioned anything to you. If the news was really bad, maybe he...I mean, maybe it made him drink more and..."

"Oh, *hija,* I remember that day like it was yesterday. He was renting a little house up the road where he lived with Claribel and Jorgito. He received an international letter. I believe it was from California. I called and he came over to get it. He sat out back reading it while I stood at the kitchen window and watched his face change from excitement to desperation. And then he did something strange. He pulled a lighter out of his pocket and burned it, burned the letter just like that."

"Did he say anything?"

"He didn't even come back inside. He went around the side of the house toward the road." She lifted her hands out of the tortilla dough and stared at the sticky mess on her fingers. "That was the last I saw of him," she said in a soft, distant voice. She moved to the sink to wash her hands.

I felt horrible for taking her back to that day. I put my hand on her shoulder. "Forgive me."

She let out a big sigh, but she seemed determined not to cry. "Like you I have wondered what it was. He burned the letter like it was evil and had to be destroyed. Maybe it is better that we don't know."

"I never should have brought it up."

"Forget about it. When I'm sad, I find it's best to work. Let's get back to the tortillas."

We covered the *masa* with a towel and let it sit while we went out on the thatch-covered patio. Out in the fresh air she breathed deeply, and with the smile of a magician, removed a vinyl tablecloth—brightly colored with a fruit motif—from what looked like a small round table. Then she scooted the table to the center of the patio, and I saw a tube connected to a tank of gas in the corner. It was a modern version of the ancient *comal,* she explained, used for making tortillas since the time of the Aztecs. With each movement her mood improved.

From a pine cabinet, which Vitico had made she pointed out, she removed what looked like a small metal stool. When she raised the lever, I realized it was the tortilla press. Her actions were precise and joyful, those of an artist about to create—lighting the *comal*, lining the press with sheets of plastic, setting up everything at the proper angle and distance.

We brought out the tub of *masa* and set it on a tiled counter. She smoothed back her hair and grabbed a hunk of the dough, rolling it in her hands to form a ball. After glancing at me to be sure I was watching, she put the ball in the press and used all her weight to flatten it. Then she peeled off the thin round tortilla and slapped it on the *comal.* It cooked quickly, and just as she flipped what was beginning to have the telltale uneven, speckled surface of a tortilla, the phone rang, breaking our contemplation of the golden brown underside.

"Fifteen seconds, no more. Take it off and put it in the basket under the napkin," she said and hurried into the kitchen.

I did as I was told. Then I grabbed some *masa,* rolled it in my floured hands and put it in the press. I flattened the thing with conviction. And then I opened the press to find not a perfect round tortilla, but a sticky mess. I had forgotten to use the plastic lining. In a panic I looked around for something to scrape off the dough before Abuela came back out.

When she stepped from the shadows of the kitchen into the bright light of the patio, the joy of teaching her granddaughter how to make tortillas had again been interrupted, and her face was lined in worry. "What is it, Abuela?"

"That was Claribel. She's coming to see Jorge."

"That's good, isn't it?"

"*Sí, pues...*"

"Well, what?"

"It was something she said, something important she wanted to talk to Jorge about. She's been hinting at taking Jorge to live with her in Mexico City. I can't stand the thought. The city is full of crime and dangerous things. One time she came down here with one of her boyfriends. He was shifty and nervous. All he wanted to do was talk about motorcycles, so he and Vitico went off to do that. All the drugs up there, the gang killings. I don't know how mothers ever let their children leave the house."

"Does Jorge want to go?"

"He might think he does. I know it's kind of boring here, but we're the only family he has known. He hardly knows his mother."

"She *is* his mother," I said and then immediately regretted it.

She looked at me as if I had just slapped her hand. She was about to say something, but changed her mind.

"I'm sorry," I said. "It's none of my business. He's so lucky he's had you to raise him. I wish I had been so fortunate." I meant it. At least after losing his father, Jorgito had been raised by kind and loving grandparents. But I also thought he deserved a chance to know his mother, a chance that had been taken away from me.

She floured her hands and grabbed some of the yellowish sticky dough. She rolled it in her hands like I imagined the fears were rolling around in her head. She squeezed and patted them away. "I suppose it won't be long before I'll be all alone here. But we can't worry about that now. We have tortillas to make."

"Oh, Abuela." A strand of her hair had fallen loose, and I tucked it back behind her ear.

At lunch Vitico didn't eat much and complained of a headache. I suspected a hangover. Abuela was composed, though I knew she was worried about Claribel's impending visit and frantic that she might try and take Jorgito away. She had called again to talk to Jorge when he got home from school.

"Mami promised to take me out to dinner in Ciudad Robles," Jorge announced, and then turned to me to explain. "That's the biggest town in the area and they have a good restaurant." His attitude turned from excited to cynical. "I hope she doesn't bring one of her boyfriends. That last one was a loser." His expression again shifted to serious. "She wants to talk to me about something important."

Abuela's face tensed up and she put down her fork. Vitico emitted a slight moan and rubbed his forehead. A truck rumbled out on the main road.

"All right. Family meeting," I threw out as if I knew something about a functional family. They all stared at me like I was crazy. Vitico gave me a warning look, but I proceeded. "I think we all know what Claribel wants to talk about."

"No, we don't," said Vitico, a combination of anger and pain twisting his unshaven face.

I ignored him. "Jorge, what do you think she wants to talk to you about?"

"*Por favor, hija,*" said Abuela. "This is not the time."

"I think she wants me to come live with her."

"There," I said. "Everybody knows what it is, but nobody wants to say it. Why don't we just talk about it?"

"Who are you to bring this up? Up until a few days ago you ignored the fact that any of us existed. Now you want to stick your nose in family decisions?"

Vitico's words stung me with a force that seemed to have more behind it than the situation at hand. Nursing a hangover or not, he was angry with *me*. I wondered if he was feeling strange about our night in the hotel. Maybe there had been a fight with Ana. Something else was going on.

"*Mijo*, don't talk to Rebecca like that. She is part of the family. She is Jorge's sister."

"It might be good for him to get out of this town...like Miguel did. I wish I could."

"You are free to do what you want. You're not a prisoner here," said Abuela. She got up, turned her back on us and stood at the sink. She opened the water faucet, which made a loud squeak, and began to scrub the pans with a force that could take off the outer layer of metal. Vitico blinked at me defiantly, as if everything was my fault. His sweet face had turned to one of a monster with puffy cheeks and black bags under his eyes. I was seeing the flip side of his jovial, flirty personality. Then he hung his head and moaned again. He got up and went over to the sink, putting his hands on Abuela's shoulders. "*Perdóname, mamá.*"

Her shoulders relaxed, though she didn't say anything.

"Wait," said Jorge. "Isn't this about me? Don't I get an opinion?" Everyone turned to him as if they had just remembered he was in the room. "I don't want to go. Not now. Maybe someday."

Abuela dried her hands on her apron and rushed to hug him. "You are the smartest of all of us. You are my wise prince. I know some day you will leave my house, but don't make it too soon."

"I want to finish school here," he said, looking uncomfortable with Abuela's arms still wrapped around his neck. "It doesn't make sense to change in the middle."

While the focus was on Jorge, I got up, went to my room, and closed the door. I still felt burned from what Vitico said. It hurt because he was right. I wasn't really part of this family…or any family. I might as well go back where I came from. At least there I knew who I was.

I dragged my suitcase out from under the bed and flopped it open on top of the covers. I pulled clothes off hangers from the closet and grabbed the things from the drawers Abuela had cleaned out for me. There was a knock on the door.

"Rebecca, can I come in?" It was Jorge.

"I'm a little busy right now."

"I have something to show you."

I opened the door and saw him holding a large coffee-table book on Gaudi architecture.

"Tio asked me to show you this." He looked over my shoulder and saw the bag on the bed. "What are you doing?"

I blew out an extended puff of trapped air. "I think it is time for me to go home."

"He didn't mean it."

I backed up into the room and motioned for him to come in. I didn't want Abuela to hear our conversation. I had no idea how I was going to tell her that I was leaving. "He's right. I can't just push myself into this family."

"You're not pushing. Tio Vitico has been acting weird lately. I think he kind of likes you."

"Jorge, he's my uncle."

"I know. Anyway, it seems like Ana's jealous."

"This is crazy. I really need to go home."

"I don't want you to go." He spoke softly and looked down at the floor. "Nobody does. It would make Abuela really upset. I like having a sister."

He definitely had the sweet gene. I put my arms around him and pulled him into a hug. I knew he was uncomfortable, so I made it a quick one.

"Let's look at the book. I'll decide later what to do."

We sat on the bed with the book resting half on his lap and half on mine. He was familiar with the pages and pointed out details as he explained about the architect's life. He told me he had done a report on Gaudi at school.

In the mirror over the dresser, I saw Vitico pass by on the way to the bathroom. He stopped a moment to look at us. I was sure he saw the suitcase.

When we finished with the book, I asked Jorge to show me where they kept it. "I want to read more later."

"Does that mean you're staying?"

"I don't know."

He led me to the small bookcase in the corner of the living room. As he slid the book into its place, I spotted the bright yellow binding of a book that I recognized from the past. It was one more in a series of stabs from my childhood that had shaken me in recent weeks. *Curious George* it said. I pulled it from the shelf and opened to the inside cover with a chill running through me. I knew what I would find. "To my dearest Rebecca, I hope you will always remember your Tio Jorge." It had been a gift for my fifth birthday. When I went to live with Gran and Granddad, I was allowed to take a few of my things, but many of my childhood treasures stayed behind. I guess Papi thought that the book wouldn't meet Gran's approval, so he didn't let me take it. I was surprised that he had brought it with him to Mexico.

"Papi used to read that book to me," said Jorge, "but translated it into Spanish. He told me it belonged to my sister, and he hoped I would meet her some day. I always wondered about 'Tio Jorge.' I asked Abuela and she told me he was a friend of my father's. She said he was a good man. Where is he now?"

"He lives somewhere in California. I'm going to find him when I go back."

"Do you think I can visit you some day?"

"I would love you to."

Vitico walked into the living room with a great weight on his shoulders. He stood with his hands cupped in front of him and waited until I looked up and acknowledged him with a nod. "Can we go for a little ride?" he said.

"If you promise not to drive like a maniac. Let me do something first." I went to my room to put my clothes back on the hangers and in the drawers, and put my suitcase back under the bed.

We took the road in the direction of Tio Jorge's old place, but pulled over after a couple of miles where it began to climb into the green hills. We followed a short path to some rocks overlooking the valley. He pointed out Abuela's house, and then brushed off a flat rock so that we could sit down.

"I'm not very good at this," he began, picking up some gravel and throwing it pebble by pebble over the edge. "It was stupid what I said."

"You had a point, but it hurt the way you said it."

"I'm sorry. Not having a great day. It's not your fault. Well, maybe some of it is. Things were okay with Ana before you arrived. Then I started to see her through your eyes and things weren't so good."

"I never said anything against her."

"I saw the way you looked at her."

"You deserve better."

"There you go again. You make rash judgments about people you hardly know."

"It's something I'm working on. It must come from the way I was raised, I mean after I started living with my mother's family. You can't imagine what it's like living on a plateau of privilege and affluence. We're up here and everybody else is down there," I said, pointing to the corrugated tin roofs down in the valley. "It distorts your point of view about other people. It's not how I want to be. Look, if you're happy with Ana, it's none of my business. I'm leaving soon and things can get back to normal."

"I saw your bags. I felt terrible."

"Jorge convinced me not to leave right away. The last thing I want to do is hurt Abuela. But I do have things I need to do back home."

"You're right. I don't really love her."

"I never said you did or didn't. I said it was none of my business."

"I used to have this sweetheart in high school. I was crazy about her. Her name was Eunice. She was smart like you. Went on to study medicine."

"Where is she now?"

"She's doing her residency in Mexico City. I don't think she's married. Last time she was home, we went out for a drink. I still felt that spark, you know."

"And what about her?"

"I couldn't tell. She's all caught up in her new life. I'm like yesterday's news for her."

"Maybe you should go visit her. Tell her how you feel."

"You're just full of good ideas about other people's lives. What about you? I never heard you mention anyone in your life. You could have a ton of boyfriends if you wanted."

"I'll take that as a compliment, but I don't want. I can't. I have to get things sorted out in my life. Anyway, it's none of *your* business."

"Yes, it is. I'm your uncle. I have to look out for you."

"Does that include sleeping in my bed?"

He glanced at me sideways and shrugged his shoulders. The sweetest smile took over his face. We were both enjoying the forbidden fruit, the air of sex between us. We didn't have to act on it, just let it sit there and warm to a nice body temperature, but go no further.

"I'm glad you're not leaving right away," he said.

"Me, too," I said. It only takes a few words to put the world back in balance.

On the ride back down the hill, I held on to him tightly and rested my forehead against his back to avoid the wind in my face.

Claribel arrived at the house on a sultry evening, the air still full of electricity after a torrential downpour and lightning storm. Jorge and I were playing cards, but every time there was a noise outside, he would look up from the game toward the door. Vitico had escaped to the computer, and Abuela, who always found something to do in the kitchen, moved around in her domain.

In spiked heels Claribel clicked across the tiles of the living room. It was hard to imagine how she had made it from the uneven pavement of the driveway to the front door in those shoes. She wore tight jeans and a low-cut, sleeveless tangerine blouse. Her hair was dyed jet black and cut short. She had multiple piercings in her ears filled with an array of hoops and dangling objects. Her eyebrows were tattooed on. The simple gold cross round her neck seemed out of place.

She was effervescent in her attempt to play the doting mother. Jorge accepted her eager kisses with an awkward grin, and then she greeted Abuela and Vitico with enthusiastic hugs. When she was introduced to me, she stuck out her hand, not as if she were greeting the daughter of her ex-husband, but as if I were a visiting dignitary from a faraway planet. "So very lovely to meet you," she said with a nervous twitch in her eyelids.

She withdrew from us as quickly as possible and whisked Jorge, clad in his best jeans and a blue shirt that Abuela had carefully pressed, off to their dinner date. He had gelled his hair and spiked it. The hair, coupled with the anxious expression on his face, made him look liked a spooked cat as he went out the door.

When Claribel brought him home several hours later, her bubbly behavior had gone flat. Her eyes darted from one to the other of us, nailing us as co-conspirators in the plot to keep her son away from her. She asked Vitico to walk her to her car.

He came back in and looked around the room for Jorge before he spoke. "She didn't believe," he said in a low voice, "it was Jorge's decision not to go live with her. She screamed at me and called us everything in the book."

Vitico, Abuela, and I huddled like a team after a successful play.

## 9: Rebecca

I could feel the heat from the idling bus on my bare legs as Abuela, Vitico, Jorge, and I lolled in the sweet sorrow of goodbye. Most of the other passengers had already boarded the Mexico City bus, and I was just about to initiate the final hugs, when Abuela pressed a small object wrapped in cloth into my hand.

"What's this?"

"Something I wanted you to have."

I unfolded the square of black velvet and saw a gold band.

"It was your father's, his wedding ring."

It weighed nothing, and yet it seemed as if my hand might fall to the ground.

Vitico rolled his eyes to the cloudless sky and stepped in, slipping a hand under mine. "Let me help you put it in a safe place. You don't want to lose it on the bus."

"I'd better go," I said once he re-wrapped it, and I tucked it into the pocket of my jeans. The sudden gift, the heat from the bus, and the sun bearing down on us made me feel faint. A prickly mix of love and sadness danced over my skin. I quickly grabbed Abuela in a strong embrace. "Gracias. Gracias por todo."

Vitico put his arm around me and helped me to the door of the bus.

On the trip to Mexico City, and then the flight back home, emotions passed through me in waves, leaving me weak but with little choice except to go forward. It wasn't enough that I had told them all that I was going to find Tio Jorge. Now I had Papi's ring burning a hole in my pocket. The words from his letter came back to me: "Please find him and give him the letter. I must live with knowing that I did not fight for the two people I loved the most." Perhaps I should do only that, hand over the letter, and abandon the notion of clearing his name, dragging up the past. I even asked myself if I really wanted to right a wrong, or if I was out for revenge. Maybe I just longed to see my grandparents and Uncle Jimmy squirm in the residue of their past misdeeds. What they did was clearly wrong, but was I, Rebecca (could I change my name back?) Delon, ready for the task? I took out the ring and slipped it on a gold chain I wore around my neck where it encircled a heart pendant that Conchita had given me for graduation.

Still, uncertainty, my constant companion, plagued me. I was about to meddle in someone's life that none of us had heard from in sixteen years. Since Tio Jorge hadn't made contact with me or the family in Mexico, I had to conclude that he wanted to be left alone. And yet, if it had been him at my graduation, it was possible that he was moving toward making contact. It was up to me to bridge the gap.

The usual summer fog greeted me as the plane made its final descent over the placid gray waters of the Bay into SFO. Though normally thrilled by the approach, I was unmoved by the twinkling lights of the city and its bridges, and the puffs of snowy fog creeping over the coastal range.

I fingered the smooth gold band that hung from my neck. What would he think of me being in his house, sleeping in his mother's bed? How much of this had he foreseen? Was I simply following a preordained plan? Step one, the letter. Step two, trip to Mexico. Step three, find Tio Jorge.

I touched down in San Francisco exhausted, my mind still reeling with questions. In the damp evening breeze with waves of fog trailing after it, I stood in front of the terminal, hoping Julia had gotten the message to pick me up. A few minutes later, she pulled up in her red Toyota Corolla with the still unrepaired huge dent on the right rear side. She gave me two quick honks, which annoyed me. It was clear that I had seen her and was already throwing my bag on my shoulder. Julia often did little things that bothered me, the kind of things that drive roommates to the point of fantasizing murder, like refusing to put CDs back in their cases or forgetting to buy toilet paper. Yet she remained my best friend. Now more than ever I needed someone to talk to, though I wasn't sure how much I should tell her about my plans. We hadn't had a chance to talk much in the last month, and when I had told her I was going to Mexico, I simply said it was time to meet my father's family. I had refrained from telling her about my father's letter.

"How did it go?" she said after a quick kiss.

"Let's see. I slept with my uncle. I fell in love with my little brother. My grandmother taught me how to make tortillas, which I guess makes me a *tortillera*, and someone told me in slang that means I'm a lesbian."

As if the other information were trivial, she screamed, "You have a brother?"

I filled her in on the details. We laughed a lot, and a couple of times I was close to tears as I recounted the twists and turns of the path into the heart of my Mexican family. I told her about the childhood book I had discovered and the old pictures of my father, learning how to dance salsa with my uncle, and helping my brother with his math homework. She let out a giddy scream when I recounted in detail how I ended up sleeping in the same bed as my uncle.

"God, Julia, I feel so lost. They are wonderful people. I wanted to be part of that family instead of the one I have here, but I hardly know them. You have no idea of the fucked up things my Delon grandparents have done."

"Yeah, I know, like buying you a BMW and sending you to Stanford."

"Shut up. Okay, I'll give you the Stanford part. I'm happy for that, but I don't need the car. It's just part of the payoff for the shitty stuff they did."

"You told me about your sleazy uncle and your Grandma bad-mouthing Mexicans, but you never finished with the story about the guy at graduation."

"It was just easier to stick with the story I had originally been told, that my mother died in an accident, and my father went back to Mexico to help his ailing father. Over the last few years I have learned what really happened and my grandparents role in it, but I kept it to myself."

"Even from me? I tell you everything."

"Jules, I was ashamed. It was hard enough for me to make friends. I always felt that if people knew the true story of my life, no one would like me. It was only in Mexico, with the Mexican side of my family, that I began to feel good about who I was. My father had a lot of problems, but he had a wonderful human side that I was able to see in his family. I'll tell you everything someday. I just can't do it now."

"I wish you felt confident enough to talk to me."

"What I can tell you is that an injustice was done to the man I think I saw at our graduation. I would like to do something about it. And when I do, you are going to hear screaming from Ashton Lane all the way to our apartment."

"Speaking of Ashton Lane, your grandmother has been calling me. I didn't pick up because I knew she was going to ask me where you were."

"How long does it take to drive to Monte Rio?"

"A couple of hours, depending on traffic in the city. Are you taking off again?"

"I have to go meet someone."

"Tell me it's not the mystery man in the bad suit."

"I have to talk to him."

"Oh God, Becca! At least let me go with you."

"I need to do it alone."

I had parked the BMW in my grandparents' garage while I was in Mexico. I stopped by to pick it up at a time when Gran wouldn't be there. Conchita's questions were innocent enough, but if Gran walked in, it wouldn't be so easy to ward off a much more skilled inquisitor. For a moment I imagined the pleasure I would feel at seeing Gran's face if I confessed to her that I had gone to meet my Mexican grandparents and that I was on my way to find Tio Jorge. But that pleasure would have to wait. I needed to be on my way. My eyes kept darting to the driveway where Gran would pull up, and Conchita seemed to understand my dilemma. She hurried me out the door saying, "We talk later. *Vaya con Dios.*" It had been a long time since I felt that I was going with God by my side.

I eased into the new car smell of my silver 328i with a feeling that it didn't really belong to me, didn't fit into any part of my life. Considering what I was going to do to my grandparents, I would have to return it, though for now I intended to take full advantage of it. That I was going to use it on my journey to find Tio Jorge seemed like poetic justice.

I turned the key and it came to life with an elegant purr, the power of a giant cat waiting to leap into action. I knew little about cars. They got me from one place to another. I had had my own car since high school, a hand-me-down really, Jimmy's Mazda that he had gotten tired of after a few months. But as I felt the smooth idle of the engine, the authority of the door when it closed, and the solid feel of the leather steering wheel in my hands, I knew the Beamer was a special car. My eyes swept over the gauges and instruments, and an image of Vitico jumped into my head. In my fantasy scene, instead of returning the car to Granddad, I gave Vitico the keys and told him it was his. I saw him running his hand over the dashboard and patting it like a baby, taking off at high speed and roaring down the highway with me in the passenger seat telling him to slow down. And then I relived waking up with his arm draped over me, the excitement I had felt that morning in the Hotel Tropicana. The whole flirtation thing with my uncle had been on the edge, and yet in a strange way brought us closer together. I could say with a certain relief that we had worked through the feelings and come out better for it, or at the very least we hadn't done anything stupid.

I glanced into the rear-view mirror and saw a car come up fast behind me and swerve into the other lane. It shook me to see the man's annoyed expression, and I realized I was driving too slow. I stomped on the accelerator, but then quickly had to hit the break as I came up on another car and couldn't change lanes. The basket on the passenger seat nearly sailed onto the floor. I reached over and caught it just in time. It was full of sandwiches, carrot and celery sticks, grapes, cookies and soda. I had told Conchita I was going to visit a friend in Monte Rio, which she must have thought was on the other side of the world as she moved around the kitchen filling the basket. She opened and closed the giant double-door Frigidaire and rummaged through cabinets until she had the basket full to the brim.

I chose mid-morning to drive through San Francisco to avoid rush-hour traffic. I navigated the endless flow of vehicles along 19th Avenue and the winding stretch through Golden Gate Park. When I got to the Presidio, the former military post, it was bathed in fog so thick that the old cypress trees shivered, and the hillsides wore the fleeting mist like a skirt. At the Golden Gate Bridge, the tops of the towers, held upright by looping cables as thick as tree trunks, were hidden from view by the puffy low clouds. At the foot of the towers, along the walkways, little people scrambled to get a view of the Bay. When the rest of the country was sweltering in August heat, the tourists walking across the bridge were burrowed into heavy jackets and sweaters like turtles retreating into their shells. Their bodies were bent, finding an equilibrium between falling forward and being held upright by the wind. A few bridge-trekkers refused to believe the chilly temperature as they made their daring pilgrimage across the landmark in T-shirts and shorts.

On the other side of the bridge, I passed through the rainbow tunnel and came out into mostly sunny skies, which by the time I got to the bottom of the hill in the flat part of Sausalito had changed to clear blue. I watched the outside temperature gauge climb rapidly to 82 degrees while I moved through a series of emotional climates that paralleled those of the Bay Area's microclimates, from foggy doubt to partially clearing excitement to azure sky giddiness. I put on a Coldplay CD and turned up the volume. After a couple of songs I changed to a CD that Vitico had made for me. It had a series of salsa songs for me to practice my steps. As I couldn't very well move my feet in the car, I fast-forwarded to Julieta Venegas. He had included Julieta's new album because of the night in the cantina. Between the Mariachi tunes and the salsa, a song of hers had come up on the jukebox. I asked who it was and he told me a little about her. Her use of the accordion grabbed me, taking me back to junior high when I had decided for some bizarre reason that it was my instrument.

One night Conchita and I were watching her favorite
Saturday night Latin music program when a group came on
playing four accordions. The music seemed so happy it
made me want to jump up and dance around the room. The
next day I decided that I had to learn how to play the
accordion. Gran said she refused to have one of those gypsy
boxes in the house. Around that time I happened upon an
article in the entertainment section of the paper that the
San Francisco symphony was going to do Tchaikovsky's
*Orchestral Suite No. 2 in C Major* with parts for the
accordion. To my grandparents surprise I announced that I
wanted to go to the symphony. They were so pleased that I
was showing some interest in high culture that they took
me the next weekend. When the third movement of the
piece came up, I made sure they noticed the accordions.
Granddad chuckled and later told Gran that I had won.
"Buy her the accordion," he said. The next day I had a green
pearl Hohner Corona II and I was signed up for lessons. I
was never much good at it, but I still loved to take it out of
the case from time to time, hold it in my arms, move my
hands over the smooth spaces, and punch the buttons.

Now driving along with the brilliance of the late-
morning sun and the melancholy whine of Julieta's
accordion, I plunged into the memories of my Mexican trip.
As Abuela, Vitico, and Jorge got farther away in time, their
images in my mind waxed even sweeter. The freedom of
the road, the sun, my warm thoughts all joined together to
make my doubts fade away. My mission to find Tio Jorge
and expose the lies of the past grew into a quest of great
importance. I would be doing something that I knew would
have made my father happy. I would show my

grandparents that what they had done to Tio Jorge and my father was wrong. And I felt like it would prove to the world I was ready to be an adult, that I was doing something with my life.

I had my phone propped up in the cup-holder between the seats and when I saw the screen flash with Patricia's name, I attached my Bluetooth headset and answered it.

"I got your message," she said. "Where are you?"

"On my way."

"Did you get anybody to go with you?"

"No. I decided it was best this way. Gives me time to think."

"I didn't hear much from you in Mexico."

"It's another world down there. There was so much going on, and I was caught up in it, but at the same time I felt like an outsider. It did give me strength, however, to go ahead with my plan."

"You are going to need George on board...if you find him." She always referred to him as George even though I continued to call him Tio Jorge. "Have you considered the possibility that he won't want anything to do with it?"

"Of course. In fact, I'm anticipating some resistance. I'll just have to use the Mexican charm I inherited from my father." I was trying to sound confident though I didn't imagine that people would normally describe me as charming. I was sure though that it was buried somewhere inside me, ready to sprout from my Mexican roots. It had been buried too long under the Delon inclination for detachment.

"I'm not doubting your charm, but from what you told me, don't count on having the same effect on George as your father."

"Hmmm. I suppose you're right." She was being kind about the charm, and also seemed to have an inside understanding of George and my father's relationship. From the first meeting I had a suspicion about her own sexual orientation. I had a feeling that her stiff lawyer's demeanor was hiding a deeply emotional being looking for an outlet. I wasn't inclined to be her outlet, though I did like her and wanted us to be friends.

"I'll call you as soon as I have news. We'll get together and talk about Mexico."

I moved into yet another climate, lazy mid-afternoon uncertainty, as I pulled into Horizons Mobile Home Park outside of Monte Rio. Growing up in Hillsborough, I was imprinted with the notion that trailer parks were just a step above shanty towns, and the residents were perhaps more lamentable in that they had made the deliberate choice to live in them as opposed to ghetto-dwellers who often had few options. It was a surprise, then, when in the first block I came upon a BMW identical to mine parked next to a huge triple-wide surrounded by flowering shrubs and beds of multicolored petunias. An intricately patterned stone walkway approached a giant redwood deck. It was my first time in a trailer park and I stared in amazement. I somehow wanted it to be squalid, a trashy cluster of rundown trailers I could rescue Tio Jorge from.

The speed bumps forced me to crawl along as I read the street names—Brookside Lane, Fairweather, and Belleview. My GPS led me to the address I had for Tio Jorge,

27 Sunset Drive. Sunset was at the far end of the park and I noticed that the homes were getting smaller and older near the end of his street. I stopped in front of one of the most modest and oldest single-wides and verified the address. It was faded blue with drawn shades. There was a small cactus garden in front and a large tomato plant heavy with ripening fruit on the side.

With the engine turned off and the gear in park, my hands still had a sticky grip on the wheel, and my breathing was irregular. There were no people in sight, no children, no dogs, no life. I punched the window button and let the glass slide down into its pocket. I took in air and felt the silence envelop me. It smelled of ocean brine.

There was an old-model yellow Mustang parked under a rusty carport, an aggressive muscle car. For moment I thought it must be the wrong address. I couldn't picture the image I had of Tio Jorge—a dapper gentleman graying at the temples, in a three-piece suit, the man I had seen at my graduation—in a car that looked set for a drag race in Modesto. Perhaps he had moved without leaving a forwarding address. I could turn around and go home. But as I stared at the car, a scene flashed in my head. I remembered driving to the beach with Papi and Tio Jorge in a candy apple red convertible with white interior. It was an old car and must have been rented from a classic car company as I only remember seeing it that one time. I also remembered Papi inventing a ditty about Tio's fondness for old cars. "Tio likes old cars, old cars, old cars."

In the red convertible we rocked along the highway and sang the line over and over, probably driving Tio Jorge nuts. My father turned around from the passenger seat and said I looked like a beauty queen in the back. Miss Hollywood he called me. I was wearing heart-shaped sunglasses that he had bought me. My long black hair was whipping back in the wind. His smile was radiant and I soaked it up like a garden does the spring sun.

We arrived at the beach, a great expanse of gray sand. It was sunny but cool. We walked along the water's edge. I was between Papi and Tio Jorge, holding both of their hands. Papi was closest to the water and he would occasionally push us scampering inland to avoid a foamy wave creeping over the sand. As it receded it left, for a brief moment, a shiny surface of glistening pebbles and bits of shell. I wanted to stop and pick up the shiny pebbles, but my hands were engulfed in theirs and it seemed rude to try to extricate them.

"Swing me," I cried, and they lifted me up between them, swinging their arms back and forth as I tucked my legs under me and hung like a pendulum. I never tired of the game and repeatedly begged them, "Swing me, swing me." I was extremely happy that day. Papi laughed and it was one of the rare times that Tio Jorge, normally so serious, laughed as well. Later he broke away from us as if the happiness was too great, and ran toward the rocks that ended the beach. "Let's catch him," said Papi, and we ran hand-in-hand after him.

On the way home in the car, I was cold and Papi took me up on his lap in the front seat where I snuggled into him and fell asleep. I still had my heart-shaped glasses on.

I came out of my reverie and looked over at the tomato plant again. A black cat slunk around the plant and disappeared under the car. It was the only sign of life on the planet.

I got out and walked along the side of the Mustang. It was relatively free of nicks and scratches. I touched the faded yellow, and it felt cool and ageless. After climbing the three steps up to the stoop, I stood self-conscious and vulnerable outside the door. I rapped on the screen, which rattled and gave off a flimsy aluminum sound. There was no answer. I stared at my car parked on the street, thinking how easy it would be to escape.

I tried to open the screen, so that I could knock on the hard door. It was locked. I rapped again and felt the tinny rattle in my bones. After another long wait the door opened a few inches.

"Yes," a voice said. All I could see was a tall, thin shadow.

"Tio Jorge?" My voice was brittle.

There was silence. The door creaked and moved an inch toward closing. And then the shadow spoke. "I'm afraid you're mistaken. There's no one here by that name."

In trying to hide, he was revealing himself. I remember voices. I remembered the many stories he read to me as a child. It was the voice of Tio Jorge, though stripped of its spirit. When he had read to me so many years ago about The Dancing Bear or The Ugly Duckling, his voice was strong and expressive. Now it had no legs. It crawled out of his throat. "All right. George. I'm looking for George Edwards."

"As I said, you're mistaken."

"It's Rebecca."

The door creaked a fraction toward opening and then silence. I thought I could hear him breathing. "I don't know any Rebecca or George...or that other person. Please, go away." He closed the door with an ominous click, and then I heard him put on the chain.

"I saw you at my graduation," I shouted through the door. "I'm not giving up. I'll come back tomorrow." I felt bad about harassing someone who wanted to be left alone, but now that I had found him, heard his voice, and yes, been hurt by his denial of me, I wasn't going to skulk away. I would, though, give him a little time.

I got back on River Road and went into the town where I passed under the neon sign saying, "Welcome to Monte Rio, Vacation Wonderland." I found a room at the Village Inn under towering redwoods and with a view of the river. It was much fancier than I needed, but I wasn't ready to start looking at my budget. I knew that tightening the reins was coming soon. If I persisted with Tio Jorge's case, Gran and Granddad would surely cut me off.

Though the conditions of my Village Inn room were much better, the turmoil I felt took me back to the first night at the hotel in Mexico. I was full of anticipation about a connection with my past, my lost years. If I could just get Tio Jorge to talk to me, I could unlock doors. The thoughts kept me from sleep, and I resorted to flipping through TV channels. After a few hours I fell asleep, but woke up later to the flashing shadows of an old movie in black and white on the screen.

The next day, his car was gone. I sat on the stoop, determined to wait as long as I had to. He wouldn't be able to get in his house without confronting me. Every so often the neighbor's curtain would draw back, though the figure stayed far enough away from the window that I couldn't distinguish any features of who was spying on me. After a couple of hours I wondered if I had driven him away, that he had been so bothered by my sudden appearance he left town. It was time to talk to the neighbor.

The woman who answered the door acted surprised, giving no indication whatsoever that she had been watching me for the last two hours. She was stocky and in her sixties, her hair dyed an unnatural blond and cut short. She wore cheap-eye-plan glasses, baggy blue jeans, and a light gray sweatshirt. "Excuse me, I was waiting to see your neighbor. I wonder if you know when he might be back."

"Simon?"

"The one who lives right there." I pointed to his trailer.

"That's what he said his name was," she said as if she suspected that it was not. "Don't associate much with nobody." She leaned in close and spoke in a low voice as we stood on either side of the doorway. "I got some mail a his addressed to George somebody. Never seen nobody else but him there and the previous owner was named Mildred Parks and she was a friend of mine. She died a few years back. I took the letter over and set it by his door. Guess it was his. We invited him to some neighborhood functions. We play Bingo every Friday. But he never came to a one. You'd think a man like that'd get lonely. Then again it's his business. You can't force nobody." I could tell she was barely getting revved up and could go on indefinitely with her gossip. I brought her back to topic.

"Any idea where he might have gone?"

She scrunched up her face and studied me. "Like I said, he keeps to hisself. I don't keep track of his comings and goings. He don't take that car out much though, except to go shopping. You a friend of his?"

"Friend of the family. Haven't seen him in many years. I was in the area and thought I'd look him up. Did he have a bag or anything with him when he left today?"

"It's not like I stand at my window watching him, but I just happened to be out watering when he took off. It was early and he did have what looked like an overnight bag. I wondered about his cat, but I guess he's got that cat door. We've had some problems with raccoons, so I hope he don't find his house full of 'em when he gets back." She sniggered at the thought.

"I see," I said, backing away. "I guess I won't wait then."

She leaned toward me again. "Ya know, oncet when I was comin' back on the coast from Gualala—my sister lives there—I saw his car parked by the beach. Musta been north of Jenner. It was a cold, foggy day, and I didn't know why anyone would want to go to the beach, but it was his car for sure. He weren't in it. Don't know if that's helpful, just that's the only place I knowed him to go."

"Thanks. You *have* been helpful."

She stood in the doorframe with pursed lips and watched me get in my car. I didn't start it right away, but sat and pondered the tip she had given me. After a few minutes she closed her door, and I got back out on the road. I followed the river toward the sea. The water was low and its banks were exposed like a woman lifting her dress above her knees. The road curved and narrowed as it passed through redwood groves and stands of long-needle pine. The lofty and dense trees forced a hush on the land as cabins nestled in the forests peered out like lonely eyes. As I got near the mouth of the river, it widened out, and the surrounding land turned back to the barren brown and gray of late summer. The sky had wisps of fog running across it, and I could see whitish jagged rocks sticking up where the river met the ocean. They stood as a warning gate to the road I traveled.

At the mouth of the river was a town called Jenner with its few houses perched on the steep hills. I passed through the hamlet and headed north, making several stops at places where you could pull off. None of them seemed to have access to the beach far below, or looked like a place where someone might get out and take a walk. I looked down at the river where it met the sea. It seemed confused, backing up on itself as the tide pushed in. A huge bank of fog sat on the horizon. I returned to my car when a biting wind made standing on the cliff too cold.

After a couple more stops, I decided that the search was futile, and I looked for a place to turn around. The road dipped down and I pulled in where a sign said, "Sonoma Coast State Beach, Russian Gulch." Another sign warned, "Caution: Lock your car. Keep valuables with you." It was too narrow to turn around, so I kept going to the parking lot. The gravel crunched under my tires and birds scattered as I crept along. In the lot was a single parked car—an old yellow Mustang. I pulled into the space next to it and saw that he was not in his car.

There was a wooded area between the parking lot and the beach, and the trailhead was next to a portable toilet. I didn't like the idea of leaving my car, but I had him trapped. He would have to talk to me. I zipped up my heavy wool sweater and headed for the opening in the brush. The plants pushed in on either side, and in a few places I had to step over fallen branches. I heard a crow cawing and saw the telltale reddish leaves of poison oak, the prickly thorns of blackberry. My Hillsborough heart pounded wildly as I imagined murderers and rapists at every turn. I kept walking and thinking the beach couldn't be that far away, but the surf still had a distant muffled sound. Had I taken a wrong turn? Why was it taking so long?

After a few more minutes on the trail, I came out on a dry rocky gulch that I guessed had to lead to the beach. I regretted wearing heeled sandals. I had wanted to look attractive when I met him. They were killing my feet, and when I got to a more sandy part, I took them off. The bed opened up onto a wide pebbly beach. Midway between two steeply rising charcoal-gray cliffs, a man sat on a piece of driftwood and stared at the ocean. I approached him like a barefoot supplicant, my head bowed in deference, sorry for the intrusion. He turned toward me and then back to the ocean. I stopped at a short distance, not knowing what to say.

He spoke first "I guess I was foolish to think I could escape you. You are your father's daughter."

"I'm trying to be. It is something new for me. I guess you could say Miguel is working through me."

He nodded. There was the tiniest hint of a smile, but with the mention of my father's name, his eyes blinked with the sadness of a man unable to escape his past.

"If you want, I'll walk away and we can pretend I never found you."

"No, you won't. Sit down."

I sat on the sand, leaning against the log he was resting on, at his feet, respectful. There was a long silence. We contemplated the waves of the cove. I imagined that both of us saw a turning point in our lives, and yet we were petrified of what might be around that corner. I felt the urge to lean against his leg. I was exhausted, the weight of the last sixteen years having caught up with me.

In an almost unintelligible voice, he whispered, "Oh, Rebecca."

"Can I call you Tío Jorge?"

"I prefer George. What I said yesterday was in a sense true. Tío Jorge is gone, buried. We begin anew. I'm George." He reached his hand down over my shoulder. I shifted my body to shake it and looked into his eyes, the same steel-blue eyes I remembered from my childhood. They sent a chill through me. His hand was a little rough, from gardening I supposed, and warm. We stayed clasped for a moment longer than a regular shake. He looked at my face, and I knew what he was thinking. His eyes watered.

"My God. Look at you. Your father is all over your face. I saw it yesterday even in the low light at my door. It left me devastated for the rest of the day. Now in this light it is shocking...and comforting at the same time. I've tried so hard to forget the past. I would have loved to be one of those amnesia victims you see so often in the soap operas. I'm an addict of *telenovelas,* Mexican soaps. I tried to forget everything, even my name."

"Yeah, Simón?"

"Who did you talk to?"

"The neighbor. The one that's glued to the window looking out on your house."

"Oh, yes. Judy. I guess that tells you how exciting her life is that she has to watch me. The name is a joke really. In street Mexican, they say Sí-mon, like 'Yeah, man.'"

We fell into safe conversation, avoiding the topics of his imprisonment, the fateful summer of my childhood, my grandparents. I hadn't mentioned Papi's letter yet. I told him about my trip to Mexico, though. I gave him news of Abuela and Vitico. After a long pause, I told him that Miguel had a son named Jorge. He made a choking sound, but recovered quickly. He said the lawyer in Mexico had written him about Miguel's death, though he hadn't mentioned a son. I talked about what a delightful young man Jorge was and about his dilemma of staying with Abuela or going to Mexico City to be with his mother. I immediately felt the ping of regret for mentioning the mother.

"He married again?" He tried to hide the pain in his voice.

"I don't think it was exactly a marriage. He had a son."

"A son named Jorge."

"Abuela and Vitico spoke kindly of you," I said.

"You talked about me?"

"Getting to know them convinced me that I had to find you. I take that back. Not convinced me, but gave me strength. I had to do it because Papi asked me to."

He thought for a long time. I knew he was hesitating about diving into the topic of my father. "And how did he do that?"

"He left me a letter and some things with a lawyer who contacted me when I turned twenty-one. You know, I think he knew he was going to die young."

George looked stunned by my words, as if he were living the moment of learning of Papi's death all over again. "His death is still not real to me. I imagine him walking the trails of Parque Escondido with his sketch pad, coming up with new ideas."

"What's he wearing?"

"A cowboy hat, jeans, blue work shirt and some construction boots I gave him. That's how I'll always remember him."

The light was fading in slow increments, the sun hidden by a thick gray cloud of fog. The constant refrain of the surf gently pounding the sand and then being sucked out over pebbles lulled us once more into silence. In the middle of this dream, I felt a gentle hand touch my shoulder.

"We should go before darkness comes. If you are hungry, there is a lovely restaurant in Jenner overlooking the ocean."

"Are you sure? I've already intruded on a good part of your afternoon."

"We could make it a twenty-first birthday celebration."

I shook my head. "You remember my birthday?"

"Of course. Birthdays, graduations. It's scary how much you can find out about a person through the Internet. Of course the birthday I didn't need to find on the Internet."

"I wish you had talked to me at graduation."

"And then what? Would you have invited me to sit with your grandparents? Wouldn't that have been fun."

"It was just over a month ago, but it seems light-years away. So much has happened."

I followed him in my car back through Jenner to the restaurant at the end of the river. The hostess seemed to recognize George and gave us a table by the window. The fading milky light fell on our table as we stared out to sea. River's End Restaurant, perched on a bluff right at the mouth of the river, was known for its spectacular sunsets, but the fog rolling in only allowed us a gradual diminishing of sunlight. The vibrant hues pictured on the menu cover were left to our imagination. On the table between us was a bottle of Napa Valley Zinfandel and two half-full glasses, which we hadn't touched except for the splash he tasted to accept the wine. I was waiting for him to say something or at least take the first sip. He picked up his glass, and I stared at the reflection of the struggling flame of the small candle next to the bottle.

"Everything I think of saying sounds too damn heavy, so I'll just say happy twenty-first."

I lifted my glass and we clinked. "Thanks, George."

"I hope you had a good one."

"They always talk of twenty-one being a milestone. For me it was an earthquake. The earth is still shaking."

George nodded as if he wasn't sure he wanted to hear exactly how my birthday had been so unsettling. He had his hand wrapped around the glass, and he looked at it oddly. "It's been a long time since I've had a good glass of wine. I don't normally drink. For me it's a social thing, and since I am never social, I never drink. I don't find it much use as a palliative."

"You mean like my father did."

"I don't criticize anyone for it. Certainly not your father. He had his demons to quell. My father, too. It was his drunk driving that killed my parents. Considering the important people in my life that I have lost to alcohol, I guess I should be dead set against it."

"It's funny how some people can control it and others can't. I think I'm more like you. It's never done much to help me with my problems."

He put his glass down and took a deep breath. His left hand was flipping the fork over and over. "Do you resent your father for abandoning you?"

The question shocked me not for its content, but because I had purposely avoided anything heavy about my father. I thought it would be difficult for him and then he just threw it out there, the burning questions of my life.

"I did for a long time, and I suppose even now there are remnants of it. These last couple of months and particularly the trip to Mexico helped me get beyond the hurt. As you say, he had his demons." It was my turn to lift my glass and I pointed it at him. "I might ask you the same question."

He took a large swallow of wine and looked at me over the rim. I knew he was wondering how much I understood about their relationship.

"You don't have to answer that," I said, "but I want you to know that I have a pretty good idea of what you meant to each other. He told me some things in the letter. So you don't need to feel like you have to hide anything."

"He didn't abandon me. If anything, I abandoned him. In prison I made him stop the visits and letters. It seemed the best idea at the time, though it nearly killed me. I had nothing to live for. God, I didn't want to get into this."

"It's almost impossible not to. But we should maybe get to know each other a bit more."

"You're wise for—"

"—for my age?"

"I'm not being condescending. You're obviously a smart, mature, and attractive young woman. I admire your strength. I know it hasn't been easy for you."

"When your childhood is ripped from your life, you grow up fast. But if we start talking about all that shit, the night is going to get depressing pretty fast."

"I am completely in favor of talking about something that's not depressing. I just wish I could think of something."

"Tell me about Parque Escondido. How did you get the idea? Vitico told me it had something to do with Barcelona."

"I was in college studying art when my parents died in the crash. I inherited not a fortune, but a good deal of money. I was an only child. I dropped out of school thinking I would return one day. I never did. After the funeral, I headed for Europe and squandered a lot of money traveling first-class, staying in fancy hotels, buying drinks for whoever would talk to me in bars and clubs. In Barcelona I thought I was in love, but I was so bewildered by life in the fast lane that I didn't know what I was doing. I mentioned that alcohol didn't do much for me, but cocaine did. I developed rather a serious habit. An older gentleman who owned an art gallery took me in and put me to work. I pretended to know something about art. The job allowed me to learn Spanish and attempt to develop my art. My medium was sculpture, particularly metal arts, terribly impractical but fun. The man, Jose María, treated me quite decently and was very patient. I was too young and unbridled to be much of a partner to him, though we managed to make a go of it for five years."

"Have you always been attracted to men?"

He blinked and hesitated. He acted as if he had already revealed too much, but then decided to go on. "In college I dated girls, but in my travels around Europe, there became no doubt where my proclivities lay. Barcelona was a wonderful place to delve into the gay experience, but the vapid life of discos and drugs soon became tiring to me, and much more so to Jose María. I still felt something was missing from my life. In the afternoons I wandered around the city looking at the fabulous architecture. It was when I saw the Dragon Gate at the Güell Pavilions that I become fascinated with Gaudi. I came to discover that the city was full of fine examples of his work. I loved that people alternately called him genius and insane. The Dragon Gate was a functional gate, but at the same time a ferocious metal beast that conjured up a mystical kingdom that might lay beyond it."

"It sounds like the gate at Parque Escondido."

"Actually the gate at Parque Escondido is an iguana, but of course I was inspired by Gaudi. Since iguanas are common in Mexico I wanted to make it more local. My gate is lot less elaborate than Gaudi's, but having focused on metal sculpture at school, I was fascinated with the way he made objects practical and at the same time whimsical and decorative. It was the complete antithesis of the functionally oriented Bauhaus movement, which came later and still has a tremendous influence on modern style. But in Gaudi I had found a kindred spirit to my way of thinking about style. So I went to Gaudi because of his metalwork, the fanciful streetlamps, gates, fences, chandeliers, and grillwork. But I came away with an appreciation of all his work, his concepts like using the natural physiology of the animal, vegetable, and mineral kingdoms. Particularly enchanting was the way he used tiles in this scheme. Since organic forms are curvy rather than flat or linear, he had to develop his own method for using tiles. It was called *trencadis*—broken pieces of tile to cover the surfaces as a mosaic. He got the decorative effect of ceramics combined with the iridescence of the glazed surfaces while at the same time remaining true to organic forms. Sorry, this is sounding like an art lecture."

"No, it's fascinating. It helps me understand much better what I saw in Parque Escondido."

"Where everything came together for me was Park Güell. He took a barren piece of land and made it into a work of art, all the while integrating his use of natural forms into a natural environment. That's what I was trying to do in Mexico. When I left Barcelona, I traveled all over Latin America. By the time I got to Mexico, I was tired. During my travels I thought about creating my own park. I had the inspiration and the money. All I needed was the land. I was traveling through central Mexico when the bus broke down in Acalán. While they were working on the repairs, I wandered up into the hills above the town. As you've seen, the town isn't much, but the surrounding countryside is magnificent. The higher up you go into the mountains, the more beautiful it becomes. I began looking for land to buy right away. It took another year to purchase the property and get things started. What I had in mind was crazy, a monumental task in rough terrain. I needed lots of workers. The town, suffering from high unemployment, was able to provide them. And that's how I met your father."

At the mention of my father, his face went through an immediate painful change. We had tried to steer away from emotional topics. His eyes had shown light as he explained about Gaudi and his project. But we had come full circle to where our conversations would always end up, the common thread—my father.

"Aside from being very handsome and quite charming, I saw right away that he was bright. He was doing the manual labor like the rest, but he would carry a sketchpad and hurriedly draw pictures when he had an idea. I had hired an architect from Spain, who would come every few months to check on the work. I invited Miguel to our meetings and found myself relying more and more on his judgment. He became my right-hand man. When I asked him why he had never gone to the university, he said that his family couldn't afford it. He had gone to work in the fields to help his father. I knew he wanted to see the world and I decided to send him to school in the States. I also knew I would miss him terribly, but I had to do it. In the end, that decision led to a series of devastating events." He sighed heavily and let his head drop.

"Here we are again."

"It's not always a good thing to take the boy out of the country."

"In his letter to me, he expressed how strange he felt growing up in the town, like he didn't belong."

"He was a rose blooming in the desert, a phenomenon. But when you try to transplant the rose to where you think it should thrive, you destroy the magic of its existence."

"Hey, it wasn't a total loss."

I made him smile. "Yes. He loved you very much. There were some good times. I visited you all in California as much as I could. I was selfish. I should have let him go."

"Did he ever tell you not to come?"

"As the years went by, he was the one encouraging me to visit, planning events where I would be included much to the chagrin of your mother."

We were getting very close to the topic of that summer. I had a desperate need to hear his side of the story, but it seemed too soon. Our eyes met and I believe he sensed my dilemma. We finished our dinners in silence and ordered dessert.

"When do you start law school?" he asked.

"In September. I have just a few weeks of freedom left."

"And when are you heading back to...are you still living in Hillsborough?"

"Oh, God, no. I have an apartment with some friends near Stanford. I mainly go to Ashton Lane to see Conchita."

"Don't tell me. She's still with the family?"

"She's a trooper. She's been giving me secret Spanish lessons. Anyway, I suppose I should head back in a day or two." I reached down for my purse and pulled out the letter. "My mission isn't quite finished. I don't know when is the appropriate time to give you this. In the safe deposit box, there was also a letter for you."

I held it out in the space between us. The candle flickered in his eyes as he stared at the thick envelope. The waiter arrived with the dessert and stood apart, gaping at us. George took the letter with a trembling hand and stuffed it in his jacket pocket.

"Mine was written a couple of years before he died. I suppose yours was written around the same time."

"I'm not sure I should read it," he said in a hushed voice, staring at the chocolate dessert as if it were a dead rat.

"I felt the same way, but in the end, how could I not?"

George was very subdued the rest of the dinner. He followed me to the Village Inn in Monte Rio to be sure I got back all right, but I was more worried about him. I thought I had made a mistake to give him the letter so soon after meeting, on a night when he had drunk for the first time in years. I kept asking him if he was okay to drive and he insisted he was. I probably should have given him more time to get used to the idea of having a connection to Miguel in his life. Yet as long as the letter sat like a brick in the bottom of my purse, I felt like we couldn't go forward. I wanted to relieve myself of at least that part of my mission, and it felt good to put it in his hands. There was also the possibility he might again retreat into his shell and I wouldn't have another opportunity.

George was still preoccupied when we said goodnight. As we stood awkwardly in the cold night air of the Inn parking lot, he had one hand in the pocket where he had put the letter and I imagined that he was caressing it, still not convinced it was real. When it came to the moment of separating, a handshake seemed too cold and a hug too familiar, so we didn't do anything. He took a step back, and then his eyes lit up as if something just occurred to him. He said he wanted to take me out for lunch the following day, and that I should meet him at his place around noon.

# 10: George

I removed the letter from my pocket and placed it on my desk. It seemed to glow in the spotlight of the desk lamp, begging to be read. I switched off the light and crawled into bed.

The wind made my home creak and pop as the warmth of the day was conquered by the cool night. And my emotions, too, were in a battle—the joy at seeing Rebecca as a mature and astute young woman against the raw pain of digging up the past. It was some comfort to know that the tragedy of losing both her parents at a young age hadn't destroyed her, but at the same time I felt responsible for all the hurt she had suffered. Despite her maturity and her courage in seeking me out, beneath the surface she must harbor some bitterness for what she had lost. She didn't seem to blame me, but I wasn't sure if she fully understood what happened that tragic summer.

Little Rebecca loved her mother, but she adored her father. I always believed that the heartbreak of her mother's death was somehow less painful to her than being abandoned by her father. Those years when she waited for him to come back from Mexico, in each one the hope being pared down a bit, could only have weighed on her. When the final blow of his death reached her, she must have been devastated. The full impact of her pain I could only guess at since my relationship with her ended when they put me into the squad car and I looked back and saw the adult-like worry in her face. I remembered how her father held her in his arms, using her to ground himself against the events that were eroding his life.

Perhaps the most painful part of that summer was that it led to a deterioration of Rebecca's relationship with Miguel, that perfect union of father and daughter. It was always a joy to watch them together. His eyes would soften when he was near her and she would curl up in his arms like fog cradled in a mountain valley—separate entities with a seamless connection. It was almost unnatural how she would never do anything around her father that might make him angry or feel disappointed in her. With her mother it was quite the opposite. I only had a few opportunities to witness Rebecca with Helen when Miguel was absent. But in those times, she would deliberately try her mother's patience, do things she knew she wasn't supposed to do, even use different language and a more assertive tone of voice.

I was on one of my visits, a few months before the last one where Helen met her death. At the time Miguel, Helen, and Rebecca were living in a small house in San Jose and had picked me up at my hotel. It was a warm, sunny spring day when we pulled up in front of the restaurant where we were to have brunch. Miguel dropped us off and went to park the car. Rebecca had wanted to go with him, but Helen insisted that she stay with us. Rebecca didn't make a scene in front of her father, though her disappointment was obvious. Miguel looked at her puckered face and told her to mind her mother.

Helen had chosen a trendy brunch café on Santana Row. There was a large crowd that spilled out onto the sidewalk, waiting for a table. Several were drinking mimosas. A friend of Helen's from high school burst from a large group waiting under the shade of a bottlebrush in full pink bloom and rushed over to Helen, calling her "Darling." In the distraction Rebecca wandered over to a store window next to the restaurant that sold handcrafted toys. I stood halfway between Rebecca and her mother, keeping an eye on her.

When Helen turned around to show off Rebecca to her friend, she was befuddled at not finding her daughter right behind her. If there was one thing that got Helen's ire up, it was to be caught off-guard in public. Her gaze fell accusingly on me, and I pointed toward the window. "Rebecca, come over here," she shouted.

Rebecca ignored her mother and continued staring through the window, her hands stuck on the glass and her nose pressed up against it. "Rebecca," Helen repeated. "Come here." Again the girl ignored her, though she moved her nose away from the glass and looked in my direction.

"Tio Jorge, I want to show you something." She beckoned with her little hand.

Helen winced. She hated that Rebecca called me Tio Jorge, especially in public. She always called me George and suggested on numerous occasions that her daughter do the same. Helen touched her friend's arm and made a comment that seemed to express the exasperation of having children.

The friend let out a high-pitched cackle, and Helen loped toward Rebecca in determined strides.

"Didn't you hear me? I was calling you." She grabbed the girl by the arm and started pulling her away from the window.

Rebecca wrenched her arm away. "I want to show Tio Jorge something."

"I'm sure George is not interested in toys. Now come on. Daddy will be here in a minute." She took hold of her arm again more forcefully.

"You're mean."

"I am not mean, Rebecca. I am your mother, and when I call you, I expect you to answer."

Rebecca's dark eyes burned with an intensity that made me sympathize with Helen who seemed to be at a complete loss. Then Rebecca saw her father coming around the corner and her mouth in a split-second went from twisted to gleeful. She ran to Miguel and jumped in his arms. All was forgotten on her part, though Helen still stood with her shoulders raised like a cornered raccoon. She glanced at me again as if it was somehow my fault.

"What's going on?" said Miguel.

"Your daughter," Helen answered with frustration. She turned and walked back toward the restaurant.

Miguel looked at me, and I shrugged my shoulders. I couldn't get involved.

What I realized was that the extraordinary relationship between father and daughter was not in opposition to Helen, nor needed to shut her out. It was, on the contrary, dependent on her, part of the triangle that needed three sides. She was the foil to their love. When he came to visit me those few times in prison before I sent him away, he talked of feeling lost in so many ways. He had needed Rebecca and Helen...and me to feel complete. Each of us fulfilled his complex set of desires in different ways. With only Rebecca still with him—when he was allowed to see her—and her depending on him so much emotionally, he felt overwhelmed. Things were out of balance. He told me how inadequate he felt, and I said he was being ridiculous, that he had to give her whatever he could. She would be thrilled with any attention he might give her. I also told him that he should focus on her and forget about me. I thought I was releasing him from the extra pressure of having to deal with me being in prison. But later it seemed that I pushed him further into that vast sea, drifting, feeling incompetent.

I also came to the conclusion that I had cut myself off not to be selfless as I pretended, but to protect myself from the pain of having a family that I could not be with for years, if ever again. Miguel and Rebecca were all I had of family, as imperfect as the arrangement was. As long as I could visit them from time to time, I had the illusion of being part of something. The land in Mexico and the Parque Escondido project fulfilled me in many ways and occupied my time, but there was still a part of me that desired human touch. If I couldn't have the physical reality of those two loved ones, however fleetingly and occasionally, I thought it better to have nothing. I couldn't stand the thought of pining for visiting day when they might or might not show up.

I heard of Miguel's death only months before I was to be released. It was a shock made crueler by the notion that perhaps I could have kept him in the States, closer to his daughter if I had allowed him to remain part of my life. Possibly it could have saved him, or was I giving myself too much credit?

The wind continued to rattle my trailer and I heard the cat door thump. I rose up and even in the darkness the letter glowed. He was in the room.

When I got out of prison, I could have contacted Rebecca. I thought about it. Yet so much time had passed. She had been raised by the grandparents that hated me. I was sure she wouldn't want to see me. And then there was the guilt of being at least partly responsible for her father tumbling into the depressive state and alcoholism that killed him. So when she came to my door, I was rocked by so many conflicting emotions that it was easier to let my commitment to isolation guide me. I denied her and closed the door. But even as I heard her car pull away, I had a feeling that it was just a matter of time. The spirit of Miguel had never stopped tracking me and now it had a physical agent in Rebecca. I played the game of trying to escape, though she found me without the least trouble.

# 11: Rebecca

"I'm not going to talk about the letter," said George in a hardened voice. His eyes showed the damage of a sleepless night and he looked as if he had aged several years.

I hadn't been prying. I hadn't even mentioned the letter. We were in Guerneville in a booth at Pat's Restaurant. He kept shifting his position, setting off a series of squeaks and groans from the plastic upholstery.

"I wouldn't ask you to."

"Well, your eyes…"

"Let's drop it. I will not ask you to talk about anything you don't want to talk about." I had planned to bring up reopening the trial, the second part of my mission, but I could see that it was not the time.

"You make it sound like I am a mental patient or something."

"George, please."

"I was doing just fine. I didn't need this." He was staring at the menu, gripping it like a shield between us.

I focused on the glossy picture of hotcakes dripping with butter and syrup. It made me sick to my stomach. "I'm sure it's not easy."

"Oh, what do you know?"

"Wait a minute." I pushed his menu down onto the table so that I could see his face. "What do I know? What do I know? As a five-year-old girl everybody I loved was taken away from me. From then on I was raised in a house where I was not loved and with an uncle that tormented me. I was treated like an exotic pet. I went to schools where everybody looked different. You think I don't know about pain?" Out of the corner of my eyes I saw people staring and the tables around us had gone quiet. I lowered my voice. "I'm sorry you went to prison for a crime you didn't commit. But look at you. You have turned into a bitter old man. You would rather wallow in self-pity than do something about your life. Excuse me. I've lost my appetite."

I got up and walked out of the restaurant. In my car I banged the palm of my hand against the steering wheel in anger, but mostly at myself, that I had let my temper get the better of me. I had gone to all the trouble of tracking him down and was just beginning to gain his confidence. Seeing me again must have been a shock. I should have cut him more slack, put up with his bad mood until it blew over. On the other hand I wasn't ready to march back in and apologize. We both needed time to contemplate this new relationship in our lives.

I started the car, made an illegal U-turn, and tested the power of the engine. On the stretch between Guerneville and Monte Rio, I drove recklessly. I was lucky that there were few cars on the road.

At the Village Inn, I started packing my clothes. And then I unpacked them. Was I just going to run away? I said things that were out of line and he would probably never forgive me. Yesterday I had gotten him to open up and today I pushed him right back into his shell with my unkind words. It wasn't the end of the world. I would have to go after him and get him back. There was a knock on the door, which I assumed was the maid who I had seen with her cart a couple of doors down.

George stood at the door with his hands crossed in front of him. He leaned forward, his mouth twisted with the words he was about to say. "What makes you convinced I didn't do it?"

I stared at him a moment, not quite sure what he was talking about. And then I let out a gnarly laugh. "Are you kidding me? Do you honestly think I would be here if I thought you killed my mother? Anybody with a brain the size of a pea could read about the case and see that you were railroaded. And I know my Uncle Jimmy better than about anybody—if he said something was true, there's a good chance it was a lie." George stood teetering in a flash of bright sunlight. I pushed the door fully open. "Please, come in. I'm sorry for what I said. That was terrible."

He shuffled into the room and looked around. "It's true though, what you said. You've had it rougher than me."

"No, I haven't. And I *can't* imagine what you have been through. It's unconscionable what the Delon family did to you. One of the reasons I'm here is because I want to do something about it."

"Like what?"

"Reopen the case. Get Jimmy to say he lied. Bring a civil suit against my grandparents. It was all their doing. Whatever it takes to clear your name."

"No."

"No what?"

"What's done is done. They'll just bring up dirt from the past. Even if Jimmy retracts his statement, they'll still think I did it."

"Things have changed in the last fifteen years."

"What do you mean by that?"

"It wouldn't be such a big deal that you and my father were together. Gay men have rights, can even get married in some states."

George winced. "Your father wasn't gay."

"He loved you. He told me that in his letter. I also know you had a physical relationship. Call it what you want. I should have said two men can get married now—gay, bisexual, straight, it doesn't matter."

"I suppose you think your generation has transcended labels and found the key to sexual freedom."

"Not at all, but we're a hell of a lot closer than your generation. The point is, you were sent to prison unjustly and I was robbed of my one remaining parent...and maybe the possibility of being raised by two men who loved me."

"That's what your grandparents feared most. But to be honest, I'm not sure that would have happened. Your father was fearful about being open."

"At least let me have the fantasy that I would have lived with my father and you would have played some role in my life. That is what was taken away from me and I can never forgive my grandparents for that."

"So you are going to make them pay?"

"God, I would think you would be happy to see them go down. They ruined your life."

"Are you sure I'm not just being a bitter old man wallowing in self-pity?"

"That was unfair. I was angry. It's not about getting revenge. It's about setting things right."

"Are you sure?"

"Well, motives are never black and white, but we do have right on our side."

"I can't give you an answer right now. I have to think about it."

We went across the street to a café and had a quiet lunch. That afternoon I drove back to Palo Alto to give him time to think about my proposition. In the next week I didn't hear from him. I called him a couple of times, but he didn't pick up. He had no answering machine and no cell phone. I could only communicate with him if he deigned to answer the phone or if I showed up at his doorstep. I had the feeling that he had crawled back into his hole.

Patricia called several times. She was anxious to go forward with the case, perhaps a little too enthusiastic as we hadn't even discussed how I was going to pay her. Motives are never black and white. I suppose she hoped to infuse her life with a bit more excitement than the regular family law that she had been practicing. What else she hoped for I could only imagine.

Conchita was rolling out the dough for a pie when I came in the back door to the kitchen. After a greeting kiss, I revealed the mystery friend I had gone to visit.

"*O mija,* why you don tell me? How is the poor man? I suppose he very angry wit me."

"I wish he were more angry. He's mostly sad. He lives alone and seems to have no friends. Doesn't talk to his neighbors and lives in a mobile home. He asked about you."

"Really? I think he be angry me."

"And why is that?" I had the feeling that Conchita knew things she still hadn't told me. She hid her face by turning around and pressed the roller into the dough.

"I don know. Maybe cause I work for the family. He always very nice to me, bring me things from Mexico. I feel bad I not help him."

"Could you have helped him?"

"Oh, you know. Tio Jorge lawyer want me to testify, but I scared. I no legal then. *La Migra* maybe send me back to Mexico." She had the dough irregular and cracked at the edges. She balled it up, slapped it around in her hands, and started again.

"Conchita, will you look at me?" I moved to her side, and she turned toward me.

"*Sí, hija,* what you want me say?"

"What you would have said if they made you testify under oath."

Her eyes started to tear up. "You don know how every day I must think of sin I make, how it hurt me know it was in my hands to save Tio Jorge and I not do it cause I fraid. But I no lie. *La señora* no let police talk to me. That day she tell me go into town."

"What happened, Conchita? What could you have told the police?"

"I know Jimmy in bed when he say he out there on cliff and see Jorge push Helen. He never get up so early in his life. When they come running to house, say about accident, *la señora* send me to wake up Jimmy. I go in his room very dark, smell of cigarette and drink. He dead to world. No way he see what happen. I so surprise when friend tell me after trial that Jimmy say he see that, his words make Tio Jorge go to prison. I don't believe it. I feel so bad. You think I bad person, *hija.*" She was sniffling and wiped her cheeks, leaving a trail of flour in the crevices of her lined face.

"No, I don't think you're a bad person. You didn't know. But what if I told you that you now have a chance to tell the truth."

She stopped sniffling and looked at me with pursed lips. "What you mean?"

"I'm going to reopen the case, prove that Jimmy lied, show that Tio Jorge was falsely tried. I need you to help me."

"*O no, hija, la señora* go crazy. She kill me."

"Conchita, you're legal now. You can work anywhere you want."

"Not so easy. I work here all my time in this country. Where I can go? What I do?"

"Just think about it."

When next I talked to Patricia, I reported the lack of progress—George was incommunicado and Conchita was still afraid of my grandmother. She had spent a greater part of her life terrified of her employer.

"What about Jimmy?" said Patricia. "He's an adult now. He must feel some remorse. He could say he was coerced by his parents, distraught over his sister's death. All we need is for him to recant his testimony. Could you talk to him?"

"Jimmy feel remorse? That's a laugh. He's an idiot, but he's not stupid enough to bite the hand that feeds him."

On the drive up to Monte Rio, Conchita twitched in her seat and kept moaning, "I don know, *mija.* I don know." I was ready to open the car door and push her out. She was terrified of going against Gran, but the immediacy of meeting with George was the greater fear, imagining that he would be a vengeful monster who blamed her for being sent to jail. She was making this trip, she kept telling me, only because I asked her.

George was charming from the start, much more so than he had been with me recently. He inquired after her family, speaking in excellent Spanish despite the fact that he rarely used it. She talked about her last trip to Mexico and how things were changing so rapidly, how he probably wouldn't recognize it. They talked about me and how Miguel would be so proud. It made me uncomfortable, but I had to feel pleased because it was a conversation that I never expected to hear in my lifetime. Their musings about the past brought back memories from those early years, and I realized that Conchita had been George's only ally in the Delon household. She had encouraged in small ways my closeness with Tio Jorge.

Since Conchita and George appeared comfortable, I began to gradually edge our talk toward that summer. "I remember the day they took George away. They still hadn't told me about my mother. I couldn't understand what was going on, and nobody would tell me anything." Conchita again became agitated, twisting her hands and breathing irregularly. "We know that Jimmy lied at the trial. Conchita told me that Jimmy was in bed when he was supposedly witnessing the...what happened. Without his testimony there would have been no case."

"Señor Jorge, don hate me," Conchita said, switching back to English.

"It wasn't your fault. I'm sure if you had been given the chance, you would have told the truth. No one knows better than me that Señora Delon can be very intimidating. I don't know how you have worked for her all these years."

"I don know, too, but I think is coming to end. I have the chance to do something. This beautiful daughter of Miguel is going help me do the right thing. As for Señora Delon, it is time to leave. I think this for long time."

I looked at Conchita with surprise. "You mean...?"

"Yes, I am ready."

We all looked at each other, three misfits about to take on the powers that be. Conchita would be defying her employers for the last thirty years. I was challenging my own flesh and blood, the people who had given me food and shelter, and if not a great amount of affection, at least what they thought was protection from the evils of the world. George would be forced to relive that horrible summer, with really little to gain except a clearing of his name, which most likely wouldn't change his life much. Of the three of us, he seemed the most bothered by the proposition, sinking into a moody quietness. All this was forcing him out of the solitude that had become so important to him. I understood that, and yet I couldn't help thinking that there was something else, something deeper that concerned him.

On the way back home I told Conchita that I would ask my friends if any of their mothers were looking for help. I spoke confidently that she would be able to find work soon. I also asked about her payday, thinking that she might want to wait until after receiving her money before giving notice. We discussed strategy.

Conchita turned to me as if she had had a revelation. "I think I go back to Mexico," she announced. "My sister lost her husband last year. I can live with her. One of my brothers is sick and another can no longer work. I have money in the bank. It is time. Of course I stay here as long as you need me."

The thought that Conchita wouldn't be nearby to comfort me when I was sad, sit me down with a cup of coffee and a piece of pie and listen to my troubles, hit me hard. But I could understand her desire to return to her home. Her mention of brothers and sisters back in Mexico also upset me. I realized how little I knew about her personal life. I got a sinking feeling that I had been as bad as my grandparents, as if employees weren't real people with real stories, just fixtures that the rich adorn their houses with.

"Conchita, I'm embarrassed that I know so little about your life. You never told me how you got to our house. All those years you took care of us and I know so little about you."

"I never tol' you cause it make me bery sad. You want me tell you, I tell you. I think is time you know."

She was married as a teenager to Juan Carlos, one of the younger sons of 10 brothers and sisters. He had little chance of any help from his family and work was scarce. In the first year of their marriage, he made the trek to the border, hired a coyote to cross, and ended up working the picking fields in the Salinas Valley of California. Soon after he left she found out she was pregnant. At great risk he came back for the birth of his son. The child was underweight and weak from the beginning with unexplained fevers and diarrhea. Juan Carlos was worried, but he needed to get back as the peak of harvest season was coming.

To recross the border he didn't want to spend the money on a coyote. A friend had told him how to hook up with small groups that went through the desert. Conchita warned him that it was risky, but he was stubborn, saying he couldn't afford the safe way and at the same time leave her the money that she was going to need.

A week after Juan Carlos left, the little boy died in his sleep. As Conchita told the story the tears flowed freely down her cheeks. "Long time I no tell the story, but the pain is always here." She pointed to her heart. I stopped at a gas station mini-mart to get some water.

"Wait, that's just the beginning," she said to me as I got back in the car with the plastic bottles of cold water. It was a hot day and she put one of the bottles up to her cheek to cool her tears. I held one to my forehead, and the condensation dripped down my face.

After the death of her son, all she could think about was getting away from the memories, out of the town with its poor sanitary conditions, which she blamed for her baby's death. More than ever she wanted to be with her husband. She used the money she had saved in a jar on a high shelf of her kitchen, plus what he had left her, to make the trip. It was strange that she hadn't heard from him, but often weeks would go by without talking, when he was very busy or didn't have the money to call.

Luck was on her side and she got to Salinas in just over a week. She found the house where eight men from her town lived, one of them her cousin. The cousin told her that they hadn't seen Juan Carlos since he left for Mexico. Conchita fell into a rough wooden chair and thought she would die. Her cousin made her some coffee and helped her contact agencies that could help her. She imagined her husband wandering through the desert dying of thirst, but the cousin assured her that he was probably picked up, maybe even sent back to Mexico. She waited a few days and then called Mexico. There was no word. She took a Greyhound bus to Southern California and talked to a group that looked for survivors in the desert. They had no Juan Carlos from her town in the records and sent her to the morgue in Pima County, the central location for unidentified bodies of men who had died in crossing the Arizona desert. None of them was Juan Carlos. She was crying again as she told of her agonizing search. I tried to concentrate on my driving so as not to fall into weeping myself.

"I beg the Virgin to let him live, but she no listen to me," said Conchita, nearly choking on her tears.

She went back to Salinas. The cousin's sister worked in Hillsborough for a rich family and knew of a woman who was looking for a live-in maid. It was Gran. She had just fired the last one and was desperate. Helen was still a little girl, and Jimmy had just been born. The moment she met *la señora*, she knew it would be a difficult position, but she needed the job.

"You never thought of remarrying? Having more children?" I asked.

"How can I think of finding new husband when I don know where is Juan Carlos? I wait and wait. Every week I call the house in Salinas. I call Mexico. Nothing. I feel a great hole in my heart. Anyway, with the pain of losing my baby, I no want another child. Your mother and Jimmy become my new family. Helen was lovely girl, very strong and with hard head. *Madre mia,* she difficult sometime, but good girl. Jimmy, I don know what happen. Even when baby he always a problem. When I try teach him be good, he run to *la señora* and say I mean. For better or worst, they become my children."

We pulled into the back of the house by the four-car garage. The doors were open and I saw Gran's Cadillac. I then looked up and saw the curtain drawn back in Gran's bedroom. In the pose of a temple guard she stared down at me with hard cold eyes. I turned to Conchita and said that I wasn't coming in. Before I could escape, Gran was out the back door, marching toward the car. I rolled down the window and felt a blast of heat mixed with her indignation. She laid her manicured hand on the car door.

"Rebecca, what's going on?"

"What do you mean?"

She glared at me a moment as if I were an insolent child. "You know what I mean. No returned phone calls. Secret trips. I called the bank and found out you used your visa card in Mexico. Mexico," she repeated as though I had gone to visit the devil. Conchita had gotten out of the car and stood by the kitchen door watching us, biting her lower lip. "You didn't tell me. I had to call the bank to discover that out of the blue you had taken off for parts unknown."

"I'm twenty-one now. I can do what I want."

She pounded her hand on the frame of the open window, her fuchsia-colored nails nearly grazing my shoulder. "When have you ever been a prisoner? You've always had a lot of freedom, maybe too much. But this sneaking around I find a bit juvenile. And today, your whisking Conchita off to who-knows-where without a word to me, spending the whole day away. I believe I deserve more respect. What in God's name were you doing in Mexico?"

"I went to meet my other family."

"Your family is here. When have they ever shown any interest?"

"How could they? Even if they had written, I suppose the letters would have been intercepted." My cheeks burned as I said it, but it was followed by the calming satisfaction of getting something out in the open. She took a step back and folded her bony arms in front of her.

"Everything I did was for your own good."

"I don't have time to discuss this now."

"You're not coming in the house? I think you own me an explanation."

"No. You owe me...and many. But now is not the time." I wasn't feeling strong enough to confront Gran. I was anxious to have that conversation with her, but on more equal ground, when I was feeling stronger, and not in her house. I started the car with the thought that I wouldn't have many more opportunities to hear the engine purr before I relinquished it. I felt a tinge of guilt that I still needed it for a while. "Very soon we will have a nice long talk. Goodbye, Gran."

She stood as tall and solid as a garden statue while I pulled out of the driveway. As her shadow receded I felt the blood resurging, my strength coming back. I put up the window and felt the clunk as it locked into place. Cool returned to the gray, new-smelling interior.

A week went by of secret negotiations with Conchita. She wanted to give notice sooner rather than later, before she lost her nerve. We waited until the day after she received her check. While Gran was at the hairdresser, we packed Conchita's things. I was shocked at how little she had after so many years in her small room off the kitchen. Most of it fit into the trunk, though we had to put a couple of boxes on the back seat. We sat at the kitchen table drinking coffee while we waited.

Through the French doors we watched Gran maneuver her giant Cadillac into the garage. She came toward the house with a steady, upright gait until she passed my car where she paused and squinted at the contents in the back seat. She glared toward the house, and then marched the rest of the distance to the back door.

She left the door open as she approached us sitting at the table. We rose up to greet her.

"Are you picking up some of your things?" she said to me. "I've been meaning to tell you that you should go through some of that stuff in the attic. I'm collecting items for St. Vincent de Paul and I don't want to mistakenly give away some of your things."

"*Señora,*" Conchita began with a trembling upper lip. Gran winced as I had seen her do a thousand times at the way Conchita addressed her. "I must leave."

"Conchita, I think it's high time you learned English. Mrs. Delon would be more appropriate." She looked from one to the other of us at we stood at attention.

"Gran, did you hear what she said."

She sighed and let her right hand float up, a question mark in the air. "Half the time I don't know what she's saying."

"She's leaving. She will no longer work for you after today."

"Of all the cockamamie things. You're not serious."

"Yes, *Señora*...Mrs. Delon. I go."

"I suppose it's more money. I will talk to my husband."

"No, is not money. I need go."

Turning her gaze on me, she said, "Did you put her up to this? Because I don't understand a thing."

"No, is my idea."

"Just like that. After all we have done for you, you are going to leave me in the lurch. I have a luncheon here next Saturday of the Garden Society. Twenty-five people for lunch. You can't be serious."

"Gran, there are agencies. I'm sure you can find someone to take over."

"Of course I can get people to take over, but I need someone to orient them, tell them where things are, make sure things run smoothly. I don't have time to do that. Surely whatever little problem you have, Conchita, can be resolved after the luncheon." She stopped and took a breath, filling herself with righteous anger as if she realized that there was the slightest bit of begging in her voice. "I can't believe I am even listening to this. I have things to do and I imagine you do, too, Conchita. It doesn't look like you have started dinner."

Conchita had a grimace on her face, but she stood strong, much taller than her five feet two inches. She looked toward the stove. I could see her mind taking an inventory of what was in the refrigerator, though she didn't make a move toward it. Gran had turned around and was starting out of the room.

"Gran, you're not listening," I shouted. My voice sounder shriller than I expected, and both Conchita and Gran were startled. Gran did a pirouette.

"What in the world are you shouting about? This conversation is between Conchita and me, and it is finished."

"No, is not finished. I am finished. It is time I go. My things are in the car." Conchita said.

Gran looked at Conchita in shock. She didn't know what to say to her, so she turned on me. "Young lady, you certainly have been on your high horse lately. Your disloyalty I will blame on youth and the impetuous nature that you have never been able to control. But encouraging disloyalty in Conchita is something I absolutely can't abide. It is beyond compare. Conchita, if you walk out that door, there is no coming back."

Conchita was still strong with one leg ready to move out the door, though the other looked like it could buckle into a kneel. I took her by the arm and gave her the extra push she needed to get out of the kitchen.

"So that's it then, a fine how-do-you-do. You give them everything and they turn on you," Gran said, looking up to heaven.

"Gran, you are being overly dramatic. Conchita has decided to leave. End of story."

Gran reached for the counter with one hand and grabbed the pearls at her neck with the other. She made a low matronly roar, pushed herself off, and stomped out of the kitchen.

Conchita was torn in the car, a great sense of relief mixed with worry about the future. "What I have done?" she said with her head down.

"You did the right thing."

"That was terrible. I don thing I can testify...her sitting there looking at me."

"Yes, you can, and you will. When this is over, you will feel much better, like you have done the right thing. I promise."

"I don know. Mr. Delon always so good to me."

Her bringing Granddad into the conversation shook me. I wanted to think of him as an evil accomplice to Gran, yet Conchita's words gave me a sense that it wasn't true, that he was somewhat of a victim like all of us in Gran's war to get her way. I wondered if back then he had protested at all, or simply gone along with what I was sure had been Gran's idea, her vengeful reaction to the loss of a daughter. I knew they were both devastated by my mother's death, and not being a parent, I might lack the capability of understanding what a loss of a child can do to a person. They found a way to blame Tio Jorge, but the real culprit was my father who had taken their daughter away.

I was unsure, though, why they had been so insistent on raising me. I think the signs were there, even at the age of five, that I couldn't replace their golden girl, that I would be something of an embarrassment in their circles, that physically I would always be a reminder that their daughter had married a Mexican.

## 12: George

It was my beach. I claimed it as mine because I did not abandon it in hard times, for in fact, that was when I frequented it most. I went on days of dense fog, wind, and cold—days when no one else wanted to be there. There were many times I sat in fog so thick it drizzled from the sky. Only a storm could keep me away. I would go prepared—layers of clothing, waterproof jackets, scarves, hats, and gloves. I brought thermoses of hot tea and food to nourish me. And for my mind, I brought books to read, often a sketchpad. On days of bad weather I usually had the beach to myself, and if I had to share, it was with the occasional fisherman or hearty dog-walker.

On a midwinter day of damp cold air, when the fog was low and heavy, I pulled into the parking lot of Russian Gulch Beach to find that someone was in my regular spot. There were any number of other places to park, but cantankerous old fool that I was, I was irked that a large green Chevy truck was occupying my place. It must have been a newcomer, as the regulars, those few who showed up from time to time on dreary days, respected my spot. And as the truck had a "Dog is my copilot" bumper sticker, I surmised that I would have to contend with a romping dog in addition to a stranger's company on the beach.

When I emerged from the scrub and brambles that one had to pass through to get to the beach, a chilly wind cut through me and I caught the smell of rotting marine life. In a distance was a lone figure off to one side of the cove, grasping a fishing pole. The dog, an Irish setter, ran up and down the beach among large clumps of seaweed, chasing birds. Gulls and cormorants took flight while sandpipers ran with rapid skittish steps in front of the galloping strides of long reddish fur.

I settled into my place, a piece of driftwood that formed a natural lounge chair. A thick branch stub acted as a backrest and at its base was a flat part of the trunk that served as the seat. The man, some thirty yards away, turned once to acknowledge my arrival, and then ignored me. His dog was busy with the birds, so I was left in peace. I warmed myself with sweet, hot, milky tea and ate some rolls that I had stuffed with cheese. I followed the little sandwiches with red seedless grapes, which I popped in my mouth as I read a collection of Flannery O'Connor's short stories. No matter how destitute you imagine your life to be, you can read her characters and come to the conclusion that your life is a stroll in the park by comparison. I finished a deliciously grotesque story about a traveling bible-salesman who stole a young girl's artificial leg. I popped another grape in my mouth and giggled.

It was early afternoon and the sun broke through for five minutes before it was gobbled up again by the bank of fog. I tried to sketch a small flock of brown pelicans flying in formation. I wondered how the lead bird was chosen and sketched it larger than the others. When I bored of drawing, I watched the fisherman cast and recast his line with incredible patience. It tired me and I slid down onto the rough sand, leaned my head against the trunk, and took a nap.

I woke up to a hairy beast sniffing my face.

*"Rudi, ven acá,"* I heard the man shout.

I sat up abruptly and saw him walking toward me. He had the pole, a net, and a tackle box in one hand and a small cooler in the other. A few wisps of dark, curly hair had escaped from under his striped stocking cap and he had a couple days' growth of beard on his handsome face. He wore a heavy wool sweater in navy blue and baggy jeans.

"Sorry," he said from a few feet away.

*"No hay de que."* I rarely spoke Spanish, but something, perhaps his addressing the dog, or the way he looked, made me answer in the language.

*"Entiendes español?"*

*"Sí, pero hace tiempo que no hablo."*

The dog continued to sniff around my bag.

"Rudi, leave the man alone."

"Really, it's no problem."

"I think he woke you up. Sorry again." He started to walk toward the trail to the parking lot and Rudi dashed in front of him.

"Is that your green truck?" I wanted to say something to him and it was all I could come up with.

"Yeah."

"Used to have one like that. Chevy, isn't it?"

He walked back toward me and smiled. He had a joyful smile. "What do you drive now?"

"Mustang. Old one." I couldn't believe I was talking to him about cars as if it were something that mattered.

"I love Mustangs. I'll check it out when I leave."

"I'm about ready to go myself. The cold has seeped all the way to my bones."

"Come on. We can walk together. Need help up?"

He set the cooler down and offered me a hand. Though I wore gloves it was still the closest thing to physical contact I had had in a long time and it sent a little shiver up my spine. We stood eye-to-eye and I realized that he was almost as tall as I was.

"You come here a lot?" he asked.

"Might say that."

He pointed his fishing pole toward the water. "I check out different beaches where I think the fishing might be good, depending on the currents, the tides, the season."

I gathered my things and we started toward the parking lot. As we got into the brush, it became much quieter, the roar of the waves muffled.

"I'm Alberto, by the way," he said over his shoulder.

"My name's George. *Mucho gusto.*"

He stopped and turned around. "*El placer es mío,*" he said with a wink, and then quickly continued on. It happened so fast I wasn't sure it was a wink. My years of being a hermit made these moments of human interaction surreal. I had the distinct feeling that he was being a tad flirtatious, but I immediately dismissed it as preposterous.

"You live around here?" he asked.

"Monte Rio."

"I'm in Forestville. Got a little place. Just me and my dog." The fact that he lived alone was more information than was called for. "You don't sound like you're from here," he said, "I mean, originally."

"No. Back east."

"I grew up in Mexico."

"Is that so?"

Whereas on the beach we had to nearly shout above the ocean noise and wind, here in the bushes it seemed that a whisper could be heard. A crow cawing in a nearby tree sounded amplified. What little light there was came filtered through the trees and I had visions of being on a trek through the wilds, Alberto as my guide. I watched his form as he moved gracefully along the path, maneuvering the fishing rod without catching it on anything. Where branches obstructed the way, he moved them aside and held them until I passed. Rudi barked and ran after something that rustled in the underbrush. There was a fallen tree over the trail that we had to climb over, and he waited until I had cleared it, a half-smile on his lips. My heart was pounding wildly as if we were being chased.

The trail opened up onto the parking lot where our vehicles sat side by side. We were back in the light of day. Hearing the cars along Highway 1 and seeing them creep around the mountain curves at a distance brought me back to reality. We weren't alone in the wilds anymore. At a short distance were people in their cars and more in the town of Jenner. Alberto put his fishing equipment in the back of the truck while Rudi roamed the parking lot searching for signs of food and other animals.

"Nice car," said Alberto.

"I bought it on kind of a whim. A neighbor was selling it."

"It's in good shape. What is it an '80, '81?"

"'80."

"I've got a couple of beers left. Would you like one?"

Beer was something I associated with hot weather, Mexico. I never drank it in California, and didn't relish the idea of drinking one in the cold. Yet I said, "Why not?"

He popped open a couple of Tecates and gave one to me.

"Why don't we sit in the truck? It's a little cold to be standing around out here." He looked over at Rudi and saw that he was still entertained.

We had moved from the wide-open beach to the hush of the underbrush. Now as we closed the doors to the truck, we were in a new intimate environment, a vacuum, cut off from the world outside. We were sitting close enough that I could smell the dampness of his wool sweater. It was all like a strange dream. Nothing seemed related to my actual life. It was reality through antique wavy glass.

He turned on the radio. It was set to a Latin romantic music station and Selena was singing from beyond the grave, "*Ay, ay, ay, como me duele.*"

"That's an old one," I said.

"You know it?"

I nodded. Selena was popular with the guys in prison, that song in particular.

"They play a lot of old stuff in the afternoon." He chugged the last of his beer and opened another one. "This is the last one. We'll have to share it."

"Still working on this one."

It was warm in the truck, but the beer didn't taste good to me. I had to force myself to drink it.

"You're not a real beer drinker, huh?" he said, giving my upper arm a light punch with the beer in his fist.

"I used to be...in Mexico."

"You've been to Mexico?"

"I lived there."

"Tell me about it."

I regretted bringing it up. The memories were so fraught with images of Miguel. I focused my descriptions on the land, where it was, nothing personal. I let my words drift into the mundane of what landscaping I had done and then stopped to finish the last of my beer. I looked over at him and saw Miguel in his eyes. "I should go," I said.

"Not yet. You have to help me with this last beer."

"I'm sure you can handle it."

"I know I can handle it, but I want to share it." He was staring at me as if trying to communicate another message. "Come on," he said, resting the can on my thigh. "I get lonely sometimes. Don't you?"

"I would think a guy like you would have plenty of girls after him." I spoke the words mechanically. My leg was twitching and my throat was dry. I took the beer and drank a sip.

"I failed at all my relationships. I don't know. I always end up alone."

I handed him the beer. The afternoon light was fading. The windows were steamed up. The music pulled little strings attached to the heart pounding in my chest. "I really need to go."

He put his arm on my shoulder and touched the back of my head, caressed it gently. "Don't go," he whispered.

A garbled laugh escaped from my mouth.

"What is it?" he said.

"I was just thinking. Back in high school, whenever we accidently touched another person or bumped into them we would jokingly say, 'Don't touch me unless you mean it.'"

"I mean it." He pulled my head onto his shoulder and continued massaging it. Little explosions were going off in my body. I felt like the desert receiving the first plops of rain after a long drought. It was magical and terrifying.

## 13: *Rebecca*

George and I came out of the Guerneville Post Office in the kind of jaunty mood you get after doing something quirky. We were friends again and had just mailed a postcard to Abuela, Vitico, and Jorge. I imagined their faces in reading it. The card was a picture of the wide beach at Jenner dotted with driftwood. I told them the beach in the picture was close to where I had found George (Tio Jorge). Although George was reluctant at first, I got him to write something at the bottom. He put "*Saludos*" and then signed his name.

We were on our way to have lunch just as a pickup truck pulled into a parking space and a young Latino man got out. George stopped, the cords in his neck rigid, his body stiff. He stared at the man. It was the first time I had seen him react to anybody on the street. He normally walked with his head down and didn't seem to be aware of anyone. I, on the other hand, during the times we had been together, hadn't let the large number of attractive Russian River men pass by without a notice. I knew a lot of them were gay, but I wasn't sure about this guy. George was in a trance.

The young man was in a hurry, a couple of large envelopes tucked under his arm as he juggled his keys, sunglasses and a paper coffee cup. He wouldn't have noticed us, if George's stare hadn't been so piercing. When their eyes met, the man broke into a smile.

"Hello, George. How are you?" He shifted everything to his left hand and then stuck out his right. Noting the smile and jovial tone of voice, I wondered if George was quite the recluse he claimed to be.

Taking his hand languidly, George mumbled, "Hello, uh...Alberto, isn't it?"

"You remembered." He grinned at me and offered the hand that George had quickly dropped.

George emerged from his stupor to introduce us. "This is Rebecca...my niece."

I was amused at his need to indentify me as a relative. At the same time it felt good that he was making me part of his family. Alberto's handshake was firm but gentle, a workman's hand. His deep brown eyes peered into mine as if we shared an ancient bond. And then it became obvious to me why George had been so flustered. Alberto had a square jaw, olive skin, deep brown eyes, and a shock of wavy chestnut hair like my father. He was taller, though, almost as tall as George, and in great shape. His jeans were tight and splattered with paint. The tail of a creature tattooed on his upper arm crept down from under the T-shirt sleeve that gripped his right bicep. He continued to hold my hand as he searched for something to say.

"I'm on my lunch break," he said, moving his gaze to George and withdrawing his hand. "Always seems like there are other things to do besides eating lunch."

George was still dumbstruck. "Yes, I guess so."

"We're on our way to lunch ourselves," I said. "Pat's down the street." It was a millimeter short of an invitation to join us.

"I'm just going to pick up a sandwich at the deli after I mail these letters." His face was frozen in a grin, letting his eyes dart back and forth from George to me. None of us knew what to say. George shuffled his weight from one foot to the other. He had his hands stuffed into the pockets of his khaki pants. His mouth was half-open as if he were about to speak.

"Well, it was nice running into you," said Alberto.

"Nice to meet you," I said in a dry tone.

He took a step toward the Post Office entrance.

"Wait," said George, snapping out of it. "I mean, you could join us." His invitation sounded like a rusty nail being pulled out of a plank. I held my breath.

"I wouldn't want to intrude."

"No intrusion. No intrusion at all." George spoke as if he was trying to convince himself.

"Ha, ha," Alberto laughed nervously. "Well, then. I could meet you there if you want to go ahead. Got to mail these." He took the letters from under his arm and waved them in the air. One flew off, landing a few yards away. I ran over to retrieve it. When I returned it to him, he smiled at me mysteriously again. I moved toward George and took his arm.

"See you in a few," Alberto said.

George walked stiffly, his body still tense.

"I suppose it was rash of me to invite him. Perhaps it wasn't a good idea," he said.

"What's with you, George?"

"He's a fisherman."

I wondered if he was a fisher of men. "And?"

"I met him at the beach. He has a dog."

"Is that what he does for a living? Fish, I mean?"

"He seemed quite taken with you."

"Oh, I don't think so. From your reaction I might think you were interested." It was one of those prying observations that I knew he hated, but I didn't mind saying it. I wanted us to get things out in the open, to share adult feelings in the new configuration of our relationship.

"My dear, being interested in someone is not something I have allowed myself for a long time. There's no place in my life for that, and besides, directing my desires at him would certainly fall on fallow ground."

"He seemed quite friendly, happy to see you."

"Maybe because I had an attractive young woman in my company."

"I appreciate the compliment, but I think you are reading way too much into it. Latin men like to flirt."

George made a little snort. "You got that right."

"Was my father a flirt?"

"I wasn't thinking of him."

"How could you not?"

"Did you notice the resemblance?"

"I'm not blind."

"To answer your question, no. Your father was much too earnest. But then, he was very young when I met him. It was a different time."

We were sitting in a booth staring at the menus when Alberto came in, though I don't think either of us was really looking at the daily specials. I had a million questions I wanted to ask George, most of them about my father. I also had a few about the man who was about to join our table.

Instead of coming right over, Alberto gave us a little wave before going to the restroom. When he emerged and came to the table, the waves of his hair were shiny with dampness and smoothed back from his forehead. I noticed the antiseptic smell of the bathroom soap. He hesitated a moment about which side of the booth to sit on before plopping down next to George, who slid as far as he could into the corner.

I hate the awkward silences of meals with people you don't know, so I searched for polite questions to ask Alberto. Though George and Alberto seemed by their first greeting to have a friendly connection, it was obvious that George knew almost nothing about him. We learned that he had a cabinet-making business. As the boss, he told us, he didn't have to rush back to work. George asked about Rudi and Alberto told us that his dog stayed at home during the day, had a big yard where he could run in Forestville. I looked at his hand and saw no ring, just little tufts of dark hair on each knuckle. As people walked by, I tried to gauge if he gave more attention to men or women, but he mostly stayed focused on the table. Alberto turned the conversation to George, trying to draw him out. He asked how long he had lived in Mexico. I jumped in to save George from talking about his past and asked Alberto where he had been born. He had an accent, though not strong. He told us he was from Hermosillo, Mexico, and had been in the Bay Area about ten years.

Though I sat directly across from Alberto, he had been politely avoiding looking at me too much, turning sideways to talk to George. Then he raised his eyes with an enigmatic smile on his unusually thick lips and focused on me. "And what about you? Are you Mexican?"

"On my father's side, but I grew up here in California. My paternal grandparents live in Central Mexico not too far from Querétaro."

While we waited for the coffee, George, who had been fidgeting throughout the meal, got up to go to the restroom. Alberto let him out, and then leaned back and stretched his arm along the back of the booth. I could see more of his tattoo, a dragon with intricately rendered scales and twists of its body.

"Is George your uncle on your mother's side?"

I looked at my hands interlaced on the table, wondering how much I should tell him. "He's not really my uncle. He was a friend of my father's. I always called him Tio."

He raised his eyebrows and stifled the smile. "They were good friends, I gather."

I froze, and then felt my face redden. "Why yes. Did George mention him?"

"Not exactly, only said that I reminded him of someone."

I took the paper napkin from my lap, brought it up to the table, and twisted it into a knot. I stared at the food stains on it.

"Sorry, if I hit a nerve."

"It's just that my father passed away a few years back. It was hard for both of us."

"I'm truly sorry."

George stood over the table like a headmaster who had caught two students cheating. I lifted my coffee cup to drink and Alberto stirred his as he scooted over to let George sit on the outside. We fell silent again as if we had tired of the strict diet of acceptable subjects, but the hidden ones, the bits of forbidden fruit, collected anxiously in the back of our throats.

"I should get back to work."

"We'll walk you to your truck," said George.

"It's not necessary," said Alberto.

"After this meal, I'm sure it will be a lazy walk for us," I said. We had all ordered the lunch special of meatloaf, mashed potatoes, and peas. "You're probably in a hurry."

"Nonsense," said George. "He's his own boss, remember?"

I kicked George under the table. My original curiosity had waned under the strain of touching on the past. It happened every time I met someone new, the uncertainty of how much to tell. In this case, with George's unusual behavior added into the mix, I felt that further conversation would only be strained.

The waitress brought the check and Alberto insisted on paying for it. The three of us walked out together and then strolled down the main street of Guerneville. Alberto, perhaps tired of our reticence to speak, was suddenly a chatty teenager, commenting on everything—the way the afternoon heated up the minute the fog burned off, the two young women in tank tops and jeans holding hands, the older man with chaps and pierced nipples, the motorcycles gunning their motors in the street, and the brave families who joined the parade. It was August, vacation month at the Russian River, giving us a great chance for people-watching.

As George had suggested, Alberto was in no hurry to get back to work. In front of the shops in the center of town, he reverted even further to being a little kid. He pointed at things in the windows and made silly comments. George and I were wet rags to his enthusiasm, so I couldn't understand why he dragged out the time to be with us.

At the pharmacy, George said that he had to go in and get something. He suggested we keep walking, that he would catch up. I wanted to kick him again for leaving me alone with Alberto a second time.  He was much too charming and good-looking. With a lot of the same qualities that I had admired in Vitico, he had gotten my attention, and there wasn't the barrier that he was my uncle. At the same time I could think of a thousand reasons not to let myself go, not the least of which was an as-yet-undefined friendship with George. For all I knew, they were secret lovers. It reeked of stay-awayness.

Alberto stopped to look at a floppy top hat of multicolored velvet in the window of a curiosity shop. "Look at that hat. Who would be caught in broad daylight wearing something like that?"

To be contrary I said, "I think it's kind of cute."

"Okay. Give me your number."

"What?"

"In case I see someone walking down the street in that hat, I want to call you and tell you what the person looks like. I'll tell you if they look cute or not."

"I don't think I need to know that bad."

"Or you just don't want to give me your number."

"There's a lot you don't know about me."

"Thus the number for future conversation during which you might enlighten me."

"I'm going through a lot of stuff right now."

"I figured."

"Is it that obvious?"

"You and George are two of a kind."

"We are?" I knew I wasn't the jolliest person around, but it disturbed me to think I was in George's league.

"He's a good man, but he carries too much sadness around with him."

"He has his reasons."

"And you, too?"

"Yep."

"Can I borrow your phone a minute?"

"What for?"

"I need to call the office and I left mine in the truck."

I gave him my phone and he punched in a number. A Daddy Yankee ring tone sounded from his pocket. He handed me my phone and answered his.

"Hi, Rebecca. How nice of you to call."

"You jerk. Erase that number."

"Uh-uh."

I hung up, but it was too late. "I'm serious. I won't take your call."

He ignored me as he keyed in my name.

Without looking at me, he pointed to my phone. "Go on. Put in Alberto. Or just use my nickname. B-E-R-T-O. Then you'll know not to answer it."

"Very funny."

I was again reminded of Vitico, that same annoying sassiness, which both attracted me and put me off. I didn't need distractions, and pursuing something with him could end up disturbing George. I wanted George on my side, needed to trust him and needed him to trust me.

George caught up with us, and we put Alberto in his truck. I shook his hand in a cool way and expected the flirtation to end there. Alberto's truck pulled away and George let out a big sigh as he dropped his shoulders. "That was weird," he said.

"I hope you didn't think I—"

"Rebecca, he is a casual acquaintance. Nothing more. He's charming and seems to have a good head on his shoulders. I saw you playing with your phones. Did you exchange numbers?"

"He tricked me. But I have no intention of answering his call...if he calls."

"I worry that you are letting your youth slip by without enjoying it. You might be pushing all this trial business too hard. The past is the past. We can't change it."

"I could say the same thing to you. It's not too late for you to enjoy life. You know what he said? He said we were two of a kind."

"You poor girl," he laughed. "Interesting, though, that he sensed we were both troubled by the past. If he knew the whole story, he would probably run away in horror. But don't worry, dear. You wouldn't hurt my feelings if you went out with him."

It seemed that his words belied his feelings. He was obviously uncomfortable in Alberto's presence, the kind of discomfort that one experiences being close to a desired person that you can't or won't pursue. It was very simple. If Alberto called, I wouldn't answer the phone.

Conchita was installed in my apartment, her boxes neatly stacked in the corner of my room. My bedroom was the largest in the house, allowing me to have a sofa for her to sleep on. She cleaned and made all of my favorite dishes. We both knew that keeping busy was the key to making sure she remained calm. When she wasn't scrubbing the tile in the bathroom with a toothbrush or defrosting the refrigerator, I took her around Palo Alto to show her stores where she could buy the Latin food products she liked to cook with.

Having someone around all of the time, even someone as wonderful as Conchita, was trying. But I knew it was a temporary arrangement. After she made her deposition, she would go back to her country until we needed her to return.

A few days after Conchita moved in with me, we had an appointment with Patricia. Conchita put on a shiny navy blue dress that fell just below her knees, opaque granny stockings, and sensible shoes. Her thick gray hair was combed. I had on jeans and a light sweater. I ran a brush through my hair to try to tame it, but it appeared hopeless. I felt unsure of how I looked, but I forgot it as we got in the car, and I smiled with satisfaction as I did each time the engine came to life.

"You like this car," Conchita said.

"I've got to give it up. I need to return it as soon as possible."

She shrugged and emitted a "humph" as if she didn't believe me.

We sat in the waiting room at Patricia's office and I looked in the mirror across the room, seeing what looked like a poor aging immigrant who had just arrived from Mexico and her disheveled granddaughter who had adopted a West Coast laissez-faire fashion in order to fit it, though it was obvious she never would. When Patricia came out to greet us, I felt even more inadequate. She had taken her usual appearance factor up several notches and was stunning. She wore a tweed Tahari three-button pantsuit and heels. Her hair was loose and fell in ample bouncy curls, while her makeup was flattering, but still businesslike. She was also attempting a new demeanor that I wasn't sure suited her—overly friendly with a forced eagerness.

"Conchita, I'm thrilled to meet you." She shook her hand. Then she kissed me on the cheek. "Rebecca, you're looking great as always."

I wanted to tell her she must be blind or a complete idiot, but I accepted her comment with a demure smile.

She got right to work interviewing Conchita. It was the first time I had heard her speak Spanish. It was fluent, but definitely a second-generation Americanized jumble. She told her she would ask some questions, take notes, type up the statement, and then she could sign it. As she went through the interview she occasionally glanced at me and gave me a secret smile. Once she even winked. I felt uncomfortable with the attention and had a suspicion that the new Patricia had been manufactured just for me. When Conchita excused herself to go to the bathroom, my fears were confirmed. She asked me out to dinner for the following week. When we had gotten together before, it had generally been for lunch. After an hour, the necessity of her getting back to work provided a logical excuse for separation. Dinner was taking things to a new level.

On the way out she took me aside. "We've hardly had a chance to talk since you've been back." When she spoke, she raised her darkened eyebrows slightly.

"We will," I said. "Soon."

On the way to the car, Conchita asked, "Is she married?"

"I don't believe so. Why?"

"She seem like a single woman, not so happy." Conchita in her innocent way often surprised me with her observations of people. Patricia had done her best to appear bubbly and Conchita had seen right through it.

"A lot of married women are hardly the pictures of happiness. Who is really happy these days?"

"My sister in Mexico. Even she lose her husband last year, she happy. She always see something good in life. I look forward to live with her. You come visit me, no? You better. You need more relax."

"Of course."

I *was* pretty uptight, dealing with a number of issues that still seemed out of my control, though it was not particularly unusual in my life. Now I had a new worry. With Patricia's interest in me, I wondered if people saw me as a lesbian. I told myself that I didn't care, but when a 707 area code showed up on my phone later that day, I answered it. I knew it wasn't George's number and I had a pretty good idea whose it was. I had vowed not to answer his call.

"I was all prepared to leave a message, but you answered," Alberto said with sweet surprise in his voice.

"Oh, I thought it might be George."

"I'm in the city. It wouldn't be much to come on down to where you are."

"I thought I made myself clear."

"Do you have plans for dinner?"

After a moment's deliberation, I convinced myself that it would be innocent enough. With Conchita staying with me, I had an excuse for going home right after dinner. Since he would have a long drive back, he probably wouldn't want to stay late anyway.

We had a meal, heavy on tomato sauce and garlic in an Italian restaurant. It included a bottle of wine and his staring into my eyes like an earnest teenager from across the table. I was beginning to feel vulnerable to his charms and thought it was just as well I couldn't invite him in. We sat in his truck outside my apartment and talked. Emboldened with the wine, I had the guts to ask what had happened between him and George, and I didn't let him off the hook with a simple "nothing." He went quickly from light-hearted to serious.

"I suppose I'm not like other guys you have dated."

"We're not dating," I interjected.

"Let me talk. This is not easy. If you are wondering if I like women, the answer is yes. I imagine getting married again someday and having children. I love kids. But I am not a slave to society's mores. The day I met George, I saw a beautiful person, a bit sad and in need. I was lonely. It didn't matter to me that he was a man or much older. He was someone that moved me in a way that I can't really explain. It was also the circumstances, I don't know, the weather, a lot of things. In the end nothing happened. It was George that stopped it. I knew he wanted to do it, but couldn't. It wasn't my first time...uh...experimenting. I guess I am supposed to feel dirty or something for those feelings, but I don't."

I was silent. I knew that he would take my silence as disapproval, or at best confusion, which in turn made words harder to come by. A car passed and the headlights lit up the anxiety on his face as his hands gripped the bottom of the steering wheel. I wanted desperately to say something. I, if anyone, should be able to understand him, and yet the silence rolled on, the smell of dog from the upholstery lingered in the air, our breathing was suspended.

"I can understand if that turns you off. It has happened before."

"It doesn't." The words crept cautiously out of my mouth. "My father and George...well, they had this thing that was in some ways beautiful, a connection, but it also screwed a lot of things up. Not their fault. People just couldn't handle it. Attitudes have changed somewhat, but middle ground is never easy for the people involved."

The truth was that his revelation made me more attracted to him than ever. He was honest about it in a way that my father wasn't. The gift of having a great capacity to love is not without its complications, and I supposed that not inheriting that attribute from my father saved me some pain. I had never been in love and the thought terrified me.

The one great love of my life had been Papi and he abandoned me. It left my emotions in shambles for a long time and the damage was still close to the surface. I had a feeling that finding a balance would be a lifelong search for me. For my father, not having that balance, the scales tipping toward needing so greatly various kinds of love, was what really killed him. I wondered if Alberto was as comfortable in his flexibility as he proclaimed.

"I don't want to hurt people, but I know I do sometimes," he said. "I certainly don't want to hurt you. But I have to be honest. The desire to hold you and kiss you is real. I want to make love to you."

I started to laugh and immediately caught myself, throwing my hand over my mouth. "I'm sorry. I'm sorry. That's terrible."

"Jesus, Becca."

"Believe me. I'm not laughing at you. It's that a girl dreams all her life of having a man like you, a man who is sweet and handsome and sensitive, say those words to her, and then when it happens, it's such a shock that it sounds funny. Me? This person is saying those words to me?"

"There not just words. It's true."

"I'm emotionally challenged."

"No, you're not. It's your defense."

I, too, justified myself by saying it was a defense, a front. I just had to tear down the barrier and I would be okay. But what if it wasn't just a defense? What if deep down I was inherently incapable of feeling...forever?

"Something horrible happened to me...and my father...and George."

"I wondered when I was going to get the story."

I told him everything. It poured out of me. At times I heard my voice as if somebody else were telling it, someone else's story. Yet as I got to the part about receiving word of my father's death, I began to cry like I had the day I read my father's letter. It seemed that I had cried more in the last few weeks than I had the previous fifteen years. What was happening to me? And then, there we were, the woman crying and the man comforting. He didn't try to take advantage. A part of me wanted him to, to have me, even treat me roughly. Then I could have felt disgusted with myself, refused to see him again. But he was too smart for that. He held me and let me cry. I rested my head in the crook of his neck. His hand caressed the back of my head. It felt incredibly good, the release of emotions, the resulting affection, the simple quiet of touch. It was how it was supposed to be. But I hadn't quite arrived. I didn't completely accept it as something real. The urge kept popping up to push him away and jump out of the car.

It was like he could read my mind. "Don't feel guilty about allowing yourself a little tenderness," he said.

"Oh, shut up. Just keep doing what you're doing."

It was after midnight when I opened the door to my room and saw that Conchita had left the bedside lamp on for me. She pretended to be asleep on the couch, but I sensed that she wasn't. In high school I would sometimes stay out late. Gran and Granddad never stayed up waiting for me to come home, but Conchita did. She would often be sitting at the kitchen table reading one of her *novelas,* small romantic comic books for adults. Though she always said that she had trouble sleeping, I knew that she was up for me. Her sleeping problem only seemed to materialize when

I was out. Other nights I would go into the kitchen for a late-night snack and hear the sound of gentle snoring coming from her room where she always left the door slightly ajar.

I got into bed and lay awake with Alberto on my mind. He had said he would get a hotel room instead of driving back and suggested we have breakfast. I told him to call me when he got up. I recycled the evening's events, and agonized over the possibility that I was leading him on when there was no possibility that anything was going to happen. Then my thoughts turned to the car. I had promised to give it up, and yet the mileage was accumulating. Each time I settled into the leather upholstery and sniffed the newness, I became a little more attached. I saw how people became slaves to things, fine and expensive possessions. Then they worked and lied and cheated to have more of them. As the inventory of wealth increased, their minds became smaller and focused on how to keep them. A whole philosophy developed around protecting what they had. If a daughter wanted to marry someone who didn't fit into the program, it was a threat. If a maid wanted to exert her independence, it was disloyalty to the status quo.

The answer became clear. I couldn't in good conscience keep the car. I would no doubt develop my own, and possibly equally absurd, program for life, but I didn't want to be part of my grandparents'. I would drop off the car the next day. I would ask Alberto to pick me up and we could celebrate my "freedom" with a breakfast containing massive quantities of unhealthy calories, washed down with mimosas heavy on the champagne.

# 14: Rebecca

Conchita and I inched along the freeway to the airport. Interstate 280 at mid-morning was usually a breeze, but a bad accident had traffic back up for miles. Conchita resorted to her usual twisting of hands in her lap. Every few minutes, she would take her itinerary out of her purse, look at it, and let out a sigh.

Patricia had filed Conchita's statement with the police and she was getting out of town for the long-anticipated time with her sister in Mexico.

"This car not so good, huh?" she said, snapping her purse shut.

"Don't remind me." I was driving my new used car, a Subaru that Alberto had helped me pick out. It had its share of scrapes and scratches on the outside, but it was tip-top under the hood according to a reliable mechanic. Though I still had a hefty sum in my college fund, I was going to need the money for law school. I went for the bargain.

The morning after our conversation in his truck, Alberto had picked me up as planned. He described his night in the motel as restless and I avoided asking why. He followed me to drop off the BMW. In the back driveway of my grandparents' he got out of his truck and stood gaping at the house. He kept nodding his head as if it explained something about me.

"Four garages?" he said.

"It's just a house. Let's go." I took his arm and steered him back to the truck. He went limp, hamming it up and faking a stumble as if he were delirious at the sight of such wealth. "Four garages."

"That's enough. We've got to get out of here before Gran shows up. Believe me, it wouldn't be pretty. She might think you are the new gardener and put you to work."

We had breakfast together, but it was my luck that he was a health nut, or knowing I was lusting after the glossy photo of waffles dripping with syrup and whipped cream, he ordered a veggie omelet just to spite me. To make it worse he also said he hated mimosas. The only brunch drink he could take was a Bloody Mary. The place didn't have a full liquor license, so we got buzzed on coffee instead. Even though he had ruined my plans to gorge myself in sinful eating to assuage the loss of the car, he kept me entertained with stories of his arrival in the States and starting high school with no English.

Jittery from the coffee, we set out to peruse the used-car lots. I think we outtalked the fast-talking used-car salesmen. By the end of the afternoon, I had the Subaru and Alberto was on his way back to Forestville. Future unknown.

My cell rang and it startled Conchita. I had misplaced my Bluetooth, but the traffic was going slowly enough that I could have answered it. I looked at the ID and saw that it was Granddad. It was the call I had been dreading. I couldn't deal with it, so I let voicemail pick up. When I had dropped off the car, I left a note saying that I appreciated the thought, but I couldn't accept the car. I hinted that they would be receiving some disturbing news soon and would perhaps better understand why I felt uncomfortable driving the BMW they had bought for me. Patricia told me that she had sent the letter to their lawyer expressing our intention to re-open George's case. It had been three days and I hadn't heard anything from the grandparents, so I wasn't sure if the call was about the car or news they had received from their lawyer. Neither sounded like an enjoyable conversation, and I wondered if I should hop on the plane to Mexico with Conchita.

After crawling along for several miles, Conchita and I made it to the accident site. It was a major crash and the gawk factor high. The two cars had been moved to the side of the road, but were badly crumpled. There were ambulances and several police cars, all with their lights spinning and flashing. They were putting a person on a stretcher into the back of one of the ambulances.

"I have bad feeling," said Conchita. "Maybe is better I miss the plane."

Conchita's road through life was filled with bad omens. Recently she had told me about the signs she witnessed on the day my mother died. She heard an owl hooting in the big pine tree outside her window as she was waking up at dawn. Then later Tio Jorge came into the kitchen before going out for his jog. She looked down at his feet and shuddered. He had on two different colored socks, one gray and one white. In Conchita's world that was a bad sign of high order. He laughed and said that he must have been sleepier than he thought when he got dressed. She tried to convince him to go back and change his socks, but he laughed again, kissed her on the cheek, and dashed out into the early-morning cool.

I managed to talk Conchita down from her cloud of bad juju and got her checked in at the airport. Once she had made it through security, I checked my message. It wasn't either of the two issues I expected. The bad juju was for me. Gran was at Mills-Peninsula Hospital. She had a stroke. Everything became a blur in front of me. I headed for the parking lot, but couldn't remember which level I had parked on. The only positive element of my panic was the comfort that Conchita had already gone through security and wouldn't hear the news until she arrived in Mexico. I needed to talk to somebody. Alberto answered right away.

"I was just thinking of you and here you are," he said.

"Oh, God, I don't know what to do. I can't find my car. Gran had a stroke," I wailed. "I didn't want to kill her."

"Becca, calm down. Are you saying she died?"

"I don't know. In the message Granddad just said to come to the hospital right away. I'm at the airport. I just dropped off Conchita."

"Think of the color."

"What?" I thought he was referring to some color therapy. Health crazy. New Age nut. This guy was too much for me.

"The levels of the garage are color-coded. Remember the color. I will stay with you until you find your car."

He had me close my eyes and remember the color. His voice was soothing. By the time I found my car, I was calm enough to attempt driving. He said he couldn't leave work right away, but would drive down as soon as he could. I got back on the freeway and headed north toward the hospital, holding the wheel in a death-grip to steady myself. Then I really regretted not having my earpiece. Let me be connected, at least with one person who had the power to stop the madness going on in my head. I trembled at the thought of what I might discover at the hospital. What if Gran were dead? What if my obsession with bringing up the past was the catalyst that sent a blood clot coursing through her body only to lodge in her brain? It would be me who killed her. I was furious with her, but I didn't want her dead.

I removed my sunglasses as I stepped into the hospital lobby, but put them back on as the fluorescent light reflecting off the shiny floors attacked my eyes more intensely than the light outside. My heart raced though everyone in my vicinity seemed calm, moving in a slow, dreamlike pace. The receptionist appeared to dally as she looked for Gran's information. No urgency in the world could make her hurry. The elevator, too, was part of the plot to impede my arrival as it stopped at every floor. When at last I exited the elevator doors, I came upon the sight of Granddad and Jimmy, sitting side by side, in identical postures of heavy heads supported by tense arms resting on their knees. Jimmy jumped up when he saw me and approached me with clenched fists and red-veined eyes.

"What are you doing here?" he spit out.

"Is she okay?"

"Of course she's not okay," he said mockingly. "She had a stroke. She might die. Look what you've done with your idiot meddling. Why do want to bring up all that old shit?

To clear the name of some faggot you hardly know who was fucking your faggot father."

The screaming coming out of his distorted face so close to mine was the ugliest thing I had ever seen, and I had the urge to destroy it. Without thinking I found my hand slapping him so hard that my palm stung. I slapped him for what he said, for sending George to prison, and in general for making my life miserable every chance he got. I wanted to slap him again. I raised my hand, but he flew into a rage, grabbed me by the throat, and pushed me up against the wall. He began screaming again.

"You're fucking sick. She was your mother. She was your mother. She was your mother. You don't even care that someone pushed your mother over a cliff?" His body was pressed into mine and his hands were tightening on my throat. "She was your mother, damn it." He continued to scream, but his voice became distant, the lights on the ceiling flashed. I struggled to breathe. Out of the corner of my eye I saw people in colorful uniforms rushing toward me. We were back in dreamlike mode. Granddad got there before the uniforms. He grabbed Jimmy from behind as he had that night many years before and threw him to the ground with a single decisive thrust. When Jimmy started to get up, a male nurse in purple scrubs knelt over him and held him down. Another nurse helped me to a chair.

"What in God's name is the matter with this family?" Granddad moaned as if it were the first time he acknowledged there was something wrong.

"I'm so sorry, Dadda," I mumbled hoarsely. It was the name I hadn't used since I was a little girl.

He went and stood over Jimmy. "Go outside and calm down. Don't come back until you are ready to be civil. If I ever hear another outburst like that from you, I'll flatten you. Mark my words."

"You think you still can, old man?"

"Don't push me. Get out of here." The nurse helped him up and he walked by me, shaking out his shoulders and giving me the evil eye.

They took me into the nurses' station and a doctor examined me. She listened to my breathing and peered into my eyes. They had me lie down for a while. When I came back out Granddad jumped up and helped me to a chair. His face looked decidedly older than the last time I had really taken notice, the lines deepened with the pain of the last few hours. "Are you all right?" he said.

"Don't worry about me," I said. My voice sounded gritty and I clutched my throat. "How is Gran?"

"They don't know yet. They're watching her closely. These next few hours are the most important."

"I didn't—"

"I know. I know. You felt like you were doing the right thing. You were so young when you lost your mother. You probably hardly remember. For us the pain of losing a daughter is as raw as yesterday. Gran has never gotten over it."

"I do remember my mother. I remember her teaching me to swim. I remember the rabbit-shaped pancakes she used to make me for breakfast. But I don't want to have my memories stained with an injustice."

I thought back to a morning when my life was normal. I had a mother and father, and we were staying at the beach house. My mother asked me what I wanted for breakfast and I said, "Animal pancakes!" My father's specialty was the batter. He put cinnamon in it. Mom did the cooking.

"Okay. What animals shall we make today? Bunnies?" she asked.

"You always make bunnies. I want elephants!" I shouted.

"You're going to eat elephants?" Papi said.

We laughed and joked about eating elephants. Everyone was happy. And then Gran appeared in the kitchen doorway. She wore a long quilted robe and stood there, pushing her hair up. "What's all this racket? Granddad is still sleeping."

Papi stopped mixing the batter and hung his head. I sat at the table and stared at the Aunt Jemima bottle.

"Oh, mother. Don't be a party-pooper. We're making animal pancakes." Helen went over and took her mother's arm, dragged her to the stove. "Look."

She peered into the frying pan and shook her head. "What's that?" She pointed to an elephant's trunk that had gotten detached from the body. "That looks absolutely…well, pornographic!"

"Mom!" Helen said, jiggling with laughter. "You've got a dirty mind. That's an elephant's trunk."

"Well," Gran said with her hand on her hip and a big lipsticked smile on her face. "it looks like a you-know-what to me. Let me have a go at it."

She took the spatula and turned to me. "Sweetie, I'm going to make you a whole zoo." And she did—monkeys and giraffes and a hippopotamus. I ate so many pancakes I got sick.

I thought about Gran lying in a hospital bed nearby, and the bitter person she had become. She wasn't always that way.

"What happened to us? I was just thinking of a time when Gran was different, before my mother died," I said.

He put his hands to his face and smoothed out his forehead. "I didn't know back then what she was up to. I should have known, but I didn't. The pain at the time clouded my thinking. It was several years later when Jimmy, drunk one night, confessed what they had done. Your Gran hatched the plan immediately after the accident. She told Jimmy what to say. When he first came to me with what he had supposedly seen on the cliff, I believed him. And then in the custody hearing, Gran convinced me that if we didn't do everything to get you, you would be raised by homosexuals, that your father would wait for that man to get out of prison and they would raise you. We had to do something."

"That man has a name—George—and he spent seven years of his life in prison for a crime he didn't commit."

"Believe me, Rebecca, I am not proud of any of this. When I found out the truth, I seriously considered going to the authorities. But a man has to protect his family. I couldn't tell the police that my wife and son had perjured themselves. Your father had gone back to Mexico, and yes, I had some pretty strong prejudices against homosexuals. But I am not the ogre you probably think I am. Times have changed. One of my best managers is gay. He has a partner and they have adopted two little boys. If they want to get married, what do I care? I feel bad about George, and I am willing to do whatever is necessary to make this right. I know I can't give him back those years, but anything else I can do..."

I didn't know if this was a new, improved Granddad, changed by the crises surrounding him, or the Granddad that was always there that I never had the chance to see. When I learned of how badly they had treated my father and the way they had sent George to prison, my silent plotting to bring justice began. I lumped my grandparents and Jimmy together as the enemy. Now I was being forced to recognize Granddad as a person who had his foibles like all of us, but he wasn't the villain I had made him out to be.

"I'm sorry if I misjudged you in the past," I said.

"You might not believe this, but Gran and I have loved you in our own way. We wanted the best for you. It wasn't easy for me to watch the tragedies pile up in your life. I know it was stupid for me to think I could give you things, material things to compensate. There were other things I could have given you, emotional support, but I didn't know how. I never told you how bad I felt when your father died. I should have talked to you, comforted you. Remember that time I took you out to dinner, just you and me. We went to the pizza place you liked. I wanted to tell you how bad I felt about your father, but you were so angry, so sad, I didn't know how to get through to you. The truth is that I liked your father. It nearly killed Gran that our gorgeous daughter wanted to marry a Mexican. He wasn't someone I would have chosen either, but he was a hard worker and a loving father. When your parents got married, Helen was a senior at UC Berkeley and your father a junior. I tried to convince him to stay in school. I offered to support them until he finished. Then he could get a job at my company. But Miguel would have none of it. He was determined to make it on his own. He dropped out of school and started working construction. Helen finished college before you were born. Miguel soon moved up to foreman and began to take real estate courses in the evenings so that he could get a license.  I admired his independence. When tragedy struck our family, he was just getting established as a real estate broker and beginning to make money."

"I remember moving to that house in San Jose that he bought. We lived there such a short time."

"He adored you. I can't imagine how he must have felt to leave you behind. I'm sure he regretted it the rest of his days. I'm not proud of how we treated him. Despite all these impediments, you turned into a lovely young woman. I can't tell you how proud I was the day you graduated from Stanford. Stanford! I went to Fresno State!"

He sniffed and I looked over at him in shock. I was witnessing something I hadn't seen since the day of my mother's funeral, the last time I saw my grandfather cry. The tears rolled down his cheeks and he seemed more surprised than anyone, not knowing exactly what to do when his face was wet with bodily fluid. I found a tissue in my pocket and slipped it to him.

We felt the shadow of a doctor standing over us. I raised my face and saw the somber look in her eyes. I feared the worst.

"Mr. Delon. It looks like she is going to pull through. There was damage, though we still don't know the extent of it. Most likely there will be some memory and speech problems. She'll also need help with motor skills. Again we still don't know, although signs are looking good for a slow recovery."

"Thank God," said Granddad in a still shaky voice. "Thank you, doctor."

I jumped up and shook the doctor's hand. The relief I felt was like waking from a nightmare where you were being chased by a hideous creature and finding out it was just a dream. But I was mostly happy for my grandfather's sake. After the things he told me, I had an affection for him that I hadn't allowed myself to feel for many years. I didn't want to see him hurt.

When the doctor had gone, he turned to me and said, "And I want you to keep the car. Heavens, what am I going to do with it? The minute you drive it off the lot you lose thousands of dollars. I wouldn't give them the satisfaction of buying it back from me at a ridiculously low price. It's a good car. You should keep it."

With the news about Gran, the old Granddad was back. His voice had turned businesslike and keeping the car was more based on sound financial advice rather than emotions of gift-giving. At the same time, he had let out a side of him that couldn't be completely reeled in. He had changed in my eyes. Maybe there was hope for Gran, too. I kept thinking about what the doctor said about memory. Perhaps she could come back as a less bitter, more open version of herself, the past forgotten, or at least too hazy to matter.

Granddad sent me home. When they allowed visitors, it would only be one at a time. It was an easy way of saying that maybe it wouldn't be a good idea for her to see me.

Then there was the other possibility that she wouldn't remember who I was. I also wanted to escape before Jimmy came back. As I walked down the corridors and out the front door, I scanned the area around me, imagining him jumping out of every dark corner to attack. Granddad wouldn't be around to protect me.

I got to my car without sighting Jimmy, but I did a careful check of the back seat before I got in. Then I locked my door as soon as I had closed it. I tried to forget Jimmy and concentrate on my talk with Granddad, which filled me with hopeful thoughts. I turned on the radio and tuned in La Romantica 104.9, doing the imaginary sway of my hips as the car rolled along. I remembered my days in Mexico and looked forward to being there again. My good feeling lasted until I pulled up to my house. Jimmy's car was parked in front. He saw me and jumped out. I grabbed my cell and punched in 911 though I didn't press the call button. He sauntered over and I put down the window halfway.

"What are you doing here?" I said.

"We need to talk. You can't do this."

"I could press charges. You touch me again and I will."

"Aren't we big with the lawyer-speak these days?"

"I just had a talk with Granddad and he supports me. He knows that what you did was wrong."

"The old bastard always did have a soft spot for you. I don't know why. I think one of the ladies he was plugging was Latin."

"You're crude."

"Aren't you going to get out?"

"I want you to go get in your car and drive away. We'll talk when there are other people around. I don't trust you."

"Come on, little sister, talk to me."

"I'm not your sister. I don't even want to be related to you."

"Ya know, you're pissing me off." He had his hand resting on the top edge of the half-open window.

"Get away from the car, Jimmy." I still had my finger on the call button. I looked in my rear-view window and felt my panic beginning to fade. Alberto's truck pulled up behind me and he got out.

"Is everything okay here, Becca?"

I was never so aware of Alberto's size until I saw him standing next to Jimmy. He was always so gentle. I was surprised to see him look tough, like someone you wouldn't want to mess with.

"Alberto, this is Jimmy...my uncle."

"Yeah, the *real* uncle," Jimmy said in sarcastic tone, backing away a little from the car. "And who is Alberto?" he asked me.

"He's a friend." And then to Alberto I said, "Jimmy was just leaving."

Jimmy looked Alberto up and down like he wasn't afraid of his size. "See you later, Becky." He was the only one that called me that. He knew I hated it.

I got out of the car. "I'm glad you came." Alberto stared at my neck. He touched a finger to it.

"What happened?"

I leaned down and examined my neck in the side-mirror. It was still red, and I could distinguish the finger marks. "Jimmy got a little out of hand at the hospital."

"Why, that bastard!" He started after him. "Hey!"

"Don't, Alberto. He's not worth it," I said.

Jimmy jumped in his car and started it.

"You touch her again and I'll kill you," Alberto shouted as he pulled away.

"That was gallant," I said. "I've never had someone offer to kill for me."

He hugged me. "I would, ya know. I'd prefer another way, but I would if I had to."

I settled into his embrace like we had done it million times. He was scaring me in the way he naturally usurped the role of the man in my life. I wanted to be strong enough to protect myself, yet when he showed up on his white horse, I couldn't have been happier to see him.

# 15: Rebecca

The pitch-black night was full of noises that I wasn't accustomed to, chirping crickets and croaking frogs, the occasional hooting owl. A backdrop to these sounds was the constant babbling creek. I lay awake listening, all my senses alert in a strange bed. My nose detected the not-unpleasant smells of a dog and a man close by. Yet from the sheets rose a flower-garden freshness, suspiciously seeming as if Alberto changed them just before he made his run down the peninsula to rescue me.

The dog rose, shook out its limbs, and I heard the clinking of its tags. There was a heavy arm across my back, and the darkness was dense and oppressive. Trying not to make too much of a stir, I fumbled for the mini-flashlight he had put on the bedside table in case I needed to get up during the night. With my movement he rolled on to his back and fell right into a contented snore.

I longed to be in my own bed, though with Jimmy stalking me I was happy to be far away from my apartment. Alberto insisted on spending the night with me, but had to be up early for an appointment with a client in Santa Rosa.

Circumstances, I reminded myself, rather than passion prompted our first night together.

We had gotten to his house in Forestville late. We were both exhausted, and as we pulled up to the dark house, Rudi began an angry bark and growl that seemed to chastise Alberto for leaving him alone. Once we were inside the gate, the dog smothered him with licks and insistent paws. As I stood aside, ignored, I hugged myself against a mysterious presence, something large and overpowering that I couldn't see. Alberto turned on the porch light and my eyes immediately jerked upward. Rising above us and surrounding the little house was a grove of redwood trees, stately pillars standing like sentinels in the blackness of the night. And then my gaze came back down and saw how selfish the trees were, not letting other plants grow in their shadow. The yard was covered with brown discarded foliage, scales shed from a giant sentient being. It was an enchanted house in the woods that seemed safe from Jimmy, but at the same time offered dangers of another kind. What was I getting myself into?

Alberto opened the door and Rudi rushed in, leading me across the threshold into their world. It was more of a cabin with upgrades than a house, exuding a rustic masculinity combined with the comforts of modern life. The kitchen had shiny enamel appliances and granite counter tops, though what I noticed most was that it was clean. We passed into the combined living-dining room, and as he switched on lights I saw that it, too, was lived-in, but orderly. Unlike the apartments of most of my peers, it had actual décor—rugs and pottery from Mexico, a leather sofa, framed prints on the walls. An adult lived here.

There were two bedrooms, his with a queen-sized bed, and the much smaller guest room, which also served as his office. He made the grand gesture of offering me the guest room though he told me that he had recently read an article warning against sleeping in the same room as a computer screen because of the radiation it gave off.

"If I had known, I would have brought my anti-glare filter," I joked. "I guess I wouldn't mind having company tonight."

We didn't do all the things he said he had wanted to do several nights previous. He did hold me and we kissed, cautious and exploratory kisses, then his body settled as his breathing became heavy. I lay for a minute with my head on his chest, listening to the beat of his heart, before rolling over.

I crawled out of bed, and with my little flashlight tiptoed over creaking floorboards and found the bathroom I had already awarded with my seal of approval. After flushing the toilet, I paused in front of the medicine cabinet, disgusted with my nosiness, but unable to stop myself. I opened it with the anticipation of finding evidence that there had to be something wrong with this man, a sign of such sordidness that I would have to flee from the house half-dressed in the middle of the night. I discovered a bottle of aspirin, toothpaste, deodorant, a natural shaving cream, a three-blade razor with cartridges, hair gel, Band-Aids, various ointments, and a small bottle of Aqua di Gio cologne that looked like it had never been used. I closed the cabinet and the charging light of his electric toothbrush winked at me from the shelf next to the sink. And then I saw a beautiful sleepy face in the mirror behind me.

"Are you all right?" His voice was gravelly. He put his arms around me. I was wearing a T-shirt and gym shorts that he had given me. He had on pajama bottoms and no shirt. Embarrassed that he had caught me looking into his cabinet, I turned around in his arms and buried my face in his collarbone. Taking in a deep breath of him, my resistance began to fall like grains of sand in an hourglass, one after another until they were piled in a heap on the floor. I plucked absentmindedly at the hairs on his chest, and then I felt him sigh and get aroused at the same time. We had gotten to the moment of things falling into place. "Your hands are cold," he said. "Let's go back to bed." He lifted me up and carried me into the bedroom where we toppled, a giant felled redwood, onto the bed.

He was the first man I had been with who knew how erotic a kiss could be, who took time to explore, who was led by his hands rather than his sex. The most important thing he did was to make me forget who I was, where I was in time and space. He allowed me to have the fantasy, if just for a short time, of being the ideal woman who could give and take pleasure without selling any part of her soul. The sex rose and fell, curved and climbed like a road to a high plateau, far from the cares of my everyday life that fell by the wayside.

I settled into his arms and prepared for a peaceful sleep in his hidden cabin, nestled in a redwood stand. I fell into a dream. But it soon became clear that a history of defensive habits could not be wiped out in a single night. In the very early hours of the morning, the masons of my past began to regroup and rebuild the walls. I awoke with uncertainty, a sensation that I had been diverted from my path. My real life came back to me like waves hitting the beach, one after the other bringing in more debris from the sea. My life was too cluttered to allow a new person into it. George's case and law school and Gran in the hospital and Granddad worrying and Jimmy menacing all flashed on the screen in my head in a repeated loop, demanding my attention. I would need all my strength. It was not a time to get involved with someone. I lay staring at the dark mist outside the window until it turned a milky gray.

It was early morning when Alberto stirred, planted a kiss on my head, and slid out of the covers while I feigned sleep. I felt guilty for not getting up, greeting him, giving him some sign of my appreciation for his sweetness. Instead I remained paralyzed, buried under the recurring fear that I was incapable of love while I listened to him in the shower and thought about how his body looked under the running water. Mixed in with the turmoil inside my brain was a nagging voice saying, "What was there *not* to love about Alberto?"

The smell of coffee drifted in from the kitchen and a short time later I heard the ceramic cup land with a muffled thud onto the bedside table. I opened my eyes and was greeted with a warm and curious smile.

"You don't have to get up, but I had the feeling you were awake."

"Oh, I'm awake."

"Are you feeling weird?"

I rose up, and he sat on the edge of the bed, handing me the coffee. It seemed I wasn't permitted my private neuroses, couldn't fake sleep around him, and he had correctly anticipated that I drank my coffee black. I took the mug in one hand and with the other smoothed out the hair on his arm.

"It has nothing to do with you," I said. I took a sip of the hot liquid and felt the steam rising up in my face. "And don't give me that quizzical look. You were great."

I put my cup down and pulled him back so that his head was on my chest. I dove my fingers into the thick waves of his hair, twisted it around my fingers, making curls.

"But?" he said.

"But nothing. I'm sure everything would be perfect if I had a lobotomy, if I could be just a body with no mind."

"I like your mind."

"I'm not sure you would say that if you got a good glimpse into the nether regions. It gets pretty spooky in there."

"Take me on a tour. I can handle it." With a groan he started to pull away from me. "But it will have to be later. I've got to go. Business calls. I'll be back in a couple of hours."

When he had dressed, he came in to say goodbye. He was casual rather than romantic, again anticipating that I was still struggling with the sluggish creatures that inhabited my head. I heard his truck start and I burrowed down in the covers, hoping to go back to sleep. After a few minutes of tossing in bed, I grabbed my cell phone and called George.

"How about some breakfast? I'm up in your neighborhood."

"Why am I not surprised?"

"It's not what you think. I mean, it's partly what you think, but more complicated. I have some news about Gran. You'll have to come get me, though. I'm carless."

"And where's the young man?"

"Working. He rescued me from the talons of Jimmy. Details at 11:00."

"News about Gran? Talons of Jimmy? Girl stuck in a wildman's cabin? Sounds like we're going to have a juicy breakfast."

We sat in our regular booth at Pat's and I filled George in about Gran.

"You were smart to call Alberto...in more ways than one," he said with a wink.

"You make it sound like I tricked my way into his bed."

"I'm sure he was more than willing. I saw the way he looked at you from the beginning."

"Did it bother you? I don't want there to be any—"

"What happened between Alberto and me, I should say what didn't happen between Alberto and me, was a fluke, barely more than a kiss. He was mildly drunk. There was never any potential of it going anywhere. I am genuinely pleased I was instrumental in bringing you two together."

"We're not an item. I don't know if there is potential for us, either. Yes, he's handsome, affectionate, thoughtful, intelligent, and..."

"Go ahead and say it—sexy."

I felt my cheeks getting hot. We looked at each other across the table, knowing we had kissed the same man, wanted the same man. We had both suffered so much loss in our lives, it didn't seem fair that I had "won" Alberto, that I had the distinct advantage being a woman in a society where heterosexuality was the norm. I felt overwhelmed by sadness that George and my father hadn't been able to find happiness together. Clearly there were a lot of things in life that weren't fair, a lesson I learned at an early age.

"It doesn't feel right yet. Maybe it never will."

"Just enjoy it. Let it be."

"I have so much coming up. I can't get involved."

"If you have told him everything and he is still pursuing you, that means he's got the strength to do it. You are a strong woman, Rebecca. But no one is so strong that she can't benefit from another strong person by her side."

"I still have this notion that if I depend on him, it makes me weak. I don't want to be one of those women who has to have a man to be complete."

"Think of it as complementing, not completing."

"I'm almost ashamed to admit how thrilling it was when he showed up to save the day. Jimmy was out of control. Our sweet Alberto turned into a macho man. He was fierce."

"That's what I'm talking about. He was there when you needed him."

George drove me back to Alberto's and we slowed to a crawl halfway up the driveway. He stared at the sunlight that pierced the redwoods and fell like a spotlight on Alberto's truck. Then he swept the property with a melancholy gaze, perhaps a nostalgia for his place in the woods of Mexico or a regret that he hadn't accepted Alberto's invitation that day. I asked him if he wanted to come in, but he thought not. Before he could pull away, Alberto and Rudi came running out of the house.

"George, where are you going? Stay for a while."

George brought his thumb up to his mouth and chewed on his nail. No excuse seemed to come to mind and he turned off the motor. "All right. Just for a minute. I have to get back."

Alberto grabbed him in a bear hug and I worried that George might die of embarrassment as if he were a teenage boy being embraced by a perfumed aunt. Alberto wouldn't let go until George unstiffened his arms and loosely wrapped them around Alberto's back. After releasing George, he put his arm around my shoulders, but I moved out of his embrace as we started for the door. I still felt awkward being affectionate in front of George.

"I'll make some coffee," said Alberto.

George continued his wide-eyed sweep of the surroundings. "This is quite a place. So peaceful."

"My hideaway. At times it feels too isolated, kind of lonely."

George glanced in my direction with raised eyebrows and a half-smile.

"You've got Rudi," I offered. Hearing his name, Rudi came over to me and looked up with curious, soulful eyes. I wondered if he was jealous. I petted his head, but he shrugged me off and went back by Alberto's side.

"That's right, ol' boy," he said to the dog. "Don't know what I'd do without you."

He stepped aside and held open the door while George and I filed in. The living room, which earlier in the day had felt so cozy, now seemed cramped.

"Have a seat," said Alberto. He moved the pillows, and his action sent particles of dust dancing above the Navajo blanket thrown over the back of the sofa. George continued standing in the middle of the room, head bent forward, staring at an armchair. Alberto shook his head and went into the kitchen to prepare the coffee.

"I feel out of place," said George.

"I suppose we all do a little. I think Alberto is happy to have you here, though."

We sat on the warm leather at opposite ends of the couch leaving the middle for Alberto. The smell of brewing coffee drifted into the room. "He's quite domestic," I said for no reason, to fill the silence. "Much more so than I am."

"He probably didn't grow up with servants," George said with a laugh.

"Don't be mean."

"It's just a fact. There's a learning curve like everything else. You'll get the hang of it," he said.

"Of what?" Alberto said. He came into the room with a tray of coffee mugs, milk and sugar.

"Domesticity. I think Rebecca is impressed by yours."

"Men who live alone are forced to learn. Right, George?"

"Women, too," I protested. "It's not like we are born with a special gene that makes us prepare the perfect cup of coffee or want to scrub toilets."

"You're right about that. My ex was the prime example. I did more than my share of housework. She hated it," said Alberto.

"One thing I did learn from Gran was an appreciation, or you might call it an obsession, for cleanliness." I thought of Gran in the hospital and the gnawing guilt that I had put her there came back to me. "I'd better call and see how she's doing."

I took my cell phone in the kitchen, leaned over the sink, and looked out the window at a deer grazing on the tall grass down by the creek. I punched in the number and caught Granddad in the cafeteria. He said Gran was recovering, that she was lucid and spoke a few words, but it was hard to understand her. It seemed that her speech would be permanently affected. He asked where I was, and I told him I was at a friend's house in Sonoma County. I told him why. I felt bad for giving him more to worry about, but I thought he should know about Jimmy's behavior. I wanted to keep the police out of it and I was sure he did, too. On the other hand I refused to be bullied.

"This is intolerable," he said. "When Gran comes home, we are going to have a family meeting. The four of us are going to sit down and not get up until we have resolved everything. If Gran can't contribute to the conversation, she will just have to listen. Are you with George?"

His out-of-the-blue question amazed me. Gran must have told him of my visits to George in Sonoma and he had surmised that I had gone to him to seek refuge. Again Granddad was showing me another side, talking about family meetings and drawing conclusions of where I might go in times of crisis.

"I am not staying at George's, though he is here with me now. I spent the night at a mutual friend's."

"A male friend? Not that it matters. Only curious."

"Yes. He's just a friend."

"Tell George that I also want to have a meeting with him. We will get to the bottom of this."

"The bottom of this?"

"I mean I am prepared to settle this matter."

"I want you to know that George is not pushing for any kind of settlement. He has been reluctant since the beginning."

"You may think I'm an old fart with my head buried in the sand, but I do understand that this is your baby, what you're trying to do for George. I don't say that in a negative way. I see it as something you need to do. I'm not quite as two-dimensional as Jimmy. The either-with-us-or-against-us mentality is one of the things wrong with this country right now. I would like to see us come out of this stronger as a family."

Again I was in shock. I felt like I was talking to someone I had known all my life, but never really known. Still I wasn't very optimistic about creating a warm and cozy family unit after so many years of shaky and defective relationships.

"Rebecca?"

"I'm here. I'm just thinking."

"You don't need to say anything now. Tell George what I said. We'll talk soon."

"Tell Gran I...I...hope she's feeling better."

I returned to the living room with a twisted expression on my face. They were looking at a coffee table book on Navajo rugs.

"What is it?" said George as if he feared the worst.

"Gran's okay. Granddad wants to meet with you."

"I'm not sure I'm ready for that."

"He's different. It's like he has woken up from a long sleep. He gets it."

"You mean he's ready to throw money at the problem?"

"No, I see a fundamental change in his way of looking at the world. Or perhaps it was there all along, but repressed by Gran's overpowering presence. In the hospital he told me he supported his gay manager's right to marry."

"Are we talking about the same person?"

"I know. It's hard to believe."

"I'm not even sure I support all this gay marriage stuff," said George. "In my day we were trying to create something new, not emulate the failed institution of heterosexual marriage. When I got out, I saw that there had been a shift in the way the gay community viewed marriage, not that it mattered much to me anymore."

Alberto smiled a secret smile. "George, you talk like you are over the hill. You are not. There is someone out there for you."

George's face grew taut. "There was." I felt both honored and sad that my father was his one true love, but like Alberto, I wanted to see him get on with his life. "Not everybody is into the hottie culture. You have so much to offer."

"Spoken with the true idealism of youth. Reality is a different story. And if by some miracle someone came along, I'm not sure I would know what to do."

"It's like riding a bicycle, George," said Alberto.

## 16: George

The lazy fog waited until early afternoon before retreating to a holding pattern just off the coast, allowing the sun to break free. I felt the Craftsman cottage become in an instant infused with light through the handcrafted, multi-paned windows and the faux stained-glass skylights. Shirtless and in running shorts, I lingered at the bedroom window fingering the lace curtains and looking out at the big house. Reflected in the glass were a few white hairs sprouting on my chest, and my leg muscles ached, no longer recovering from my daily jog the way they had when I was younger. Still my heart beat with a young man's anticipation.

Across the manicured lawn was a much larger version of the guest cottage with a low, overhung roof, and two massive square pillars leading to the wide porch. It stood like a wall against me, skirted in flowering lilac, something out of a magazine, so perfect as to render it lifeless. Everyone called it Helen's house. It had been left to her by her grandparents, built in the 1920's as a beach house when they had enjoyed considerable prosperity. The house had opened its broad mouth and swallowed Miguel yet hadn't quite found a way to digest him. No one had, certainly not me. Only little Rebecca could hold him in the palm of her hand.

I awaited Miguel's visit with a curious mixture of excitement and dread, excitement for what I knew would occur and dread for the inevitable separation afterwards. It was Helen's afternoon to play tennis with her girlfriends at the club in Carmel. Rebecca was down for a nap. There was a light knock on the door. I didn't bother saying, "Come in." The door was never locked. Nor would I comment on Miguel's insufferable need for formality. Despite the lazy weekend afternoon and the quickly rising temperature, Miguel wore stiff jeans and a sport jacket over a starched long-sleeved shirt. The longish waves of his black hair had been tamed with gel and the expression on his face resembled a teenager ill-prepared for a blind date. I detected a whiff of cologne as he crossed the threshold, but I wouldn't repeat that he needn't have bothered with perfume, that I liked his natural smell just fine. There were things I knew would never change, some of them I didn't want to, like Miguel's transition when the door closed, his shoulders dropping and the crack in his demeanor producing the threat of a smile, the need to kiss hanging about him like a buzzing insect.

We never knew if it was Helen who had become suspicious and set up the trap, or if a spy in the house had called her at the club and told her to come home right away. We heard the slap of her sandals on the wood floor of the cottage, but it was too late. She opened the bedroom door and saw us sharing a cigarette in a tangle of naked limbs. She left the door open and bounded out of the house with the grace of a gazelle. Miguel leapt off the bed, grabbed his jeans and stabbed his legs into them. "Oh, God, oh, God," he moaned. I lay back and took another drag on the half-finished cigarette to keep from bursting into laughter. I could only find a relieved amusement in the horror. There would be no more wondering if she knew. And that itself was liberation.

By late afternoon the feeling of liberation had paled. There had been no communication from Miguel, leaving me to muddle over the uncertain prospects of our future. I replayed a thousand times Miguel's panic and flight from the house, the taint of desperation soiling the perfect contours of his face and dulling the shine in his dark eyes. In my anxious state I went to the window several times, but the big house stood as before, not giving up any of its secrets.

In the early evening there was a sudden flurry of activity. Doors closed. Cars started up. They were leaving for the dinner to which I had been invited. I knew it was not the best decision, but I came to the conclusion that I should attend. I dressed quickly and headed to the restaurant in my rented Miata convertible.

Helen's family and some family friends sat on either side of a long table at the Old Fisherman's Grotto Restaurant. It was Jimmy's sixteenth birthday party. There was curiously an empty seat at the end of the table where Miguel and Helen were. Helen's mother looked up from the other end with a slightly admonishing smile for my lateness, but nothing more. It seemed that she hadn't been told of Helen's discovery, and Helen had allowed my seat to be held as to not disturb the propriety of the occasion.

Margaret gestured for me to sit down and went back to occupying herself with Rebecca, seated near her grandparents with the other children.

"How dare you show up!" Helen hissed from behind her menu as I slipped into the seat.

"Not now," Miguel pleaded.

"On what planet do you live that you would think you are still welcome?" Helen continued.

"Let it go, Helen. We'll talk about this tomorrow after we get back from the Aquarium," said Miguel. Miguel and I had planned to take Rebecca to see the fish. Helen had suggested that we go without her. She was bored by the idea, claiming she had been there hundreds of times.

"Aquarium! Ha! There will be no Aquarium trip. I don't want him anywhere near Rebecca. If he had any decency, he would be out of town by now."

"Helen, please," said Miguel. He nodded his head toward the other end of the table.

I remained quiet but burning inside. I glanced down the table and wondered how long it would take before the quarrel filtered down to Helen's parents. Her father appeared oblivious as he cupped his hands in an imitation golf stroke, no doubt recounting his day on the course.

"You want me to run as if I committed a crime? I have been a part of his life a lot longer than you have, and I have no intention of disappearing." I spoke softly, but gathered strength as the words came out. "It was time you knew."

"You make me sick."

"Sick? You surprise me, Helen. I thought you were a little more open-minded with your tattooed lower back and all your Berkeley friends with their pierced eyebrows."

"I don't give a shit what people do in the bedroom. But not in my fucking house, not with my fucking husband."

Miguel pleaded with his eyes that I not say anymore. The rest of the table had gone quiet. Jimmy gaped at them with a twisted smile as if he knew exactly what the conflict was about.

"Why don't you do us all a big favor and leave?" Helen said loud enough that the whole table heard.

"If that's what you want," I said and looked expectantly at Miguel, but he dropped his eyes and said nothing. I stood up and threw my napkin on the table. "I bid you all a good evening," I shouted. I walked a few paces and turned around. "Jimmy, I forgot to wish you a happy birthday. You must be very proud." I was fairly certain that I had found my spy.

I got out to the parking lot and took a large gulp of ocean air as I leaned against the car, delaying my departure with the fantasy that Miguel would come running out of the restaurant after me. It didn't happen. Driving back on Highway 1, I decided that after my jog in the morning I would pack up my things and go back home to Mexico.

The chilly fog was draped over the coastal trail as my shoes hit the path. It caressed the sage scrub and manzanita, and gently stroked the windswept cypress trees that looked like cartoon cut-outs, exaggerated examples of trees caught in a constant howling wind. Overhead, seagulls weaved in and out of the damp grayness, screeching and gliding on the wind. A small animal rustled in the brittle underbrush and scurried away.

I loved the early morning run, the serenity of it, nothing but the sounds and smells of nature and the workings of my body as it pumped life into my limbs. I had passed the first half-mile of pain and now my muscles were kicking in. My body was like a machine producing the internal warmth against the gusty wind that buffeted me, first from the ocean, then swirling around to get me from the back.

But the regular pounding of my feet, the bath of cool dampness, the twists and turns of the trail, and the steady but labored breathing couldn't keep my mind from the previous day's events. This would be my last jog along the cliff, along the path that I had discovered some years before on my first stay with the family at their weekend home. I would remember my runs as my time of solace from the stale air of tension these visits created, the strain of hiding. Now that we had been found out, it was up to Miguel to find a way to come to me. The intimacy of the cottage would be history, banked in my memory against the months of loneliness until the next visit, if there was one.

The cliff trail was still high above the water, but would soon be dipping down to where it was only a few yards above the beach. I heard the metallic chink-chink of a towhee and then spotted the dull brown bird perched in a gooseberry bush. As I approached, the bird adjusted its long tail and took flight. What would Miguel do? Would he fight? There had been no fight in his eyes the previous evening when I had stormed out of the dinner party. There had been nothing. After nearly eight years, nothing. Nothing of the joy when I first told him I would take him on as a worker on my land in Mexico. Nothing of the elation several years later when I told him I was sending him to study architecture in California. Nothing of the delight that crossed his face when the door was shut and the clothes came off. Nothing of the ecstasy that distorted his face in moments of raw sex or the calm pleasure in the quiet times afterward.

The tension in my legs shifted as I started down the gentle slope to where I would be closest to the ocean, where the roar of the waves would be loudest. Ahead was the part of the run where my muscles would be tested, the steep climb to a lookout. I slowed my pace at the low flat point and looked out to the beach, empty except for the gulls and sandpipers doing a snake dance among the tubes of kelp littering the sand.

At the point of the trail midway between the two cliffs, the wind gusted about my head and seemed to whisper counsel. "Let him go," it said. "Let Miguel have his American dream."

I always doubted that Miguel would ever leave Helen, but now I felt it, as the wind put it into words. Helen was the key to Rebecca, and his daughter was everything to Miguel. And no matter how many presents I showered on the little girl, I would never be more than a surrogate uncle, never the second father I sometimes fantasized.

I was three quarters of the way up the steep trail before I became conscious of my progress and noticed the pull in my legs. I made a final push and emerged onto the flat top of the bluff. I gasped for air and felt my sweat turn icy as a cooler wind struck me. After a few strides, I became aware of another presence. I looked up and was startled by a lone figure, a woman gazing out toward the ocean. She was huddled into a thick turtleneck sweater with a blue silk scarf tied under her chin. She wore what looked like stretch ski pants and sneakers. At the sound of my feet, she turned toward me. It was Helen. I stopped and ran in place, gradually letting my feet slow until they were at rest. We stared at each other, our shoulders leaning slightly forward as if there was going to be a shoot-out.

"What are you doing here?" I asked.

"Why are you destroying my family?" Her voice was shrill and her jaw clenched. She gripped a stick the thickness of a riding crop that she must have picked up on the side of the trail. She had the look of someone about to raise the branch and beat me senseless.

"That was not my intention."

"You're disgusting. Miguel told me you've been preying on him since he was a teenager."

"He didn't say that."

"I suppose he feels some vile obligation to you for what you did for him. He doesn't need you now."

"I wonder if you know what your husband needs, if you know him at all."

"What do you know, just waltzing in and out of our lives from time to time? Miguel's weak. He wants to make everybody happy. Leave us alone!" she screamed.

"You're upset."

"You're damn right I'm upset!"

"We all need to talk, but not like this. Not now."

"Talk? Are you insane? Like I'm going to accept this?"

She became frightening in her anger. Her blue eyes were piercing and she was having trouble breathing. Wisps of fog broke away from the main cloudbank and swirled around us. I glanced at a sign ten feet beyond her that warned people to stay on the path, away from the unstable cliffs.

"Helen, move away from the edge."

"Don't worry," she said in a gnarled voice between gulps of air. "I'm not going to jump. Wouldn't give you the satisfaction."

"Move back from the cliff. It's dangerous." I took a step toward her.

"Stay away, you pervert." She stepped back and brandished the stick to protect herself. She was an arm's-length away from me.

"Helen, please."

And then the unreal began. A chunk of the cliff started to give way. Her feet scrambled, like a Charleston dance-step before starting to go down, her legs quickly disappearing over the edge. She dropped the stick. "Oh, my God," she screamed. Her hand grabbed at the edge of the precipice, but the dirt and gravel came away as her weight pulled her down. It all happened in a split-second. I reached out. It was too late. Her hand fell out of sight. A long scream shattered through my brain and then nothing but the surf pounding the shore. I dropped to my knees and crawled to the edge with a prayer that a ledge had broken her fall.

At least that was the story I had told Miguel and the police, and had gone over so many times in my head that it seemed real. There were no witnesses, despite Jimmy's testimony—no record, no videotape, nothing to corroborate or refute my story. But there were moments in prison when the walls closed in on me and I sank to lows that I thought I would never crawl out of, times when another version of the events seeped into my brain to torture me.

In crime they talk of temporary insanity. It seemed that Helen and I were both temporarily insane at that moment on the cliff, driven by our love of Miguel and our frustration with him. It could have gone either way. It could have been me down on the rocks. That she hit me with the stick was certain because there was a mark on my neck. There must have been some kind of struggle. The time between when she raised the branch to hit me, once maybe twice, and when she went over the cliff was a matter of seconds, muddled seconds of confusion and fog, blind anger and fear. Had I simply defended myself from her blows, or was there a thrust of my arm, a push if you will, that sent her over the edge? I had replayed it a hundred times in my head and each time I was no more certain what actually happened. Yet during one of my low times I had to conclude that I was responsible for her death just as she might have been responsible for mine. The tragedy was a difference of moments, inches, a few degrees of strength, but I felt the guilt was mine. I dove into it and wallowed in it like a pig rolling around in its own filth.

I had never been religious, but Jim was on a redemption kick, ranting daily about the need to confess. I told him one day that I had doubts about the innocence that I had always professed. We talked about that moment of insanity that must occur in every violent crime. He said that in his case there was no doubt he did it, but the actual pulling of the trigger and the blast knocking the man back against the wall, the screams of his wife were still fuzzy to him.

After talking to Jim I made the disastrous decision to write Miguel and tell him my thoughts, saying that maybe the story I had told him wasn't exactly the truth. I told him that though I meant no deliberate harm to Helen, I had most likely been responsible for her death. A week later I got news of his death, and I calculated that his accident must have happened soon after getting my letter. I was devastated. It was a few months before I was to be released and I didn't know if I should kill myself then or wait until I got out. On the outside I would have more options to make sure I did it successfully. Again Jim got me through the crisis. He brought Ramon, the Brazilian, into it, and they wouldn't leave me alone for a minute. They kept telling me I had made it through seven years of hell, and freedom was coming. I owed it to myself, and to them, to get through it. I did.

When Rebecca first proposed reopening my case, I was dead set against it, in part because of the letter I sent to Miguel. Her plan to prove Jimmy's testimony false could discredit the DA's case, but I was worried about my letter getting into the wrong hands. In the end I agreed to do it because it meant so much to Rebecca, and she seemed so convinced that she was fulfilling Miguel's wishes. I had served my time and it wasn't going to make much difference to me anyway. What I hadn't counted on was the call I got from Jim a few months after he came to visit me.

"Hey, buddy, how's it going?" he said.

"Oh, you know."

"Something's going on, isn't it?"

"What do you mean?"

"Got a call from the DA's office in Monterey. They want to talk to me."

"About what?"

"You."

"What did you tell them?"

"Nothing. What's up?"

"Rebecca, the daughter. She found me and has this notion that she wants to reopen the case and prove that I was convicted on false testimony."

"Should have just let it lie. You served your time. You were fucked over, but it's done."

"You're not going to tell them?"

"My release was conditional. My parole officer told me I better cooperate."

"Christ!"

"Cool out. I don't have to tell what we talked about in prison. Anyway, there's always that gray area."

"I don't want you to lie."

"We've been over this. If we don't know what the truth is, it's not a lie."

"The gray area."

"Yeah. The insanity."

"Yeah."

"You know, I wanted to ask you something when I came to your house, but I was embarrassed. I'm having a hard time getting back on my feet. I hate to ask you, but if you could give me a little help, I would sure appreciate it. Just a loan. I'd definitely pay you back."

I couldn't believe what I was hearing. He was blackmailing me. Jim, my savior. My yoga guy. My mother always told me there was no free lunch, but it still felt wrong. I was silent long enough to make him squirm a bit, though he didn't give up.

"Wouldn't need that much. You know, a thou."

"A thou." Long pause. "Guess I could handle that."

On the one hand, I could let him blab to the DA's office. What were they going to do? I was pretty sure they couldn't try me again, double jeopardy and all that. I just didn't want Rebecca to find out, at least not in some public setting. Maybe I would have to tell her someday, but it would be my choice when and where.

A thousand dollars wasn't much to me. I sent him the money and hoped it would be the end of it.

## 17: Rebecca

I walked into the oppressively formal living room of the brick house where I had grown up and my eyes fell on Gran, a collapsed matriarch, slightly slumped over in her wheelchair. Though her hair had recently been done and she was impeccably dressed in a lavender silk pantsuit, her face was notably asymmetrical, one side more slack than the other. Her eyes, though, were sharp as she followed my entrance into the room.

I went first to Granddad. He slid from the worn brown leather of his favorite armchair—the one piece of furniture in the room that appeared used—into a standing position and we hugged. It was a real hug this time. I next went to Gran and leaned down to peck her on the cheek. Her only reaction was a slight upturn on the good side of her mouth that could be interpreted as an attempt at a smile or a half-grimace.

Jimmy sat on the sofa, his elbows resting on his knees and his fine square chin cradled in his manly hands sporting golden tufts of hair that picked up the sunlight coming in the window behind him. He stared at the ground. I sat on the other end of the sofa and addressed him. "Hello, Jimmy."

"Becca," he mumbled, not unpleasantly.

The antique Arendal clock on the mantel above the cold fireplace ticked pompously as Granddad cleared his throat. His voice at first sounded like an engine trying to clear its valves of residue.

"The first issue I want to address is Jimmy's repugnant behavior toward Rebecca. Emotions have run high recently, but nothing can be accomplished by lashing out at one another."

Jimmy stiffened up and dropped his arms. "But she—"

"There is no 'but she' in this conversation," he thundered, finding his range. "Whatever your feelings about Rebecca's recent actions, there is no excuse for assault. If you lay a hand on her again, I will see that you are arrested. It is a terrible thing for a father to have to say to his son, but you need to get it through your thick skull that I'm serious. I will not tolerate this behavior. Do you understand me?"

Jimmy sat with his arms crossed and stared at his father.

Granddad returned the stare. "I need a verbal acknowledgement that you understand. Yes or no."

"Yes," Jimmy uttered firmly, still with an edge of defiance. Gran looked at her son with eyes bathed in a pool of mother-son dependence, as if trying to communicate that they had no choice but to listen to Granddad, at least for now.

"Fine. As you all know, Rebecca has been in contact with George. I admire her tenacity in pursuing what she thinks is right. In doing so she has forced us to recognize that an injustice was done."

Gran squirmed in her chair as if she wanted to get on her feet. She raised her arm and a garbled shout escaped her lips, the words unintelligible.

"Margaret, for once in your life shut up. Anyway we can't even understand what you are saying." We were all shocked by the force of his words, though I applauded his sentiment. "I know you had your reasons for what you did. If I had known at the time what you were up to, I never would have allowed it. And when I became aware years later, I was too weak to do anything. We all lost someone that day, a daughter, a sister, a mother. She was special to all of us. She was my golden girl and I will never recover from her loss. But Margaret, you took matters into your own hands as if only your grief had importance. You decided that vengeance and deceit were justified. We ruined a man's life."

"Two men actually," I chimed in.

"Yes, you could say that. Your father was another victim of the unfortunate stream of events. Three important people in your young life were taken almost in one fell swoop. No matter what we thought of George's personal life at the time, we have to admit that he was very fond of you and you of him. I understand why you would want to prove his innocence. And if you really believe that is the case, I stand by you. Only God, our daughter, and George know what really occurred that day out on the cliff. Whatever happened it was certainly Jimmy's false testimony that sent him to jail. I suppose that Margaret, in the grips of anger and depression over Helen's death, felt that assuring George's conviction and exposing his relationship with Miguel were necessary. She was adamant that we get custody of Rebecca. But that didn't make it right, and I might shock you all by saying that I sometimes wonder if Rebecca might have been better off living with her father. Maybe it would have kept him from spiraling downward. God forgive us for what we did. It was wrong."

Gran began to whimper like a scolded dog. A bit of drool escaped the lax side of her mouth. She might have been experiencing remorse, but I doubted it. More likely she was incensed that her husband didn't support her decision.

"I have already discussed with Bob the legal ramifications," Granddad continued. "I can't of course blame George for wanting to clear his name and I know there is no way he can be compensated for the time he served unjustly. At the same time I don't want anyone in my family going to jail. Jimmy was a minor at the time and I suppose we could argue that Margaret was temporarily insane due to her grief."

Gran shook her head and let out a grunt of disgust.

"Bob thought we should talk to George and his lawyer, that we could perhaps go before a judge with the facts as we now know them. He is working on a way that George can be exonerated of the crime without retrying the case. I don't think anyone wants a retrial. I am prepared to pay for everything, including any compensation."

"George isn't really interested in money," I reminded Granddad.

"I realize that and I know you think I'm one to try and solve everything by throwing money at it. But sometimes a simple apology isn't enough. If he doesn't want the money, he can give it to charity. I would feel more comfortable if there was a financial exchange that reflects my commitment to making things right. And speaking of money, I will ensure that you have enough to finish law school. I don't want you to start out with a mountain of debt. Again, it doesn't begin to make up for what you have endured in losing both parents, but it is something I can and want to do for you."

I nodded thanks.

Granddad fell silent and the room suffered for lack of the voice that had grown more powerful and resolute the longer he spoke. It seemed that we were now suspended in a vacuum capable of sucking out all our air. Gran had returned to her hangdog expression, though her eyes were still sharp and defiant. She would never admit that she had done anything wrong. Jimmy was slouched down in boredom, staring at the opposite wall, his long legs disappearing under the marble-topped coffee table. The mantel clock continued its relentless tick.

"Are we finished?" Jimmy mumbled.

Granddad gave him a long, disarming stare. "Yes."

"Mom, do you want to go back to your room? I'll call the new girl. What's her name?"

Gran raised her arm and pointed at Jimmy with a shake of her bony finger. "No, you," she garbled.

Jimmy got up and wheeled her out of the room without so much as a glance at Granddad and me.

"Rebecca, I want you to arrange a meeting with George. Unofficial. No lawyers. Just the three of us."

"Thanks again. I know this isn't easy."

He raised his eyebrows and let out a burst of air. "It's what has to be done."

## 18: Rebecca

Patricia and I hurried up the steps to the courthouse. We were late. She held the glass door open and waved me through. I tried to avoid her eyes as she scrutinized me, her head slightly tilted to the right. In the brief few steps between the top of the stairs and the door she must have noted my change in pace, the heaviness in my step, and the dull look on my face. In her indomitable style she wouldn't be happy until she got inside my head and had a look around. I moved out of her range and started down the corridor toward the room where the hearing would take place. She came up beside me and our heels beat a syncopated rhythm on the marble floors.

"This is it, kiddo," she said.

Kiddo? I didn't answer.

She lay a cool hand on my arm and stopped. "Rebecca, what is it? This is what you've been waiting for."

It was and it wasn't. I was doing everything that Papi wanted me to do. "It doesn't feel right," I said.

"You'd prefer a fight?"

"We're winning because they allow us to win."

Patricia's face stiffened. The makeup that was supposed to cover up her wrinkles seemed to accentuate them. Her hair was sprayed to excess. I preferred the old Patricia, the one that wasn't so concerned about her looks, the one that didn't try so hard. She blew a little snort of frustration out her nose, then immediately seemed to regret showing emotion. She tried to cancel it with a manufactured smile.

"That's the way the world works," she said with her hand floating upward. Perhaps the answer was up in the ornate fixtures of the high hallway, or even further up in the heavens.

"It doesn't seem fair, all that time we spent with *Napue v. Illinois, whosamabob v. Maryland* and, God, all the others. In the end, does it matter?"

"We had to be prepared."

I had been helping Patricia with the research on cases dealing with false testimony. Between that and starting law school a couple months before, I was buried in legalese. It was the time of year in coastal California when offshore winds brought blasts of dry heat from the Central Valley. I wandered around my apartment dazed by the eerie hot winds and in shock at the amount of reading I had to do for my courses. To get me through it I needed to feel inspired, to believe that justice prevailed because it was right. Everything I had learned about George's case, from the original conviction to what was most likely to be a reversal in today's hearing, showed me that truth could be bought, sold, twisted, and repackaged. Was a career as a lawyer really the road I wanted to head down?

I stared at Patricia and hopelessness took over my voice. "I can just imagine Granddad, the judge and the DA sitting over cocktails after a golf game, discussing George's case. They're playing damage control as if it were a business deal where a few wrong moves had been made. It's all about money and power."

"It's not a pretty picture. But we are getting the result we want. Anyway, you said you thought your grandfather felt real remorse for what the family had done. At least he's doing something about it."

"It's easy to feel remorse when you know that nothing bad is going to come of it. Wealth and privilege put an innocent man in prison for years and now the same connections are used to correct the past without making any of the guilty parties suffer."

"We don't know exactly what the judge is going to say."

"Yeah, right. You think they're going to send Jimmy or Gran to jail?"

We beat up the floor a little more with our heels as we continued down the hall to the courtroom.

George and Conchita were standing in the shadows near the large wooden doors. Conchita looked smart in her new gray midi-length jumper over a blue rayon blouse. Her sister had taken her shopping. With the new clothes and the relaxation she had gotten in Mexico, she looked ten years younger. George had on the same suit he had worn to my graduation. I wanted to tell him it didn't flatter him, but I saw in his eyes that he was already on the edge of fleeing in a panic.

"They're all in there," George said with a nervous bite in his voice.

"Sorry we're late," Patricia said.

"It's my fault," I said, hugging George, and then Conchita.

When we entered the courtroom, Granddad turned and smiled. He nodded as if to say that everything was all right. Gran in her wheelchair lifted her head as an animal might, sensing a possible enemy in her territory, but didn't look at us. Jimmy was next to Gran, leaning back with his eyes closed, his arms folded across his chest.

Judge Petrini moved his bulk into the room with a practiced ease and made a good attempt at a serious demeanor though there was something in his dark eyes that appeared too casual. After billowing out his robe and lowering himself into the seat, he wasted little time in saying that he wanted to question Ms. Espinosa first. We all glanced around as if we weren't quite sure who he was talking about. Conchita had always been just Conchita, and I was again reminded how the rich know so little about the help that take care of them.

I give the judge credit for treating Conchita with great respect and sympathy. He asked her to clarify the statement she had made about Jimmy being asleep in bed when the incident occurred and why she didn't come forward sooner. She reiterated that at the time she knew very little about the case. Her English was not good and she had her hands full taking care of Rebecca. No one talked about what was happening, especially when Rebecca was around. She fell short of saying that Gran had deliberately kept her in the dark.

She only learned about Jimmy's testimony later from a friend who had read it in the papers, but she was afraid to say anything then because of her undocumented status. If she had lost her job, she would have been out on the street. The questioning was brief, and she retook her seat with an obvious show of relief.

The judge then called Jimmy. His questions were direct, without coddling.

"Did you or did you not see Mr. Edwards push your sister off the cliff?"

"I already made my statement to that effect."

"I want to hear it from you personally."

"No, I did not."

"Where were you at the time of your sister's death?"

"Conchita told you, didn't she?" he said with a sneer.

"I want to hear it from you. You will kindly answer the questions I put to you. Answering under oath before a judge is not the same as making a statement."

"I was asleep."

"How old were you at the time?"

"Sixteen."

"Did anyone tell you to say you saw Mr. Edwards push your sister?"

Jimmy hesitated. Gran's head was down. He locked eyes with his father. "No. No one. It was my idea."

"Your idea?"

"Yes."

"You decided you wanted a man convicted of a crime he didn't commit."

"We don't know that he didn't do it. Just because I didn't see it doesn't mean he didn't do it."

I saw the muscles in the back of George's neck tense up.

The judge wiggled in his seat and leaned forward, suppressing a sardonic grin. "In this country, the prosecutor must make the case. Until then, the person is innocent. Aside from your testimony there was no evidence. It should have been dismissed."

He hesitated a minute when the courtroom door opened with a squeak. George turned around. His already tense face tightened a few degrees and his mouth fell open. I looked over my shoulder and saw a tall man with a gray ponytail take a seat in the back. He nodded slightly to George, and then folded his hands in his lap.

The judge told Jimmy he could step down and went on to berate the DA's office, saying that it was a travesty that they had achieved a conviction with such a weak case. He spoke sternly to a young blonde woman who represented the district attorney. She looked as if she had recently graduated from law school, and she stared straight ahead as the admonishments floated right past her, really aimed for nameless parties in the past. Most everyone involved with the investigation from the police officers to the DA to the prosecuting attorney had retired or left their jobs. The current courtroom scene was all for show. And then she surprised everyone by speaking out.

"Your Honor, may I approach the bench."

The judge peered out over the top of his barrister frames as if annoyed. It wasn't part of the plan. But he assented. They spoke a few moments and then called Patricia up. The three of them conferred a few more minutes in low voices. With worry lines on her forehead Patricia turned around and glanced at the man in the back of the courtroom. In the rest of the conference the judge spoke and Patricia nodded her head a lot. They returned to their seats, the blonde woman with a smug look on her face.

During the interlude, people had perked up. Even Jimmy came out of his slouch and sat on the edge of his seat.

When the judge began to speak again, it was clear he had lost his jovial manner. He repeated that George's trial lacked sufficient evidence for conviction, but he no longer spoke in an admonishing tone. He said that all rights of a citizen would be restored to George. There was no official apology for the time he had spent in jail. He announced the hearing was over and quickly left the room.

I turned around again to look at the man in the back. He was gone. A hush fell over the courtroom, and then everybody stood up.

I rushed over to Patricia. "What the hell was that about? There was no apology. His rights restored? That basically already happened when he got out."

"Oh, the judge felt that he could only go so far."

"Come on, Patricia. The man in the back? The long conference at the bench. Something happened."

Patricia smiled demurely at the other woman, who packed up her things and turned to leave. "We'll talk later," she said to me in a low voice, still smiling.

Granddad approached George and shook his hand. They both looked bewildered. Jimmy had Gran almost out the door and Granddad followed after them. He looked back at me with a weak smile.

I went over to George. "Are you all right?" I was dying to ask who the man with the ponytail was, but it seemed best to leave it for later.

"It's over," he said. "So glad I'm a full citizen again. I guess that means I can buy a gun."

Patricia sidled close to me, her thick briefcase bumping me. "What's that about a gun?" she said.

"My rights restored. I can buy a gun." We tried to laugh at his joke, but our hollow laughs barely jostled the air around us. We quickly moved toward the door.

Patricia, Conchita, George, and I had planned to go out for lunch, though I didn't feel much like celebrating. We headed down the hall and Patricia stayed close to me, trying to engage me in conversation about everything except the hearing. She commented on how difficult it must have been growing up in the house with Jimmy. It had been her first encounter with the man she had heard so much about. "And your grandmother, my God, that woman is scary. I feel for you, I really do. Your grandfather seems decent."

"Yes, he is." I had done my share of family-bashing, but I didn't want to get drawn into it with Patricia.

"And Conchita, you poor dear," Patricia went on. "You worked for them all those years."

"Yes, well..."

"Rebecca, you must call me when you need help with your studies. It hasn't been that long since I was in school. I still remember all the benchmark cases."

Her chatter filled the air around us and I wanted to tell her to shut up, but it didn't seem an appropriate thing to say to someone who had just helped me with the case I had spent a good part of my life thinking about. Whenever she was near, she tried so hard to be part of what was going on with me. It was uncomfortable, but particularly today. Everybody in our group seemed to depend on me to anchor them. George lagged a few paces behind. His shoulders were bent under another mystery that I was going to have to pry out of him. I was certain he knew the man in the ponytail. Conchita walked along with an expression of relief on her face, but still out of place. Though I appreciated each of them with a fondness I couldn't describe, having them all together, looking at me as if I was their guiding light, made me feel inadequate for the task.

We walked out the front door, and I spotted Alberto standing next to his truck parked on the street in front of the courthouse. Patricia stopped mid-sentence when she saw that she had lost my attention. She followed my gaze and saw the culprit. They had never met, but she knew about him. I left them huddled in a group on the stairs and went down to Alberto. He was propped-up against the door to his pickup with his arms crossed in front of him. He had on tight jeans but a nice blue-and-white striped shirt, boots, and a leather jacket aged to a buttery softness.

"Hey," I said.

"You don't look very victorious. Everything go all right?"

"Still not sure exactly what happened, but there was some half-assed admission that the original trial was essentially bogus. Not the big apology we were going for."

"Is George okay with that?"

"I guess." I didn't want to get into the story of the mystery man until I knew what was going on.

He glanced at my group and gave them a little wave. "Haven't heard from you lately."

"Been pretty busy with school and the hearing. Conchita's staying with me."

"Any of that disallow returning phone calls?" He was standing up straight now, his fists slightly clenched at his sides.

"Nope."

"What is it then?'

"I told you from the beginning not to get your hopes up."

"Getting my hopes up would be if I expected you to be my girlfriend or asked you to marry me or some crazy idea like that. No. I'd just be happy with a returned phone call and maybe the chance to see you once in a while."

"Maybe that's too much to hope for."

"Jesus, Becca." He banged his hand on the edge of the truck bed and paced as far as the tailpipe before turning sharply around and coming back to face me.

"People are watching," I said.

"You should know by now I don't give a shit what people think."

"That's just it. I *don't* know you. I know this person who for some strange reason has decided that I'm somebody he wants to be close to. What if I'm not?"

"God, listen to yourself. You don't even make sense. Look, I'm sorry you lost your parents. I'm sorry you had a shitty time growing up with your grandparents. I'm sorry your uncle is an asshole. I'm sorry you have an identity crisis."

"I don't have an identity crisis," I fired back.

"Get over it. Stop pushing people away."

"You're shouting."

"You're damn right I'm shouting. Maybe it'll make you hear what I have to say."

"Why are you so upset?"

"Did it ever occur to you that I might be in love with you?" He slammed his hand on the edge of the truck again. "Damn, you made me say it. Now you're sure to run for cover."

My little heart was all a pitter-patter and running through a field of buttercups, but not a muscle of my face moved a fraction of an inch. I stared at him as if I hadn't heard what he said. Thank God he didn't look down or he would have seen that my knees were shaking. Instead he turned around and put his arms on the cab of the truck, burying his face in them.

"All right," he said, his voice calm, but defeated. "I can see there's no getting through to you." He slid his hands down and opened the door to his truck.

I put my hand on the door, and for a moment there was a tug of war, him pulling and me pushing. "Got any plans for Christmas?" I said.

"What? Christmas? Don't play with me, Becca."

"I'm serious. I want you to go to Mexico with me. I want you to meet my father's family." He let up and I pushed the door closed. He turned to face me. "You can't go until I get an answer," I said. I loved his pouty eyes, but I kept my poker face. "Actually, why don't you come to lunch with us? We can talk more about it."

He looked over at the steps again. "Are you sure your girlfriend won't mind?"

"About as much as your boyfriend."

"Touché."

"You were kidding about Patricia, right? You don't really think…"

"She's got a nasty stare going on right now."

"Did you mean that?"

"About Patricia?"

"No, that other thing you said."

"My hand hurts," he said in a whine.

"Let me see." I took his hand in mine and squeezed it hard.

"Ouch."

"That's what you get for going all macho on me." I put on more pressure, pushing into the bone. "Did you mean it?"

"I meant it. Did you mean it about Mexico?"

"You would love Abuela and Jorge. Vitico might be difficult at first. He's kind of protective. Please come." I lifted his hand up to my lips and kissed it. "All better?"

"*Esta mujer me vuelve loco,*" he said, looking up at the sky.

"You're no Sunday picnic yourself. Let's go."

I lead Alberto up the stairs to where Patricia, George, and Conchita were engaged in conversation as if they hadn't just witnessed my little scene with Alberto. They turned toward us with secret smiles that registered George's amusement, Conchita's joy, and Patricia's disappointment.

Alberto embraced George in a tight hug. George was beginning to look less uncomfortable, but he was still a little taken aback with the affection. He also hugged

Conchita, who whispered an encouraging, "*Mijo,*" in his ear. But as I introduced him to Patricia, she stuck out her arm to shake hands like a fencer jabbing at her opponent.

"I've heard so much about you," Alberto said. "Rebecca told me about all the work you did on the case."

"She did a lot of it. She's quite a determined young woman."

I rolled my eyes. "Shall we go?" I said.

At the Dim Sum restaurant we passed around little plates that I knew had Alberto wondering if he was ever going to douse his appetite. Patricia managed to hand the food to me without once looking at me. She had been avoiding me since the courthouse steps and was currently occupied in a conversation with Conchita about the prices of food in Mexico. As a further snub she spoke in Spanish. George broke his usual reluctance to speak Spanish and joined their conversation. He seemed to have gotten over what happened in the courtroom and slid his chair closer to Patricia and Conchita, most likely assuming Alberto and I wanted to be left alone. But when Alberto overheard Patricia mention that her grandparents were from Hermosillo, he jumped into their discussion. Even enemies can put down their arms to talk about a common homeland.

I found myself in the role of the *gringa* having a hard time following the conversation of Spanish-speakers. There is something about the language itself that doesn't lend to turn-taking, and if you don't speak it well, the words can get lost in the air. From being the unwilling center of attention just a short time before, I had quickly been relegated to outcast. Under the table I put a hand on

Alberto's leg and he covered it with his own, though his attention was still on Patricia. He seemed determined not to let her ignore him. I had discovered that he hated being ignored more than anything. He would never let George or me escape into our respective dens, and he wouldn't let Patricia hide behind her façade of the aloof injured party.

I started to remove my hand from his leg, but he grabbed it and cradled it in his. Still he kept the conversation going with Patricia. I glanced up and saw the waiter bringing another bottle of champagne. I drained my glass and allowed the waiter to fill it up.

With the second bottle, the voices rose to an even higher level of clatter. If I didn't concentrate, all I heard was a barrage of open vowels and rolled r's going from person to person. I focused in to grasp that they were still on the subject of Hermosillo and that Patricia hadn't been there since her grandparents died. Alberto told her about recent developments, how fast the city was growing, the restoration projects in the colonial part of town. He spoke with an enthusiasm about his hometown that made me question what I had previously deduced as a complete adaptation to his new country.

Alberto caught me downing yet another glass of champagne and switched to English. "I think we'll have to visit my parents in Hermosillo when we go to see your grandmother over the winter break."

Patricia, who was beginning to relax and speak with confidence, quickly stiffened. She looked at me for the first time during the meal, her mouth frozen in a malformed "O". George and Conchita fell silent.

"Alberto, what are you doing?" I said with an unintended, but obvious screech to my voice. He had used the public "we." He had revealed a spontaneous invitation of just a short time before that I was already having second thoughts about. And most frightening was that he was adding on a trip to see his parents where he no doubt had it in his head that he was going to present me as someone important in his life.

"Oops," he said with a bad-boy grin. He glanced at George and Conchita, counting on their good will to counterbalance my shock and Patricia's displeasure.

George jumped in to help his friend. "What a wonderful idea! Christmas in Mexico."

"And you're coming with us," Alberto said to George.

Now it was George whose expression turned to shock. "Nice thought. But you can count me out."

# 19: George

    I was cut off from Rebecca and Alberto who had their airline headphones looped over their heads. They were watching one of those manipulative Hollywood movies heavy on loss and sentimentality that I had refused to get sucked into. I was a weeper and didn't like showing my tears in public.

    I had the aisle and Rebecca the window, Alberto graciously offering to take the center seat. I had a feeling he liked being in the middle, and I couldn't help thinking of the way Miguel needed Helen and me on either side of him. It was foolish to make the comparison. Alberto was not my lover, and I was happy that he and Rebecca were moving toward something, despite her resistance. They were holding hands, their fingers enlaced, resting on her thigh. But there was a tightness in her jaw that made me think she wasn't completely comfortable with it.

    We were on our way to spend the holidays in Mexico. I had agreed to the trip after strong lobbying from Alberto. Rebecca was also encouraging, though less enthusiastic. There was the unresolved issue of the mystery man in the courtroom and how he had influenced what happened. I had managed to avoid a private conversation with Rebecca about it. After our Dim Sum lunch, Patricia had taken me aside and told me she would leave it up to me to explain the peculiar ending of the hearing to Rebecca.

"Was the woman from the DA's office really threatening to have Jim testify?" I asked.

"She just wanted the judge to know they had a card though they didn't plan to play it.  She told the judge she had someone who could support the theory that there had been a struggle, so that maybe the conviction wasn't that far off base."

"So they were saving face."

"We all agreed we had reached a moot point since you had already served your time. They couldn't try you again. But it did make the judge a little stingy with the apology thing."

"What I told Jim in prison was fuzzy, and the truth is, if there is one, I don't know exactly what happened."

"You don't have to explain anything to me. My only concern now is Rebecca. She needs to believe in your innocence."

"What do I tell her?"

"She trusts you. I'm sure you'll think of something."

In fact I hadn't. Part of the reason I embarked on the trip was to find some way to explain. I was also curious what happened to the letter I had sent Miguel years before. I was afraid it might fall into Rebecca's hands before I had a chance to explain another one of the infamous decisions in my life.

I pulled a novel out of my bag, but it was impossible to concentrate. I fidgeted, got up to go to the bathroom, shook out my legs as I walked up and down the aisle, asked the flight attendant for water. A headache began in the back of my head and made its way to my temples. I was going back to the jungle where the story all began, back to where my world was once so large and expanding. My current life had gotten so miniscule, having gone from my whimsical kingdom in the Mexican forest to a rundown trailer with a fickle cat as a sometime companion. When Rebecca reappeared, my world began to grow again, tiny baby steps. Clearing up the details from the past was part of the painful growing process. How simple my trailer life had been. Now everything was flooding my brain, choking my ability to think clearly, creating sporadic distortions like the feeling that it was Miguel sitting next to me instead of Alberto.

In the years since leaving prison I had been marginally successful in holding my thoughts of Miguel at bay. Now they were a constant companion. One memory that wouldn't leave me was the last complete night we spent together, the time I accompanied him to Mexico City when he left to go to Berkeley. We were in a hotel near the airport and both full of doubt. He clung to me through the darkness, the sounds of jets roaring overhead, the traffic rolling by on the *Periférico*—he spent much of the night with his eyes open. I didn't sleep either as I contemplated giving him up to the great unknown, realizing that anything could happen. Yet the closeness we felt that night convinced me that nothing could tear us apart, nothing I thought. That was the naiveté of love.

When Rebecca, Alberto, and I arrived at the Mexico City airport, it was in a flurry of reconstruction and almost unrecognizable to me. It bore no resemblance to the halls I had escorted Miguel down when he left. Now there were endless corridors of advertising and expanded shopping centers that you were forced to walk through to get to the exit. It projected exactly the modern, prosperous image that Mexico wanted the world to see.

We found our rental car, a VW Jetta, and got complicated directions how to get out of town, which the rental agent insisted we would have no trouble following. Alberto took the wheel and I sat in the back. If we drove straight through, we could get to Acalán before midnight. Rebecca assured us that we didn't want to stay in the Hotel Tropicana, and we had declined Abuela's invitation to stay at the house. We had reservations at the four-star Colonial in Ciudad Robles about 10 miles down the road from Acalán.

As we headed north, traffic was heavy and aggressive. I could tell that Alberto had forgotten about this kind of driving as he hunched forward and grasped the wheel. From the years I used to drive in Mexico, I remembered how some of the gentlest, most reserved Mexican men and women would turn into fiends in the driver's seat, always in a mad rush to get somewhere. And yet everyone seemed to arrive late for appointments. It was one of the many incomprehensible things about Mexico that you learn to accept since you know you can't change them.

Rebecca had the map spread out on her lap and Alberto kept saying, "Is this right? Is this right?"

"Just stay on 85," she said.

"But I don't see any signs that say 85."

Over her shoulder, Rebecca said, "Why am I doing this? You used to live here."

"It seems like a million years ago." I looked out the window at the rows of shacks made from salvaged materials with rusty metal roofs, piles of garbage along putrid drainage ditches. "For all I know we could be in Calcutta. None of it looks familiar to me."

Patches of blue sky began to appear when we got out of the giant bowl where Mexico City sat like last night's soup gone cold, a Mexican pozole of cloudy vegetables and the bite of heavy spice lingering just below the surface. Soon we eased into a landscape that seemed more like the endless sprawl of Los Angeles, descending into the bland, quiet Central Valley. Patches of cultivation could be seen on either side of the road, though the land was dry, the few hills a muddy brown.

Once we passed the city of Pachuca, a couple of hours from Mexico City, Rebecca folded up the map.

"What are you doing?" Alberto said, still gripping the wheel with such force that the veins in his arm stood out.

"Just stay on 85, babe."

I chuckled. So they had reached the "babe" level of sweet nothings. Not honey or dear or sweetie—babe. With the satisfaction that I had helped them along the road to a small plateau of endearment, I leaned back in the seat in hopes of taking a nap. I closed my eyes, but my pounding head didn't allow me any rest.

"Look at that," Alberto said.

I sat up. In front of us was a wall of mountains, enriched to an enticing green by the late-afternoon sun and shrouded in mist at the top. I suddenly couldn't wait to get out of the arid plains and climb into the lush forests of the Sierra Madre, even knowing they would envelop me in the rough cloak of painful memories.

The longing to escape into the mountains was short-lived as only a half-hour of winding roads sent my head from pounding to spinning. I sat up straight and opened the window for air. The music was tuned to a radio station playing *rancheras,* and I imagined myself a drunk at a fiesta, the type that stumbles around, his eyes dazed by the tragedy in the music until he falls and passes out. The switchbacks on the road followed one after another and my head rolled from side to side. I was unable to focus, helpless to stop the churning in my stomach. I reached up and put my hand on Rebecca's shoulder. She jumped slightly, and then turned to look at me.

"Good God, George! What's wrong? You look green."

"We've got to pull over," I said.

As soon as there was a turnout, Alberto moved the car off onto a patch of gravel and I leapt out. I ran over to the edge and looked down into a wide green valley as it spun around in my head. Rebecca got out and started to come toward me, but I motioned her back with my hand. "Back, back, back. It could get messy."

The nausea passed and I sat down on the guardrail, gazing out over the Sierra Madre that held locked in its verdant bank the memories of my days with Miguel. In a nearby bush I heard a songbird that he used to call a *primavera.* After the workday was done and the other workers had left, we would sit on lounge chairs on the porch of the unfinished house, facing the waterfall. The golden late afternoon sun would cast long shadows, and the *primaveras* would tweet and warble in an endless loop of joy, nearly drowning out the sound of falling water in the distance. I ached for those days of innocence and peace. That was before I got the brilliant idea that I had to send him to the United States to study.

In the next little town, Ixmiquilpan, we stopped at a pharmacy for Dramamine and sat around drinking Coke to give the medicine time to have an effect. We were parked in a gas station with all the car doors thrown open. The air was hot but thin, and the sun was just getting ready to fall behind the highest peaks. Little had changed in these parts, and the years since I had been there seemed to have vanished like the wispy clouds that had veiled the sky just a short time before. Now it was a cerulean sky, low and stained with a hazy sliver of white moon. My heart heaved in a dramatic remembering of my many bus rides along this road to the Mexico City airport on my way to California to visit Miguel.

Alberto had his seat back and was taking a nap, while Rebecca kept glancing at me, checking to see if I was all right.

"I wonder if Miguel would have stayed here in these mountains, made a life for himself if I hadn't come along and messed things up."

"Oh, George, that kind of thinking is not going to get you anywhere. Besides, don't give yourself so much credit. He would have gotten out of here one way or the other. He didn't feel like he belonged."

"I'm worried about seeing Abuela, Vitico, and Jorge. They must blame me in some way for what happened to him."

"They don't. Abuela confessed to me that she knew from a young age, long before you came around, that there was something that kept him from finding happiness. Vitico, too, struggled with the notion, especially in those last few years when he came to realize that the brother he adored had a pain inside him that wouldn't go away. Jorge, of course, was too young to understand. He remembers a loving father who used to read to him, and then was taken away. He's a great kid. I know you'll get along."

"I wonder what Jorge's mother thought about Miguel wanting to name their son Jorge."

"She's a good-time girl, and I doubt she gave it a whole lot of thought. Abuela says that Claribel used to smoke a lot of pot and do God knows what else when she was pregnant. Abuela believes that it was only her everyday prayers to the Virgin of Guadalupe that allowed her grandson to come out normal."

It was late when we got to the hotel in Ciudad Robles. The rest of the trip had passed in a daze, the Dramamine doing its trick. I had curled up in the back seat with my backpack as a pillow and gone in and out of a hazy slumber.

When we had talked to Vitico from the San Francisco airport, he insisted that we call the house no matter the hour we arrived at the hotel. He sounded a little worried, but wouldn't say what was going on. I fell into an armchair in Rebecca and Alberto's room, and stared blankly at Rebecca as she made the call, not following the words, but gleaning that something was wrong from her expressions. She hung up the phone and turned toward us.

"What is it, babe?" Alberto asked.

"It's Jorge. He went to visit his mother in Mexico City and was supposed to be back three days ago. They haven't heard from him and Claribel doesn't answer her cell. It doesn't make sense, Vitico says. Jorge knew we were coming and was so excited about it."

"They're probably just having a good time in the city," said Alberto from his position stretched out on the bed.

"It gets worse," Rebecca added. "The last time they talked to him on Claribel's phone, they were at her new boyfriend's. He described the place as a mansion with lots of Hummers and SUVs in a circular driveway, a swimming pool, tennis court, a game room with a giant screen and the latest version of Wii."

"What the hell is that?" I asked.

"Video games like Playstation," Alberto said.

I shook my head and she went on.

"Abuela is convinced that Claribel has gotten involved with a drug kingpin and that she and Jorgito were caught in the middle of something."

"Poor Miriam," I said. "She's had her share of misery in life."

"She's held the family together through everything, but this could be her undoing," said Rebecca. "She adores that boy."

"We'd better get some sleep," I said. "Tomorrow might be a tough day."

"I'm sure there's a simple explanation for why Jorge hasn't returned. Let's not jump to conclusions," said Alberto.

I dragged myself up out of the chair. Alberto's eyes were closed, but Rebecca sat up straight on the edge of the bed, her hands folded in her lap. She looked up and forced a smile.

"Could you walk me to my room?" I said to her.

"Still dizzy?"

"Just wanted to talk a little."

Down the hall there were a couple of overstuffed chairs in a lounge area near the elevator. Between the chairs, set at right angles so we weren't quite facing each other, was a small table with a plastic Christmas tree covered with fake snow and colored blinking lights. What an odd place, I thought, to have this conversation, next to the symbol of Christmas cheer, with the lights incessantly pulsating frivolity.

"We haven't had a chance to talk since the hearing," I said.

"I've been so busy with school. I don't know about this law business." She sat, in fact, like a frustrated schoolgirl with her arms folded in front of her.

"I've heard the first semester is the worst."

The elevator door opened and a couple came out arm-in-arm, a distinguished-looking older man with a mousy young woman in a party dress. They stopped short, surprised to see us there, and then said, "*Buenas noches*" before moving on.

She gave me a strange look. "What is it, George?"

"Stirring up the past has its consequences."

"I'm learning that. Do I want to hear about the man in the back of the courtroom?"

"Probably not. It's kind of a double-whammy."

"What the hell is that supposed to mean? You know, I don't think this is a good time to get into this. We both have a lot on our minds."

"Precisely, and this is one thing I liked to get *off* my mind. I don't want you to hear it in some other way."

She picked at some of the fake snow and rubbed it around in her fingers. "All right, let's go."

"He was my cellmate in prison. His name is Jim. He was big on confession. Might say he was obsessed with it, a carryover from his Catholic upbringing. When you spend that much time with someone, it kind of rubs off on you."

"Where is this going?" The colored lights flashed on and off. She flicked a gold angel with a trumpet that dangled from a branch.

"He told me I had to confess."

"Stop. I don't want to hear this." She got up and yanked the plug out of the wall, sending the cheery tree into darkness. She held the cord in her hand and stared at the plug.

"You must believe that I never wanted to do your mother any harm. If anything, she—"

"Don't, George. This is not—"

"Rebecca, sit down. It's not as bad as you think." She fell back into the chair and threw the cord on the floor. "She came out to the cliff that morning. I don't know what her intentions were, probably hadn't thought it out. She was in a rage. She started hitting me with a stick. Of that I'm certain. And then there was a kind of madness. Two educated, basically gentle people struggling on the edge of a cliff. I swear I don't know what happened, what the actual motion was that made her go over the cliff. The version I told the police seemed the best to protect everyone. I never mentioned the stick and Helen's hysterical reactions, the awful things she said. And then Jim came along with his confession therapy at a time when I was feeling really down. He convinced me that I had to take responsibility for her death."

"So you might have pushed my mother off the cliff?"

"No! Well, maybe, unintentionally...I don't know."

"Just tell me the fucking truth!" she screamed.

"The only truth is that your mother died and it was horrible...for everybody. It was a disaster so powerful that the reverberations are still being felt today. It won't stop until we all die. That's why I was hesitant to dig into the past when you first came to me. It seemed better not to muddy the pond. But you were so sure this was what you wanted."

"And I suppose the confession therapy included a letter to my father."

"You know about that?"

"I know he received a letter around the time of his accident. Abuela didn't know from whom. Don't worry. He burned it." She stood up again. "This is bullshit! I've had enough of your fucking confession therapy. Look what it did to my father. And now you're at it again. Don't you feel better that you got it off your chest." Her tone had a sting to it, and she stood over me with the same intensity that her mother had that day. I imagined her picking up the Christmas tree and striking me over the head. "Why didn't you just leave my parents alone? You fucked everything up!" She turned and marched toward her room.

"Rebecca, I..."

She held up her hand and wagged it. "I can't talk to you anymore."

And there it was. In Rebecca's mind I had become not only the person I was accused of at the trial—the home-breaker, the jealous homosexual—but also the person responsible for both her parents' deaths. Terrific.


When Alberto came down the following morning for coffee, I could tell that he hadn't slept much either and knew the whole story. He smiled and put his hand on my shoulder.

"We'll get through this," he said.

"Should I go?"

"She just needs a little time. I talked her down. None of what you said shocks *me*. We talked half the night and she admitted that she has a lot more of her mother in her than she ever thought, especially the temper."

"I don't want her to hate me."

"She knows it's not worth pointing fingers at this point. Placing blame, if on anybody, ultimately comes back to her father. When she started this dive into the past, I don't think she realized how deep the waters were. Give her time."

She arrived a few minutes later with a cool "Good morning." She said she didn't want any coffee, and we got in the car to go to Abuela's.

# 20: *Rebecca*

We pulled up in front of Abuela's house before the sun had risen above the high crest of the surrounding mountains. She was at the door immediately, alert and dressed as always for a day's work, showing no signs of her anxiety over Jorge. But when I embraced her, I felt her need for comfort, woman-to-woman, her desperation that something had happened to her grandson. I was still raw from my talk with George. This was not the reunion I had hoped for. We separated and she returned to her role of motherly strength.

She took George's two hands in hers. "*Mijo,* how long I have waited to see you again. I know your journey has been painful, but it has you back to my door, just like it did Rebecca."

"Doña Miriam, you are an inspiration to us all. You look no older than the last time I saw you."

"I feel like I aged twenty years in the last few days." She sighed and moved quickly to Alberto. "And you must be the fine young man we have heard so much about. Any friend of Rebecca is welcome here." He bent down and kissed her cheek.

Vitico came into the doorframe, sleepy-eyed and with his hair disheveled. "I see you are all up with the chickens. Where's my little cucaracha? Come here. I missed you."

I felt Alberto's eyes on my back as Vitico gave me a bear-like hug.

"Vitico, let me introduce you to Alberto."

"My brother," Vitico said. He held Alberto's hand with a mysterious smile on his face. "How nice to meet you. Yes, very nice." He kept looking him in the eyes and smiling. "You treat her right or her uncle is going to break your beautiful face."

"Vitico, behave," I said. "He treats me fine, probably better than I deserve."

"I doubt that," said Vitico. "You deserve the best."

We went in and sat around the table where Abuela had coffee, fresh-squeezed orange juice, and her homemade crispy tortillas with beans and melted cheese on them. She told us to eat first and then we would talk. Only Vitico and Alberto seemed to have an appetite while George and I sipped our coffee. When Miriam admonished George for not eating, he told her that his stomach was still on a mountain road, rolling from side to side. She went to the cupboard, pulled out a tin full of herbs, and made him a special tea.

After we ate, I got up to go to the bathroom and walked past Jorge and Vitico's room. This time it was Vitico's bed unmade, and Jorge's perfectly squared, military-tight, and looking very cold. I refused to believe that it had seen the last of my little brother. There was a small niche in the wall between their bedroom and Abuela's with a statue of the Virgin of Guadalupe surrounded by flowers and lit candles. It wasn't my habit to pray, but I said a prayer for Jorgito that he might be brought home safely.

While I was in the bathroom, the phone rang and I rushed back to the table. I saw Vitico with the phone, but Abuela was trying to wrestle it away from him, "Jorgito, Jorgito, is that you?" she said.

"*Por favor, mami.* I can't hear," said Vitico. He looked at me for help. "Rebecca?"

I put my arm around Abuela and coaxed her away from the phone. "If it's him, we have to let Vitico talk, find out what's going on."

After a couple of eternal seconds, Vitico cupped his hand over the mouthpiece and said to us, "It's Claribel. They're all right."

"*Gracias a dios,*" Abuela said and lunged for the phone again, dragging me along with her. "*Donde están? Qué pasó? Donde está mi Jorgito? Está bien?*"

"*Mami, por favor.* If you don't let me talk, I won't get any answers."

Alberto helped me get her to a chair. He talked to her in a gentle voice, calling her señora, convincing her that in a few minutes we would know everything. "Look at Vitico's face. You can see that everything is fine."

Vitico spoke a few more minutes, hung up the phone, and then turned toward us slowly. Everything wasn't fine, but at the same time he didn't appear as someone about to give bad news. He seemed to be debating how much to tell of the story.

"There was a problem involving Claribel's boyfriend, Don Isidro. Isidro's driver took them to a safe place, said he didn't want them to contact anyone until they had assessed the situation. He thinks it best that they get out of Mexico City as soon as possible, but doesn't want to drive them in Don Isidro's car. She asked if we could go and get them."

"Let's go," said Abuela. She turned to Alberto and me. "You have a car."

"Of course we can take our car," said Alberto.

"*Mami,* we can't all go or there won't be room for them," said Vitico. "I think just Alberto and I should go."

"I'd like to go. I could help with directions," said George.

"Like you did yesterday?" I said. "And your stomach? You should stay with Abuela. I'm going." I didn't mean it cruelly, but there was still a sharpness to it.

"No, you're not," said Vitico. "It could be dangerous."

"Dangerous?" screamed Abuela. "You said they were safe."

"They're safe. They're safe. Okay, I'm going to tell you. You're going to find out anyway, but don't get hysterical. Don Isidro was shot down outside a restaurant when they went out to eat."

"*Dios mío!* Jorgito was with them?"

"Yes, but the driver got them out of there quickly and doesn't think anybody got a good look at Caribel and Jorge. The police might be looking for them, though, as witnesses. Don Isidro's people all agreed that it would be best not to get Jorge involved in being a witness."

"I can't believe this," said Abuela, falling into a chair and putting a hand to her forehead.

"They have a plan to take Claribel and Jorge to the Meliá Hotel downtown where we can pick them up and leave town immediately. They say it's safe, but I still think Rebecca should stay here."

"No way. I'm going. He's my brother."

As we drove down the Paseo de la Reforma we spotted the hotel, looking like a monolithic pink cake that was split open in the middle, revealing a glassy blue center. It was hard to miss. That was why they had chosen it. Alberto pulled up to the entrance and a uniformed man rushed out to open our doors. We got out, and Vitico explained to the doorman that we were just picking someone up.

The lobby was still decorated for Christmas, but it was difficult to tell where the holiday decorations stopped and the regular décor began. Thousands of lights and bold colors assaulted us in the twenty-story atrium with hundreds of rooms like eyes looking down on our search of the area. We saw Claribel almost immediately, a black cat curled up on a giant red sofa under a shiny brass gazebo. She wore a scarf on her head and sunglasses, a black leather jacket with the collar turned up.

"Claribel, where's Jorgito?" Vitico said in an accusing voice.

"He wouldn't sit still. I told him not to go far." Her voice was scratchy and worn. Though her eyes were covered, her face looked puffy. She uncurled her legs and rose to her feet, taking a few wobbly steps. I wasn't sure if I should feel sorry for her or strangle her for not keeping an eye on Jorgito.

"God, Claribel. You just let him wander off," Vitico said.

"Nice to see you, too, Vitico. How the hell are you? Have you had a pleasant last few days?

"Sorry about Don Isidro," I said.

"Thanks," she said. "He can't be far. I'm sure he wouldn't leave the hotel."

"Let's spread out, cover the lobby, and meet at the front door."

I didn't see Jorge among the many guests moving about, but as I stood gaping at a towering abstract sculpture, I spotted him looking down at me from a glass elevator descending from a high floor. He had on a hooded sweatshirt and baggy jeans, a waif in the garish surroundings and seemingly oblivious to any potential danger. I rushed around to the elevator door and met him.

"Jorge!"

He approached me with an innocent grin. *"Hermana, como estás?"*

I hugged him quickly. "Come on. We've got to go. Your mom is worried about you."

"I think she fell asleep."

Vitico came around the corner and put an arm around Jorge's shoulders. "What are you doing, wandering off like that?"

"Relax, *tío*, we're OK."

We met Claribel by the door and hurried out to the car. We still didn't know exactly what the danger was, if there was one, but our nerves were fed by the tension of the city. I felt bad for Alberto getting caught up in my family's mess and sympathized with him trying to maneuver into the hectic traffic of La Reforma. As soon as we got on the avenue, the cars came to a standstill. Nobody said anything. I was in back with Jorge in the middle and Claribel and the other side. Vitico drummed his fingers on the dashboard, and Alberto gave him a sidelong glance. He stopped. "Sorry," he said.

"All right. What exactly are we dealing with here? I feel like we're paranoid and don't even know why," Vitico said.

Claribel took a deep breath and began the story. "Isidro took us out to Aguila y Sol in Polanco, one of the best restaurants in the city. He can do that kind of stuff. We came out of the restaurant and Benito, the driver, pulled up. We were about to get in the car when two men approached. Isidro pushed us into the car and slammed the door. '*Vete,*' he said to Benny, but Benny didn't want to leave his boss standing there. He hesitated. Isidro screamed again, '*Váyanse,*' and pounded the side of the Mercedes. Benny sped off and told us to keep our heads down. We heard shots and I lifted up to see, out the back window, Isidro sprawled on the ground. Benny reached back and pushed my head down." She coughed and began to sniffle. From her jacket pocket she pulled out a ball of tissues and dabbed at her nose. "It was my fucking fault."

Vitico turned around to look at her, alarm in his face. "How's that?"

"As we were leaving the restaurant, I realized that I had left my cell phone on the table. Isidro always travels with a bodyguard, Frank, and Frank went back in to get it. Because of me he wasn't there to protect Isidro. And that's why I couldn't call Abuela to say we were okay. Benny took us to his sister's house. It was pretty far out, in Iztapalpa. It's a bad area, and I didn't like it, but he said we'd be safe there. We couldn't leave the house, and his sister didn't have a phone. She was nice, but it was horrible being stuck there. We didn't hear from Benny for twenty-four hours.

Finally he shows up and confirms that Isidro died in the hospital. We started talking about how to get us out of town. He said we couldn't go back to my apartment and that whatever we did, we shouldn't talk to the police."

Vitico was still turned around with his jaw hanging open. "And why's that?"

"He thinks they're messed up in it. It was revenge. You probably think Isidro was a drug guy. He wasn't, but he was a lawyer for the big guys. He defended a major dealer who killed a couple of cops, and got him off. The police were not happy about that, obviously, and took matters into their own hands. Benny says that they probably want to make sure that there's no one around who could identify the killers."

Traffic inched along on Paseo de la Reforma, and now that we knew the true danger, we felt trapped. At any moment the police were going to tap on the window and ask us to get out of the car. Two lanes over we saw a police car.

"My brother," Vitico said to Alberto, "we need to get out of here. Make the first right turn you can—slowly, brother. Don't give them any reason to stop us."

What had seemed like a simple adventure before, now had my heart beating wildly. I reached up and put my hands on Alberto's shoulders. "Are you OK?"

"Uh-huh."

"Sorry about all this."

"It'll be something to tell our grandkids." He winked at me in the rear view mirror, but I could tell he was worried.

I squeezed his shoulders and sat back. I realized at that moment I loved him, that he was the man I wanted to be with. And if we were lucky enough to get out of this mess, I had to remember he was the one driving. He had already seen enough of my crazy family to make the average person turn and run. But I knew he wouldn't. I caught his eye again in the mirror, and I raised my eyebrows. I wanted to say "I love you," but it wasn't the time or place. Instead I said, "Watch the road, babe."

With Vitico's directions, Alberto got us out to the highway and on the way to Pachuca. We were back on the same stretch of road we had been on the day before and Alberto had done almost nothing but drive for two straight days. Vitico called Abuela and she insisted on speaking to Jorgito, not believing that he was all right until she heard his voice.

"Why don't you let me drive?" I said.

"I'll take over," said Vitico. "You guys need to rest."

We stopped and Alberto crawled in back. Jorgito went up front with his uncle. Claribel was curled up again in her corner and seemed to be asleep. Alberto put his arms around me, and we formed an uncomfortable cocoon on our side of the backseat. In our embrace was a growing familiarity and the relief that we had left the danger of Mexico City behind as we climbed into the green hills. Alberto's head pressed its weight on my shoulder as his breathing became deeper. I watched the sun slide in and out of cirrus clouds, and I smiled when Alberto started to snore as if there wasn't a care in the world. For the first time since I was a little girl I had a family—Alberto, Vitico, and Jorge with me, and Abuela and George awaiting our return. I knew it would have made Papi happy, that it had taken a long time, but he had prepared these people to take care of me, help me through life. Even meeting Alberto had an indirect link to my father through George. I almost imagined him up there, or wherever he was, pulling the strings, guiding me along. I also knew that I would still have my times of uncertainty and doubt, that the wounds of my early years still resided just beneath the skin, ready to rise to the surface, like what had happened with George the night before. Despite everything—the vulnerability of the small car, the danger that still lurked if we were stopped by a roadside cop, and the general wariness of not knowing what was around the next bend—I had confidence that things would be okay. With Vitico at the wheel and Jorgito as his copilot, and wrapped in Alberto's arms, the vehicle was taking me into a future better than anything I had been able to imagine for a long time.

Abuela and George had spent the day in the kitchen, preparing a big feast, and on the patio, making tortillas. It seems that it had been a good therapy session as they beamed when we dragged our feet through the door. They were putting the final touches on the plates of chicken mole, chile rellenos stuffed with pork, two kinds of homemade salsa, braised vegetables, and cheese-covered corn on the cob. We had only stopped a couple of times at gas stations for crappy snacks and soft drinks, so the table was a glorious sight. Jorge grabbed a hot tortilla, rolled it up, and stuffed it in his mouth before his grandmother could stop him. Not that she cared much. He could have done anything at that point. For Abuela he had come back from the dead.

I watched with emotion as Jorgito met his namesake. It was hard for me to maintain my anger at him. Alberto, again my hero, made me realize that what George said was right. It was a tragedy that would be with us until the day we died. But no good could come of stewing in it.

George tried to act normal, polite and interested, as if meeting a friend's son that he had heard much about. But inside I knew that he was deeply moved as he looked into the eyes of Miguel's son the way he had first looked into mine that day on the beach.

Jorgito turned to me with a bright smile and dancing brows. "Can I show him the book?"

"Maybe after we eat." But when I saw his face fall I said, "I don't know. I guess you could do it now."

Jorgito took an anxious George into the living room and sat him down on the couch. We all followed and stood in a circle while Jorgito took *Curious George* from the bookshelf and placed the sacred object in George's hands. George stared at it dumbfounded.

"Papi used to read it to me when I was little, translating it into Spanish as he went along."

George looked up at Jorgito, confused at first, seeming not to make the connection who Papi was. He opened the front cover and saw the inscription he had written to me. He tilted his head and his hands began to shake. "Yes, I remember," he said, almost in a whisper. He smoothed the page and wiped off a speck of dirt. "I remember."

"I asked Rebecca if she wanted to take it back, but she told me to keep it," said Jorgito proudly.

The room was so silent that we all heard a giant tear from George's eye plopping onto the paper. Jorgito had the horrified expression of someone who thought he was doing something good, but it had turned out wrong. The rest of us gawked stupidly, trying to push back our own emotions.

He wiped his eyes and said, "Jorgito, thank you so much for showing me this. It means a great deal to me, and I want you to keep it, too. Maybe someday you can read it to your kids, or your nephews." He looked at Alberto and me, and winked.

"All right," Vitico shouted. "Who wants a beer?"

"I do," said George, and we all chimed in, including Jorgito.

Abuela looked at him and shook her head.

"Oh, let him have one, *Mami*," said Vitico. "This is a celebration."

"Let's eat," she said. "The food is getting cold."

We all looked over at the table where Claribel sat by herself, her head down, her shoulders slumped, a far cry from the bubbly, confident woman I had met on the first trip. She still wore the leather jacket, and no one had invited her to take it off. No one had spoken to her since we arrived, and though Abuela had offered her cheek for a kiss, she later ignored her with an obvious disgust for the risk she had put Jorge into. She felt us all staring at her and got up, wiped her eyes, and went toward the bathroom.

In a low voice, Abuela said to Vitico, "I want to know everything that happened. Don't keep any details from me. We'll talk after dinner."

Jorgito's head sagged at the table, and after we finished, Abuela sent him off to his room to get some sleep. Claribel went out on the patio to smoke a cigarette while George, Alberto, and I washed dishes. Abuela surprisingly let us move about in her realm and sat with Vitico in the living room, talking in hushed tones. As we bumbled around in her kitchen, she would occasionally glance at us and say, "Don't worry about that. I'll do it later."

They finished talking and returned to the kitchen. Vitico went to the door and called Claribel in from the patio. We stood in the dim light, the smells of dinner still around us, mixed with the floral essence of the dishwashing liquid. Abuela spoke. "Rebecca, I want you to take Jorgito back home with you. If there is even the slightest danger to him, I want him out of the country."

"I wanted him to come and visit. I would like that."

"I mean now."

Alberto, George, and I all looked at each other, thinking the same thing. "But Doña Miriam, these things take time," said George.

"We may not have time. I don't trust the police. Vitico knows someone who can help arrange things."

"But that could be as dangerous as staying here and dealing with the police," said George.

"The connection I have is a professional. It is safe, but it's expensive," Vitico said, his voice trailing off as if he was embarrassed to say it.

Claribel had stood off to one side, quiet but her body tense. "And what about me?" she asked in a small but desperate voice,

Abuela looked at her as though she had forgotten she existed. "You were the one that put Jorgito in this danger in the first place with those drug people."

"Don Isidro wasn't into drugs. He was a respectable lawyer. And I did it for Jorge. I wanted to give him a chance in life. Isidro could send him to the best schools. He was going to buy us an apartment in Polanco. I gave up my job to be with him and when he met Jorge, I could see he wanted to take care of him, too." She began to choke on her words, tears gathering in the corners of her eyes. "I wanted to give Jorge all the things I never could before. It was all for him." She broke into a sob.

I felt miserable for her and had the urge to comfort her. But I didn't make a move, and no one else did either. She sat down in one of the kitchen chairs and buried her face in her hands. The room was filled with her sobbing, but it seemed that no one could hear her. It was the first time I had seen the hardness in Abuela, what people often referred to as her strength. Her family was everything to her, and she had never considered Claribel family. She could dismiss her without a thought. At the same time, George, her son's lover, who she hadn't seen in sixteen years, was embraced.

It was finally Vitico who spoke. He sat in a chair opposite Claribel.

"We only want what is best for Jorgito. It is just for a little while. Maybe you could go stay with some relatives until this all dies down. But I think you should call the driver guy and find out if there is anything new. Can you trust him?"

She stopped her wailing and looked up, grateful that someone was actually talking to her. "I don't even have my cell phone. I lost it that night."

"You can use mine."

Claribel went into the other room to make the call. A collective groan spread around the room, and Abuela turned to survey the sink, stove, and counters.

"I'm afraid we made a mess of your kitchen," I said. "I'm sure things aren't the way you would like."

She put her arm around me. "Oh, *mija,* we all do the best we can."

After a few minutes, Claribel came out and pointed the phone at Vitico. "You talk to him. It's way beyond me." Vitico took the phone into the other room. To the rest of us she said, "It's hard to get a straight answer out of Benny. That guy can talk. Long story short, he went to stay with some relatives. He didn't say where. He's going to lie low for a while."

We nodded our heads and I melted into one of the kitchen chairs. The rest followed suit as we waited for Vitico to give us his impression of what was going on.

He emerged after a long conversation, rubbed his head and then stuck his finger in his ear, shaking it back and forth. "A lot more than I ever wanted to know about the police. The agents that Don Isidro's client killed were AFI, federal police. Used to be one of the most corrupt agencies until Fox tried to clean it up. Still some bad apples though. Benny thinks they went after Don Isidro rather than the client to set an example to lawyers who would defend cop-killers. Benny talked to some friends in the PGJ, Mexico City's judicial police, who are supposed to investigate the crime. They have no suspects and probably want to keep it that way so they don't piss off the AFI. Everyone thinks it was some rogue AFI agents that shot him down. They also don't want to go out looking for witnesses for fear of leading AFI to people who they might threaten or worse."

Abuela moaned. "Oh, no, *mijo.*"

"The lawyers and judges are screaming for an investigation. They are sick and tired of the violence against them for their decisions even though they might not have agreed with Isidro's client getting off on a technicality."

"This is all giving me a headache," I said. "Can you get to the point?"

"Benny's analysis is that PGJ isn't going to go out of its way to find witnesses. It should all die down in a couple of months. He's going to make himself scarce for a while."

"I still want Jorgito out of the country as much as it pains me to be separated from him," said Abuela. "I've got some savings to pay for getting him across the border."

"*Mami*, you don't have enough."

George cleared his throat, and we all turned our eyes to him. "I'll cover it. I'll do anything to make sure Jorge's safe. Rebecca's grandfather is insisting on a financial settlement even though I don't want it. I was thinking of turning the money over to Jorge anyway. There's enough for his mother as well if she wants to go."

"Oh, bless you, Tio Jorge," said Abuela, and George winced at the name he had tried so hard to run away from.

"Abuela, he prefers George now," I said.

George threw up his hands. "What the heck! Miriam can call me what she wants."

We broke into laughter except for Claribel who was deep in thought. "I don't want to go. I appreciate the offer, George. I'll go stay with a cousin in Tampico for a few weeks. Benny and I are going to keep in touch. I know you will take good care of my son. He's probably safer without me."

It pained me to see her defeated, giving up her son for nobody knew how long. In a way I wanted to see her fight for her child, stay with him, help protect him. But I knew that what Abuela wanted was probably best.

## 21: Rebecca

While Jorgito slept, we plotted his future, and in the car back to the hotel we talked about where he would live. Alberto offered his spare bedroom, but I hated the thought of him being so far away. George, in his usual pensive way, gave subtle indications that he was about to speak from the front passenger seat. He took a breath, rested his hands on his knees, and looked out the window.

"I've been thinking," he said, "it's time for me to leave the Horizons Mobile Home Park, past time. I could rent a house down the peninsula for us, a three-bedroom so Jorge could have his own bedroom as long as he stays with us."

I leaned forward, rested my arms on the back of Alberto's seat, and squeezed his shoulder so that he wouldn't feel left out. "Do you know how much a decent three-bedroom rents for?" I said.

"My dear, even without your grandfather's money, I'm a little better off than you might think. I've hardly spent any money in the last sixteen years. What I had before, plus the profit from the sale of my land in Mexico has just been sitting in safe investments, growing a bit. How would you like living with your brother?"

My heart began to swell at the thought of living with my new family. It was a dream that the old me, the cautious doubting me, set immediately to attack. My family would consist of a reclusive man who wasn't really any relation, a half-brother who I hardly knew and was still this side of a tricky border-crossing. "Who's going to cook? We'll all starve. I'm a disaster in the kitchen, and I don't think we could survive on your microwave dinners."

George turned around and spoke seriously. "Rebecca, stop putting up barriers."

"I'm not."

"First you're worried about how much it is going to cost and then who's going to cook. Details."

There was still tension between us. I felt petty and small to put a damper on what must have been a momentous decision for him. He was the one jumping a great hurdle, breaking out of his isolation, and he was doing it to create a home for Jorge and me. I should have embraced the idea, and deep down I did. But there was fear of change, new uncertain relationships, and a past full of painful memories.

It had taken many years for George to get to a place where he was ready to share his life. Perhaps a family was what he always wanted, had wanted with my father, that he had fantasized at one point living with Miguel and raising me. Providing a home for Jorge and me would be for him somewhat less than the family he might have wanted, but the closest that life could offer him at the moment.

I stared at the back of his head, his wispy hair and thin neck, and the horrible image came to me again of my mother and him struggling on the cliff. How much had he wanted my mother out of the picture? I thought of the day at the Russian River after our argument when he asked me how I knew he didn't do it. Were my efforts on his behalf what had caused so much hurt to my grandparents, put Gran in a wheelchair, made Conchita lose her job, and dug up painful memories for everyone really for a guilty man?

And then, as if he sensed my thoughts, he turned and gave me a smile, part mystery and part innocence. "It would be starting anew," he said, almost an apology. "Why not give it a try?" He glanced at Alberto. "And of course we would welcome visitors from Forestville."

"Thanks. I thought you had forgotten all about me."

"No way," I said with a laugh. I caressed the back of his head. "With a new house we'll probably need a handyman from time to time."

"That's me," he said good-naturedly. "Your Mr. Fixit on call. I just hope you and George can keep future crises to leaky faucets and broken windows."

It was too soon to think of living with Alberto. Anyway he had his business up north, and I needed to be near law school. I sat back, opened my window, and let the wind hit my face and rake through my hair. I shook my head in hopes that the wind would carry the remnants of past doubt out into the cool night air. I didn't want to meet them again.

At the hotel Alberto and I collapsed on the bed. I was oblivious to the lumpy mattress, the tinge of mildew in the air, the several varieties of insects that were probably lurking in the dark corners. It felt like it had been the longest day of my life, and I fell asleep without even taking off my clothes. We slept through until the next morning.

As soon as we walked into Abuela's house the following day, Jorgito strolled over and high-fived me. "Yes!" he said with an ear-to-ear grin.

"Hey," said Vitico. "Don't be so excited about leaving your old uncle. Your grandmother is going to miss you like crazy."

"And you're going to have to learn to make your own bed. Nobody's going to do it for you over there," I said.

"*Hermana*, don't spoil the moment. Can I go to Disneyland?"

I shook my head with a laugh. "We'll see." I wasn't that much older than him, but I felt like I had left the spontaneity of youth far behind me. He acted as if he were going on a big adventure rather than escaping from rogue police and making a dangerous border-crossing into a new country where he spoke very little of the language.

Vitico took me aside and explained that it would take a day or two to make the arrangements. Jorge would have to get to Monterey and then it would take another day or so to make the crossing. I hated cutting the visit short with Abuela, but someone needed to be on the other side of the border to meet Jorge. Alberto still had to visit his parents in Hermosillo, and I felt a sense of relief that I wouldn't be able to make the trip with him. I was sure he had told them about me, and they were anxiously waiting to meet me.

After another of Abuela's big breakfasts, Alberto, George, and I headed for Parque Escondido. It would be our only chance to go there before we had to leave. Since Vitico's and my trip there a couple of months before, the owners had given up trying to make it a successful business, and the bank had taken over the management. Vitico said that improvements had been made, though he also thought that being owned by one of Mexico's largest banks took away from the romance of the place.

The road twisted and turned through the woods pressing in on either side, and we felt the cool mountain air the sun hadn't had time to warm. We passed through the last dusty hamlet of poorly constructed houses where we had to share the road with goats and the occasional man on horseback. Just past the houses we saw a man step out into the road and another pull tight a thick rope wrapped around a tree, blocking the road. Our first thought was that it was a robbery scheme, but the two men hardly looked the role of highwaymen. The one with the rope had sun-weathered arms that strained with his effort, a tired face in the shadow of his cowboy hat, and threadbare clothes. The other who came up to the window had salt-and-pepper hair, a newer cowboy shirt with snaps, and grimy jeans. He humbly bowed his head and in a low voice said they were collecting forty pesos for road maintenance. There was nothing official about them or the way they stopped us, so Alberto in the driver's seat asked what their authority was. The man only repeated that they were collecting for road improvement.

"This is crazy. George, tell them who you are," I said.

George gave me a hushing look and took out his wallet.

"You're going to pay them?"

"Oh, what is it? Less than four dollars." He handed the man the money.

The man with the rope let it go slack, and the other wished us a nice day.

"I hope that means they have paved the last part which used to be dirt and gravel," said George.

After another mile we were on the bad part of the road, and it seemed worse than when I had passed this way with Vitico. We bumped over potholes and ruts, prayed as we went around narrow curves that nobody was coming. George began to laugh. "Nice improvements," he said. "I want my money back."

We came to the old iguana gate, and a short man in his fifties stepped out of a newly painted booth to charge us the entrance fee of fifteen pesos per person. The man looked inside the car and a bad-toothed grin took up half of his brown face.

*"Señor Edwards, es usted, de verdad?"*

It was Juan, George's old foreman during the construction on his property. George had explained to me how Miguel had taken over more and more responsibility in the managing of things, coming into conflict with Juan. I wondered if Juan still held a grudge.

George got out of the car with a pained expression on his face and went around to shake his hand. "Juan, it has been a long time. How is your family?"

"Fine. Thank you for asking. Juanito, the youngest, is now a doctor."

"That's wonderful." George looked like he couldn't wait to get back in the car.

"Of course, my old boss and his friends don't pay. I wish you welcome."

"Give my regards to your family," said George, backing away.

George eased into the front seat. "Let's go," he said. "The little weasel stole a bunch of equipment when he left my employment. Miguel wanted to go after him, but I said no. Several of the workers who were his relatives went with him. To make a big deal about the theft would have caused bad blood in the town."

"Did you know the two collecting the toll?"

"They both worked for me. Most all the men around here worked for me at one time or another. Miguel was fair with them, but he didn't tolerate any bullshit either. If they didn't show for several days without a good excuse, he fired them."

The renovations on the house had been completed, and we walked in the open double door with blue, green, and red Talavera tiles around the frame. George told us that the tile design was called Palacio Especial and had involved a week of debate before the final pattern was chosen. Every detail was a memory for him and he pointed out things, explained why they had chosen a particular feature or material. The large living room had been converted into a welcome center and reception for the bed-and-breakfast. George shook his head at the cheap pine furniture, stained to look old and the striped cushions in colors that clashed with the tiles around the fireplace.

"We used to have a fire every night in the winter. Now look at the chimney, so clean and cold. Am I being awful?"

I took his arm and squeezed it in an attempt to lessen his scowl. "It must be hard," I said.

"Let's go outside. That's the true beauty of the place. I was never all that happy with the house. It was too heavy in its design. What worked well in Barcelona wasn't so well adapted to the Mexican jungle. At one point I wanted to tear it down and start all over. When Miguel left to go to the States, I stopped working on the house and concentrated on the outside, the gardens."

We walked out the doors to the back that gave onto the swimming pool enclosed by the two wings of the house. On one side had been the master suite, guest bedrooms and study, and on the other the dining area, kitchen, and maid's quarters.

As soon we got outside we heard the waterfall. "Ah," said George. "That's what I miss."

The open end of the patio faced the falls, though you couldn't see them for the trees. A couple of children were playing in the pool, and a watchful mother looked up from her book. She was still in a robe as it wasn't yet warm, though the children in the heated pool didn't seem to mind. We greeted her as we walked past and went down the steps to the path that led to a gazebo. George was pleased that they had kept to the original idea of a wild garden, flowering shrubs and fruit trees, rough cobblestone, irregular pathways.

The pillars of the gazebo were encrusted with the same broken tiles that I had seen on the benches in my previous visit. The roof was overlapping green ceramic that mimicked the scales of a serpent. George told us that the metal benches inside the gazebo were his own design. They were surprisingly comfortable, ribbons of polished iron that conformed to the body, and the benches were in a half-moon shape to create intimacy. We sat a while and listened to the falling water.

"This is so relaxing," said Alberto.

"You poor guy," I said, putting my arm around him. "You've done nothing but drive the last three days."

"I wish you were coming with me to Hermosillo."

"I can't. George and I are going with Jorgito to Monterey and then we'll meet him on the other side. It sounds ominous, the other side."

"I trust Vitico," said George. "I believe he knows what he's doing."

"He's a good man. I wish he would find some happiness," I said.

"He doesn't seem happy to you?" Alberto said.

"He puts on a good façade and he doesn't have the devils that my father seemed to have. But still, his devotion to Abuela and Jorgito, I think, has kept him from finding his own life."

"He's got the same warmth as Miguel," George said.

"You noticed that, too, huh? Yes, under that joking exterior is a sweet and sensitive man."

"Kind of like the one you have next to you."

"All right, folks, enough of that," Alberto said. "I'm ready for a swim. You told us to bring our suits."

"But not in the pool," George said. "I have a better place."

From the gazebo we followed a trail into the woods, which intersected with a path that Vitico and I had been on the previous summer, and eventually led to the bridge where we had stood and talked. There was the mosaic-tiled lizard on the rock in the middle, glistening in the sun that spotlighted the natural pool under the falls. As it was the dry season, the waterfall was less rambunctious than it had been before, but still provided a calming sound as it slid over the moss-covered rocks and rained down on the pool.

"You mean here?" I said. "The water must be freezing."

"Refreshing," George corrected. "The water is not deep and it gets a lot of sun, so it's really not too bad."

We crossed the wooden bridge and took a trail down to the water's edge. George indicated a clump of bushes where we could change though I still had my doubts about going in the greenish water. I braced myself with the idea that it couldn't be any colder than the ocean in Northern California, which I forced myself to swim in on those days when the offshore breezes sent the temperatures into the eighties and nineties.

Alberto waded in and did a little dance as the water hit his ankles. "Yikes!" Then he dove under and came up shaking his head with a scream. "Jesus Christ!"

"That's encouraging," I said, still with my toes barely in the water.

George came from behind and dove under, his feet kicking a splash that doused me.

"Damn you," I said, causing George and Alberto to laugh.

I waded in slowly, shivered and cursed under my breath while George and Alberto waited with arms crossed over their chests. I turned around and backed into the water, taking the shock of it just as I felt Alberto's arms around me. "Not so bad, huh?" he said.

"You guys are crazy. This is torture."

He held me and I felt better with the heat of his body. After a few minutes I did become accustomed to the water and tried to convince myself that I was having a good time.

We paddled around the big rock where the lizard's beady eyes gazed at us with mistrust and then went over to the waterfall, where we let it rain down on our heads, again causing me to shiver. I had to admit, though, it was something like paradise, pictures I had seen in *National Geographic* where I fantasized being with a loved one. With the water pattering on our heads, Alberto leaned in to kiss me. The chilly water and the hollow drumming on our skulls made it somewhat less romantic than the pictures, but I knew that the memory of the day would warm it significantly.

I had managed to put behind me the night of George's confession. The place was too beautiful and the time too important to feel angry. It pleased me to see George, when conditions were just right, loosen his jaw, let his shoulders drop and become like the young man I had vague memories of at the beach with my father. I backed out of the waterfall and turned to look at him standing waist-deep in the pool. Since he had come back into my life, I hadn't seen him with his shirt off, and I was surprised that he was in very good shape, not muscular but toned. Unlike Alberto's broad chest with its glistening curls of dark hair, you could count the few hairs darkened by the water and plastered to George's chest. He looked like a boy, vulnerable and wide-eyed. His attention was drifting off into a distant memory, and I watched the tension begin to rise in his face.

Alberto splashed him. "Hey, George. Come back."

George, at first stunned, splashed back, and set off a round of water-fighting. We were children on our first outing of summer. Later our skin showed goose bumps, and we climbed out of the water onto some large flat rocks. Then we were seals basking in the warmth of the sun while the birds of the jungle called to each other. Alberto took my hand and laced his fingers with mine. I couldn't remember the last time I had felt this kind of peace.

"Are you really going to rent a house on the peninsula?" I asked George.

"Should it be near the ocean or inland? I don't mind the fog at the ocean, but it would be farther for you to go to school."

"But those days when the sun comes out are so glorious by the water. What about Half Moon Bay? It wouldn't be too much of a commute."

"What do you think, Alberto?"

"That's a great area. Wherever you guys end up, I'll find my way there."

He squeezed my hand and something felt different. The moment was pure, not followed by a counter-moment of fretting that maybe I was making a mistake, that I wasn't capable of love, all those doubts that normally plagued me every time I started to feel close to someone. I looked up into the blue sky filled with layered formations of puffy white clouds, some vertical as if rising up in a cottony explosion, and others stretched out along the horizon like snow-covered mountains. One high cumulus formation had a slightly darker edge, a shadow, and I imagined a reclining person, my father floating on it, peering over the edge and smiling down on me. I felt a powerful and uncontrollable surge of emotion rolling in waves over me. The tears began to stream down my face.

Alberto rose up on one elbow with a look of horror pinching his face. "Rebecca, *mi amor*, what is it?"

"Nothing," I said in a soggy voice. "That's just it. Nothing is wrong. Nothing."

I reached up and touched his cheek and the creases smoothed away, his shiny dark eyes still searching my face, looking inside me, wondering. In a shaft of golden light a pair of electric blue butterflies chased each other above us, dipped and dived, darted away and then came back. Their wings shimmered with an otherworldly intensity. One landed on Alberto's head and perched on a thick strand of wet hair. It fluttered its wings slowly and became still.

"Don't move. Just stay right there. Don't move. Don't move," I whispered. "George, look."

"Ah, they're back. When Miguel and I first came here, there were hundreds of them. Then they disappeared."

The second butterfly hesitated in the air above Alberto's head, and then dropped down next to its mate. It fanned its wings and came to rest.

Vincent Meis lives in San Francisco where he is a teacher, editor, and writer. And when he gets the chance, he is a traveler looking for the setting of his next story. He has published one previous book, *Eddie's Desert Rose.* His website is: www.vincentmeis.com.